Camera Ready

Dear Trish,
Hope you enjoy
this story!

Adele Royce

Camera Ready

Books in the
Truth, Lies and Love in Advertising
series:

Camera Ready

For Position Only

Princess Smile

Camera Ready

adele royce

DAGMAR
MIURA
LOS ANGELES

Published by Dagmar Miura
Los Angeles
www.dagmarmiura.com

Camera Ready

Cover photo by Merrell Virgen

First published 2020

ISBN: 978-1-951130-34-3

For my beloved husband and muse, Marty,
who is so much a part of the words on
every page of every book, story, poem.
Thank you for being my greatest champion.

One

TONGVA PARK WAS NOT exactly a Norman Rockwell painting. After dusk, it was more like something from Francisco De Goya's black period. It was not the safest path, but it was the quickest—and there was something exhilarating about the element of danger—the chance that I might not make it to the other side. A chilly breeze whistled through the rusty fig trees as I made my way through Main Street in downtown Santa Monica. The bars and restaurants were humming with chatter—the bar-hopping locals getting started for the evening. As I closed in on the park entrance, I felt my heart pulsating as I whipped my way towards Ocean Avenue. I shivered, my stilettos clacking against the cement with a compulsive rhythm.

The playful laughter of children echoed in the distance, almost drowning out the din of their parents, who were arguing close by. I glanced over my shoulder, spotting a homeless man sleeping soundly on one of the benches, and I inhaled the omnipresent scent of weed lingering in the air.

The urgent sound of moaning and groaning emanated from nearby public bathrooms. Despite my attempt to avoid looking in the direction of the noises, I spied the darkened silhouette of a man and woman engaged in vigorous sex, thudding against the wall near the door to the ladies' room. My heart thumped as I sped up. It was too late; a woman's voice screamed breathlessly, "Hey perve—next time take a picture."

I lowered my head and emerged onto the brightly-lit Ocean Avenue, giggling triumphantly as the last vestiges of a spectacular sunset shimmered before me. I stopped walking long enough to absorb the orange-pink rays stabbing through fluffy cloud formations hovering at the base of the restless ocean. The sunset was my promise of hope—of love, romance and all its trappings. I wished sunsets were never-ending, so I could immerse myself for hours—just to feel the residual sense of peace.

I was headed to Herringbone Seafood Restaurant after a day of client meetings and an exhaustive post-mortem with my boss Warren. I had been Vice President of Accounts at the advertising agency, Warren Mitchell & Partners, for two years. Although I knew I was good at my job, our fearless leader could not resist the temptation to micro-manage. Jeffrey had left the final meeting of the day in a huff, declaring that although he was a partner, he still felt like the creative director—only with better pay.

I entered the restaurant and heard my cell phone ring. I fished it out of my handbag and saw the name *Derek* lighting up my phone screen. "Hello, darling," I said, smiling into the phone. I put my hand over my other ear so I could hear him clearly. "Did you change your mind and decide to come meet us for dinner?"

"I wish," he replied. "I was just calling to let you know I'll be late again tonight. These rehearsals are running long."

"Do you miss me?" I asked, scanning the restaurant for my best friend and confidante, Marisa. As usual, she was late.

"Always," he responded. "I should be home no later than 9 p.m."

"Do you want me to bring anything home for you? I'm at Herringbone."

"Nah ... there's craft service ... I'll be fine. See you later. Tell Marisa 'hi' for me."

I approached the hostess and asked for a table for two.

"You have a reservation?" she asked, flipping her brunette bob, and casting a skeptical glance my way. She had a pudgy face and her bangs were too long.

I read her nametag. "I don't—do you think you could squeeze me in, *Claire?*" She reminded me of someone I went to Cal State Long Beach with many years ago.

Claire managed to find me a four-top, and after settling in, I neurotically pulled out my phone and began going through emails. I really wished Derek didn't have such a rigorous schedule; ever since he had joined the Los Angeles Philharmonic as first chair violinist, he worked far more hours. It was a fifty-two-week a year job, unlike his previous gig at Orange County Symphony, where he could teach music on the side at USC. The L.A. Phil was gearing up for a string of shows at the Walt Disney Concert Hall and rehearsals ran late every night. Between my job and his, we were basically crossing paths in the night, sharing some occasional snuggling, but little quality time.

While I waited for Marisa, the waitress approached me with a glass of ice water. As soon as she set it down, she said to me, "Um ... there's a gentleman who wants to buy you a drink. He's on the other side of the restaurant. Good-looking guy." She winked and smiled at me, like she was in on a joke.

I studied her, now puzzled. "Really? Well, I'm actually waiting for my girlfriend and I can't accept a drink from a stranger."

"He said you two know each other … your name's Jane, right?" the waitress offered as proof. Her long, light blonde hair was drawn into a side ponytail and she had guileless blue eyes. She seemed reluctant to give up, so I assumed she must have been tipped generously.

"Okay, fine. I'll take a glass of chardonnay," I relented, skimming the crowded, dimly lit restaurant, past the many hanging trellises spattered with Tivoli lights and faux greenery. The attempt at fairytale charm seemed to compete with the ceiling's cold white open-piped industrial facade. I turned in every direction to see if I recognized this 'stranger' who had just bought me a drink. There seemed to be no one there I knew, but with so many people, I just could not be sure.

"Right away," the waitress answered, smiling, and galloping away to get my wine.

When she delivered the drink, I sipped it slowly and continued answering emails and texting back and forth with Marisa, who was held up in traffic. I met Marisa when she was a tabloid reporter, long before she became a highly sought-after news anchor. She had recently been promoted by the network and given top billing on a nationally syndicated nightly entertainment show—*The Real Marisa Silva.*

"Excuse me." A deep, silky male voice intruded on my thoughts. I looked up and had a hard time hiding my astonishment. It was Craig Keller, the most notorious playboy in town, and managing partner of Keller Whitman Group, one of Warren's fiercest competitors. He was someone I tried like hell to bury in my mind long ago, but who still frequently haunted my dreams.

"May I join you?" he asked, sliding into the chair across from me.

I stared at him blankly and said nothing. After all, I had carefully avoided him for two full years. When I saw him at events, I made sure I knew where he was the whole time, so we would not cross paths. This drove Derek nuts. He already had an inferiority complex about Craig and, although I had never revealed the nature of our relationship because it happened before Derek and I got together, it was clear Craig made him feel small and insecure. Derek would always question me as to why, if I didn't still have a thing for Craig, I avoided him at every pass. I continually had to reassure Derek that I was no longer interested in Craig, which was mostly the truth. I had moved on. Derek and I had been living together for more than a year and nothing could come between us ... not even Craig Keller.

I cleared my throat and set my phone on the table. "I'm meeting someone."

"Whoever it is doesn't understand what a rare and beautiful creature you are," he responded, giving me a lazy smile with those perfect white teeth, "or they would have been on time."

I didn't want to tell him I was waiting on a girlfriend. I wished Derek were on his way to meet me ... to protect me from this predator who had made my life miserable just two years earlier. The only thing I hated more than seeing Craig was the fact that, at that very moment, I was thinking about my outfit and wondering whether it was stellar enough for an impromptu encounter with the man himself. I was relieved to be wearing Chanel ... a sleek hunter green sleeveless shift dress with a matching boucle puffy-sleeved bolero jacket thrown casually over my shoulders. My long auburn hair hung in loose curls. I felt satisfied that the effect had to be, at the very least, chic.

"Thanks for the drink," I said curtly. "But, if I'd known it was from you, I ..."

"Oh, come on, Ms. Mercer, lighten up," he interrupted. "Don't tell me you never think about me."

I took a good look at him. I had not seen him up close for what seemed like ages and he looked even better than I remembered. *Yes, Craig Keller, I see your glorious face in my dreams, so I guess that constitutes thinking about you. I wish I could stop thinking about you and concentrate on my live-in boyfriend, who loves and cares for me, unlike you, who sleeps with every woman you meet, and leaves a path of emotional destruction in your wake. I really hate you … when I don't think about being with you.* "What do you want me to say?" I asked, taking another sip of wine, and searching his light jade eyes thoughtfully.

"I obviously want you to say 'yes'," he responded, leaning toward me. "And in case you were wondering, I think about you all the time."

I laughed. "You must have amnesia … that happens when you get old." I was unable to resist the crack. Craig was ten years older than me with a birthday in September, so I knew he had recently turned thirty-eight. And, given what I knew about his ego, approaching the big 4-0 had to be tough for him.

Craig's eyes lowered to his suit jacket lapel and he brushed something off it. "Very funny, Ms. Mercer. I never forgot that snarky wit of yours. It's one of the things that drove me crazy in the first place."

"Of course, as opposed to the willingness to do whatever you wanted, whenever you wanted it," I retorted, pulling the bolero jacket tighter around my shoulders.

"Jane … come on … can't we be friends?" His eyes sparkled wickedly, as they always did with those long lashes. "I'd like to think I could call you for a drink every now and then … you know, just like old times."

At that moment, Marisa waltzed in, on her cell phone, fumbling with something in her handbag. When she approached the table, she took one look at Craig and said loudly into her phone, "I'll call you back."

"Well, well, well," she began, looking Craig up and down. "I see what happens when I'm a few minutes late." Marisa looked like a stunning celebrity. She was in a black Yves Saint Laurent pantsuit with a white silk blouse underneath. Her brunette hair was slicked back and pulled into a high ponytail. She wore dark red lipstick that shimmered under the restaurant lights.

"I've been keeping your friend company," Craig announced, not missing a beat. "You don't object, do you?" Even though he was speaking to Marisa, his eyes did not stray from mine.

"That all depends," Marisa replied, eyeing me with suspicion.

"It's fine, Marisa," I said quickly. "We were just catching up … it's been a while. Now if you'll excuse us," I turned to Craig, whose expression had become one of amusement.

"Of course, my dear … don't be a stranger." He swiftly pulled his chair out and rose to his feet to make room for Marisa. Although he gestured for her to sit down in the empty chair, Marisa ignored him and took the chair to my right. Craig gently pushed in the chair, gave me a little smile, turned, and disappeared into the crowd.

She plopped down hard and glared at me. It was clear she was not at all pleased to see Craig Keller. I understood why she viewed him as pure poison. As soon as she was sure he was out of earshot, she leaned in, set her elbows on the table, and cradled her chin in her hands.

"Um … was I seeing things just now?" she queried. "Because there's no way my friend would knowingly sit and talk to a man like that after everything he did to hurt her."

"Oh Marisa, it's not what you think," I protested, chuckling at her severe demeanor. "He sent me an anonymous drink while I was sitting here waiting for you. Trust me, if I'd known he was even here in the first place, I wouldn't have come in."

The waitress cut in to ask Marisa for her drink order.

"I'll take a vodka and soda with lime, please," she

requested, snapping up the menu and skimming the dinner specials. She must be on a diet, I thought. No calories except for the vodka. As soon as the waitress had gone, Marisa continued her grilling. "I wondered whether he would resurface again, now that he's about to be single."

"Single?" I repeated in disbelief.

"Oh, please … don't tell me you didn't hear. It's been all over the tabloids."

"Hear what?" I asked her.

"He's going through a nasty divorce," she revealed with a cat-like gleam in her golden-brown eyes. "His wife must have finally gotten fed up with all his philandering. Rumor is she's getting the house and joint custody of their two children."

"No shit," I blurted. "I had no clue." I looked around the restaurant again to see whether Craig was still there, almost as though I needed to observe him again—this time as a divorced man.

"So … you can imagine why I freaked out when I saw him sitting here," she explained. "I know how hard it was for you to resist him in the past." She shot me a look, eyebrows raised, and chin lowered like she was talking to a young child.

"The past is just that, Marisa," I said, thinking that for someone who was going through a divorce and custody battle, Craig did not appear to have a care in the world. But that's just how he was—his house could be burning down around him, and he would smile and offer you a cocktail—make you feel like it wasn't really happening.

"I saw how you were looking at him. Please promise me that if he goes after you again, you'll talk to me before you do anything." Marisa's dark red lips were pursed as though she were seriously worried about me.

The waitress cut in to deliver Marisa's drink and get our dinner order. As soon as she had gone, I turned to

Marisa. "*Oh my God*, could you please give me an ounce of credit here? I mean, the man broke my heart and nearly destroyed my career. I hate him ... no, I *despise* him."

Marisa studied my face for a moment. "You should be careful with using the word 'hate,' Jane," she cautioned. "You know what they say ... there's a fine line."

"You have nothing to worry about, Marisa," I insisted, tapping my fingers against the table impatiently. She was starting to get on my nerves. "And anyway, I'm living with the man I want to be with, so there's no way anything could happen. Now, please, can we just change the subject? How's Ewan?"

"Amazing as ever," she answered, suddenly flushed with excitement. "I think this could be serious ... he could be the one."

I knew Marisa would gladly turn the conversation to her English rock star boyfriend, Ewan Blade, whom she met at a press event for his band, Brave Harlots, who happened to be a client of mine. Ewan was the lead guitarist and they were having a whirlwind romance. It was the first time I had seen Marisa so excited to date someone. She was finally dating a bigger celebrity than herself.

"I know what you're thinking," she continued, stirring her drink with a paper straw before taking a sip. "But this time, it's different. Can you believe we've been dating for six months already?"

She was right. I was thinking it was a little too good to be true, especially given Marisa's previous relationship disasters. From what I knew of Ewan, he was a decent guy, very unlike most rock stars who ran around with groupies and did copious amounts of drugs. He was sort of introverted ... more like a true artist than anything else. I was happy for Marisa if he was, in fact, *the one*.

MARISA GAVE ME A ride to my car and, while driving home, I could not help but obsess over my Craig Keller encounter. I wondered whether I really did hate him or if Marisa's concerns were warranted. I had to admit, he looked totally delicious sitting across from me in his navy three-piece suit with a skinny yellow and blue tie. No man I knew dared to wear a three-piece suit, but Craig pulled it off—he had always been a snappy dresser—always looked camera ready, as Marisa often described. Even though he was close to forty, there was not a wrinkle on his face or a single grey to be seen in his glossy dark brown hair. In fact, he hadn't changed one bit from the man with whom I had once been intimately involved. I, however, had changed. I was nothing like the insecure, unstable person I was two years ago. And that was a good thing. I never wanted to be that girl again.

With the memory of Craig Keller came the terrible zigzagging of emotions, the obsession, secrecy, rage, and desire. He was the sorcerer of all things romantic until he turned vicious and brutal. He gave and withdrew affection as it suited him, quickly whipping me into a pile of emotional debris—one I had to unearth to find myself again. What I told Marisa was true. I hated him. But in a strange and awful way, I loved him too.

After my torrid affair with Craig, Derek and I got together, and life had settled into something wonderfully calm and full of happy moments. There was no way I wanted to mess that up. Still, there was that familiar side of me that was a little restless … a side that craved a bit of wanderlust and, although I hated to admit this, a slight hint of drama.

I stopped to pick up cat food on the way home and happened to be at the cash register when I spotted it. It was *LA Insider Magazine*—one of the more prominent industry rags—and there, in vivid color, was a photo of Craig and his wife. The editor had made it look like someone tore the photo in half and placed the two pieces next to each other. "Battle Royale," the headline read. I could not resist the urge to pick up the magazine and flip it to the page where the story was. Marisa was right. Craig and Alessandra Keller were embroiled in an ugly, high-profile court battle over alimony and child support, as well as custody of their children. As though on auto-pilot, I handed the magazine to the cashier so she could ring it up.

The cashier, who looked like she had not slept in weeks, eyed the magazine cover and gave me a little grin. "That guy's cute—everyone's buying this issue," she commented before swiping it and handing it to me over the counter, assuming I wanted to read it so badly, it should be kept separate from the cat food. I accepted it. "Enjoy," she said as I grabbed my bags with the magazine under my arm.

At home in our apartment that night, I took a hot shower and put on my white fuzzy robe, anticipating the contents of the magazine as though I would a slice of chocolate cake—something delectable. I would relax and pore over the tabloid while I waited for Derek to get home—voraciously gleaning details about Craig's private life.

I looked around our small apartment, thinking of all the things that had happened over the past two years. True, it was the same two-bedroom apartment I had before Derek moved in, but it had morphed into a warm nest for us as a young couple. Before we got together, it was simply a place to store my rather large and luxurious clothing collection—one that, at the time, I could barely afford. It was also where I crashed after running all over the city attending work and social events.

I sank into our well-worn Eames era grey twill sofa, which was a lot more stylish than it was comfortable, and eagerly thumbed through the tabloid. My heart raced as

I explored numerous photos of Craig splashed all over the publication, mostly posing with different women at parties. I shook my head. *What a mess.* For a moment, I caught myself feeling a little sorry for Craig. He had to hate all the intrusive, negative publicity.

I heard the door unlock, and Derek entered, carrying his violin case and some books, looking beleaguered. I dropped the magazine on the glass-topped boomerang table and stood to greet him.

"Hi sweetie … is everything okay?" I asked, approaching him.

"Yeah … just a long day," he answered, setting his violin case and books down and putting his arms around me. He kissed me on the neck. "Mmm … you smell good," he commented.

"So, do you," I replied, pulling away slightly so I could see his face. He looked boyishly handsome as always, with his sandy-colored hair, naturally flecked with golden highlights. I rested my chin on his shoulder. "I missed you today."

"Just today?" I heard the smile in his voice.

"Every day. Maybe we should go on vacation," I murmured, burying my face in between his jacket lapels. "You know, somewhere exotic … where we can have drinks with little umbrellas."

"That would be heaven," he responded, stroking my hair softly. "But it's going to be a long time before I can get off work. Probably not until summer."

We stood there, rocking each other silently in our tiny living room, until Derek abruptly pushed me away and beelined for the coffee table. "What's that?" he questioned, pointing at the magazine on the table with Craig Keller's picture on the cover.

"What's what?" I responded innocently, wracking my brain for an excuse.

He picked up the magazine and flipped through the

pages quickly, throwing it down again and turning to face me. His expression was serious. "What's it doing here?" he demanded.

"I—um, I just bought it. I have to read those magazines for work, you know, to keep up with what competitors are doing." *What a lame excuse but what was I supposed to say?*

"Don't tell me you didn't notice," he accused, studying my face—searching for some sign that I was lying.

"Notice what, Derek?" I asked, now feeling defensive and knowing Derek was not about to buy my innocent act. I untied and retied the belt on my robe.

"Your man is on the cover … he's all over that rag and he's getting a divorce. Don't tell me you didn't notice that." Derek was acting uncharacteristically edgy at the mere sight of Craig Keller. And I didn't know what to say to him. I knew he was sensitive about Craig, but not to this extent.

"He's *not* 'my man', Derek. *You* are. Look—I'll throw the magazine away if it makes you feel better." I snatched up the magazine in question and went into the kitchen to throw it in the garbage. It had caused enough trouble for one night. I returned to the living room, but Derek was already in the bedroom. I followed and found him undressing.

I just sat on the bed and watched him in silence, trying to think of something to say that would not make matters worse. Something like, 'Well, funny you should mention Craig because I saw him at dinner … he bought me a drink and told me not to be a stranger.' *No, there was no way I would tell him that.* I sighed.

We remained silent for the rest of the evening until the lights were off and we were in bed. I was the first to speak. "Okay, Derek, I'll admit I did buy the magazine because I saw him on the cover. Marisa told me about the divorce while we were at dinner. I was just curious—about him." I couldn't bring myself to call *him* Craig ... I didn't even want to say his name out loud ... especially while we were in bed.

"Did you sleep with him, Jane?" he asked, with pain in his voice, like he had wanted to ask me this forever. "Did you sleep with a *married* man?"

"So, that's what's bothering you?" I returned, sitting up and flicking on my nightstand lamp. "Why the hell did you choose now to ask me about this?" I felt my cheeks getting hot.

Derek squinted at me in the glare of the yellow lamp light, and he propped himself up on his pillow. "You never told me what happened, and I never asked. I just thought it was something you wanted to keep to yourself. Now I get why you hid it from me. You're ashamed."

"Derek, what happened before we were together shouldn't matter. I don't ask you about *your* past relationships. We are *us* ... and I frankly don't understand why you're so upset. It's not like I see or talk to him anymore."

"Then why did you bother *buying* that magazine?" He insisted, now bolting upright like he was ready for battle. "And then lying to me about it?"

"Oh, for God's sake, Derek. Let's just give it a rest ... please?" I had no idea how to make this better and it scared me. *Was Derek going to punish me for having an affair with a married man?* I know it was reprehensible, but what could I say? I could not get into a time machine and go back and do things differently.

I turned the light off and shifted in bed so that my back was now to Derek, who had no problem falling asleep within ten minutes. *Why is it that guys can sleep no matter what?* I was the one who tossed and turned for the rest of the night, worrying about being a brazen slut in Derek's eyes ... a woman so heinous, she would commit the unspeakable and sleep with a married man.

There had to be worse things I could have done. I mean, you couldn't go to jail for what I did.

༺

THE NEXT MORNING, I awakened to an empty bed. Derek, who had the endearing habit of gently waking me each day and placing a hot cup of coffee on my nightstand, was nowhere to be found. I got up and made my way through the apartment, only to find Weezer, my fat silver tabby, lying on his back under the coffee table. Derek must have risen early, showered, and left for the day.

While I searched for a coffee cup, my thoughts were tainted by the fight with Derek. *Was it really a fight? Where would we go from here? Should I be straight with him about what happened with Craig or ignore it and hope it goes away?* Something told me Derek was not going to let it go. I supposed he had a right to know but there was a side of me that felt the opposite. It was my past and it was bad enough I had to deal with it.

On my way to the office, I called my friend Katherine Blakely, who was also heading to work. Kat, as her friends called her, divorced two years earlier and had recently been recruited by a headhunter to be CEO of a Fortune five hundred company. She had sold her own software company more than a year ago.

"Hi, Jane," she said. "How's my favorite ad executive?"

"I'm good," I answered. "At least I think I'm good."

"Talk to me," she coaxed.

"Well … I need your opinion about something," I started cautiously, pumping my brakes in the rush hour traffic. This was not a topic I liked to bring up with Kat because it involved the man we had both slept with, but it had ruined her marriage and was getting in the way of my relationship, so I really needed her advice.

"Shoot," she said brightly. I overheard honking and

knew she was stuck in traffic, too, so she had a bit of time on her hands.

"It's about Derek," I explained slowly. "He's a little … sensitive about my past … about a particular element of my past." I wasn't sure why it was so difficult to spit this out.

As usual, Kat was two steps ahead of me. "You mean Craig? But that was so long ago … is it because he's finally getting a divorce?"

"Listen, Kat, I never told Derek I slept with him." I was sitting at a red light and someone was blasting their horn loudly behind me.

"What did he think you were doing with him, playing Chinese checkers?" she quipped.

"I mean, he suspected it, but he only just found out Craig was married because of the dirt on the cover of every magazine in town. I think he's more upset that I slept with a married man. That's how I took it, anyway. I don't know what to do. He's mad at me. We had a fight last night. I don't want to lose him over someone like Craig."

Kat sighed. "I swear that man has a way of getting under everyone's skin. I don't want you to end up like me, either. My advice is that you don't tell him anything. Or better yet, lie to him. Tell him you didn't sleep with Craig, but you only considered it. Tell him what he wants to hear. That's the only way he'll let it go."

"I can't believe you're telling me to lie to my boyfriend," I responded, thinking that would be a lot easier than telling the truth.

"Believe me, if there's one thing in life I've learned about men, it's to know when to hold your tongue and when to outright lie. And this, my friend, is your time. You want this to go away? Then lie to him. He'll never know the difference and he'll be much happier. You will, too. I promise."

I suddenly laughed out loud at the absurdity of the situation. "I don't know, Kat ... it's pretty risky." Something made me lean over in the seat so I could slip off my black suede pump—I hated the way the car mats scuffed the shoe on my driving foot.

"Trust me on this one, Jane," she said before hanging up.

I thought about what Kat said and just could not shake my conscience. If I lied to Derek about what happened with Craig, he might find out later. He would never trust me again and that would be a bigger problem than me just looking like an immoral guttersnipe. No, the right thing to do would be to come clean with Derek. *But would he be able to accept it?* My stomach churned at the thought that he might not.

Two

AT THE OFFICE, EVERYONE was abuzz about rumors swirling around that Warren Mitchell & Partners was planning to go public. I hastened down the long hallway, passing several open doors, catching the dissonance of conference calls, the copy machine humming, and general chatter. I got to Jeffrey's office and his door was closed. The doors were all red—the office décor was mostly red, grey, and black, with pops of primary colors here and there. It was not like Jeffrey to ever close his door. I peered up at the plaque that read Jeffrey Vance, Partner, in grey lettering. I heard his muffled voice and realized he must be on a call. As soon as I thought he had hung up, I burst into his office without knocking.

"Well?" I demanded expectantly.

"Well what?" he asked, eyebrows raised. Jeffrey was used to my emotional outbursts and occasional theatrics, but he always welcomed me into his office, even if it were just to vent about clients.

"Is it true? Are we really going public?"

"Close the door, Jane," he replied, looking uneasily outside his office, and adjusting his collar. I turned, shut

Jeffrey's door, then sat across from him.

"You have to keep this to yourself, I swear, Jane, because the message needs to come from Warren to the employees." Jeffrey's grey-flecked hair stuck up slightly on one side, giving him a little-boy quality, even though he was over forty. I remembered meeting him for the first time when I was new to the agency—just a young receptionist trying to find her way among a bunch of cut-throat advertising types. He was the only one who was kind to me on day one. Our relationship had forged into a close friendship; I considered Jeffrey my 'work husband.'

"I promise I won't say anything," I pleaded, leaning in so I wouldn't miss one word.

"It's all true," he announced, still looking around as though someone had bugged the office. "We engaged an investment bank to evaluate the company for initial public offering … started the process months ago."

"An IPO?" I asked, thinking perhaps I had not heard right. "Thanks for waiting until now to share it with me." I picked up a pair of heavy brass knuckles that sat on the edge of his desk. He used it as a paper weight; however, we had a long running joke about which clients we wanted to use them on after particularly challenging days.

Jeffrey cocked his head at me. "First, put those down," he said with a smirk. "Jane, as much as I love you, you're not a partner and the only people who knew about it were Warren and me. I was sworn to secrecy."

I set the brass knuckles down gently. "Do you think it will actually go through?" I asked, still feeling hurt that Jeffrey had kept something so important from me.

"We have high growth prospects and should meet all the revenue and financial audit requirements," he explained. "It's the only way we can be competitive in the industry and it needs to happen. Warren has mixed feelings, but I persuaded him that it's the only way."

"'Mixed feelings'?" I repeated. "That doesn't sound good."

"Jane, you know how he is. He wants to be a big national agency, but he hates the thought of losing control over the decision-making. I told him I'm tired of losing big accounts to national agencies, especially when our creative's better."

Jeffrey was right. We had lost a string of big accounts because they wanted blue chip firms, like BBDO ... or Keller Whitman Group, I thought wryly. And I knew it bothered both Jeffrey and Warren to do all the work required to pitch the accounts and never get hired. Our biggest account was Brave Harlots, but we needed more accounts like it to put us on the map.

I bit my lip nervously. "What does all this mean for us?"

Jeffrey inspected his shoulder, pulling a thread off it. "For you, specifically? It means if you stick around, you could make a lot of money. Does that sound appealing to you?"

I felt my eyes bulging. "You're kidding," I uttered in disbelief.

"No, I'm not kidding," he responded, pushing his glasses closer to his forehead. "If you stay at the agency for a while after we go public, you'll build equity shares that will amount to a huge payout."

I just stared at him, silently considering the possibilities. I twisted a lock of hair between my fingers. *Could this finally be the break I need financially?* I envisioned Derek and I moving out of our little apartment on the corner of Lincoln and Colorado—moving to a bigger apartment in a better neighborhood or even buying a house. The thought of us hiring a real estate agent and looking for a new home together filled me with frissons of excitement.

"But, Jane," Jeffrey continued. "There's going to be pressure on us for short-term growth. We'll need to be more aggressive in pitching bigger-budget clients … everything we've already been doing, just with more intensity."

I thought about Warren answering to a board of directors and could not picture it. He just liked to do things his way. I sat back and observed Jeffrey. He had grown up since becoming partner. He even started wearing expensive suits, which was not like him at all. His office was almost as large as Warren's and he had decorated it similarly, with a black leather couch instead of Warren's signature red velvet one.

"What's the timing on all this?" I asked after a long pause.

Jeffrey shrugged. "That remains to be seen. There are a lot of factors that can slow down the process and we're trying to work through them now."

"When's Warren going to let the staff know?" I asked. News like this was going to send the nervous nellies into full panic mode.

"As soon we file the S-1 form. Once that happens, it's public information." Jeffrey stood up and walked around his desk to where I was sitting. He patted my shoulder and said, "Don't worry, Jane. This is for the best. It's time you started to look out for yourself."

Later in the day, I was in my office catching up on emails and realized I had not heard from Derek. It was already after three and it was not like him not to call or text. I picked up my cell phone and turned it around in my hand. I couldn't believe I was nervous to text him. *What was I afraid of?* I was already prepared to tell him what really went on with Craig, but I was reluctant to break the silence that started the previous night. I took a deep breath and dialed his number, secretly praying he would be in a good mood.

"Derek Lowell," he answered. He was in his car, likely driving to rehearsal.

"So formal," I commented.

"What's up?" he asked coldly.

"I wanted to hear your voice, that's all," I responded, eyeing the photo I had of us on my desk. It was one of our first photos together. I was in a red dress and Derek was in a grey suit. We were attending a holiday party for the USC professorial staff. We were smiling like two eager young paramours—blissfully ignorant of the pitfalls of cohabitating as mature adults. "Why are you giving me the silent treatment?"

"I got the impression you preferred silence, based on how last night's conversation ended."

"That's not true. I do want to talk. I want to be honest with you, Derek. It's important that you understand things." I didn't know where it was coming from, but I suddenly felt like I was on shaky ground with him. Derek had a way of being overly loyal and protective and then becoming heartless on a dime when he felt in any way slighted.

There was a long pause.

"Are you there, Derek?"

"I'm still here," he said.

"Are you up for talking tonight?" I asked in a voice that sounded weak and pandering. "I mean, could you take a break from rehearsal and meet me somewhere?" I felt my heart rate quicken. It's like he was already punishing me when he had not yet heard the whole story.

He waited a moment before responding, like he was thinking about it. "I'll see if I can get out around six when they take a dinner break. Can you meet me downtown?"

"Absolutely," I replied, a little too quickly, breathing a sigh of relief. "Want to meet at Vespaio?" Vespaio was a swanky Cali-Italian restaurant on Grand Avenue, located near the concert hall, so I knew it would be convenient for Derek.

"That's fine."

"See you then. Um … I love you," I added, longing for him to say it back. I needed so badly to hear it from him.

"Love you, too," he mumbled so casually, it came off as gratuitous, and he hung up.

I fidgeted in my office the rest of the day, trying to focus on work, but I could not keep my mind off how I was going to handle the talk with Derek. When I broke everything down, it was simple. I just needed to get this over with and hope he wouldn't hold it against me.

I recalled when Derek and I first met at a Dodgers game when he was dating a pretty, young architect. I was instantly drawn to him and we struck up a fast friendship after discovering our mutual love of music. While I had a secret crush on Derek from the very beginning, I soon realized he only wanted to be friends. After he broke up with the architect, we remained just friends for two full years. But there was always something between us—some possessive aura, despite the whole 'friendship' routine. We played jealous games, bickering, and trading barbs, going for months at a time without speaking—and then becoming best buddies again. One fateful New Year's Eve, he surprised me at my apartment to tell me that he wanted to be more than friends.

At the time, I had barely gotten over the poignant breakup and subsequent confusion, courtesy of His Highness—Craig Keller. But I was ready for Derek. I was ready to be with him long term.

WHEN IT WAS TIME to get on the road and head downtown, I ran into Warren on my way out to the parking lot. He was walking and texting, looking peeved about something. He barely looked up when he passed me, murmuring, "Good night, Jane."

As a VP, I never liked to leave before six, especially when I knew Warren never left the office until eight most nights but, under the circumstances, I had no choice. My relationship took precedence over work. Now that Derek and I lived together, it was more important than ever I put my personal life first. "Good night, Warren," I responded before exiting the building.

There was heavy traffic on the way downtown and I arrived at Vespaio a few minutes after six. The restaurant and bar were already jam-packed. I bypassed the hostess station, knowing Derek was already there waiting. Derek always asked for the same table. He had probably arrived twenty minutes early to ensure he could have that exact table. I spotted him immediately, sitting at *our* table, his back to the cross-hatched glass that covered what seemed like a zillion pieces of stemware. He had a large cup and saucer in front of him—likely a Café Americano—his favorite. When I approached, he glanced up and smiled cordially yet his demeanor seemed serious.

"Hey," he greeted me as I slid into the chair next to him, instead of sitting across. I found his hand under the table and held it for a minute while I looked him in the eye, trying to read him. His sandy hair shined under the restaurant lights and his deep-set hazel eyes were clear and bright. I couldn't help but think what a cute guy I lived with ... how lucky I was and how much I had to lose if this didn't go well.

"How was your day?" he asked, eyeing me pensively, like we were total strangers.

I tried to find a place to hang my handbag but the chairs had what I called 'soft shoulders'—I always identified that style of restaurant chair as 'man-designed,' because clearly there was no thought as to where a woman would hang her purse. I placed it firmly behind my back instead. "Well, my day was sort of weird. I found out our company may go public and I'm not sure how I feel about it. You know me and change," I added. "It's something I'm never comfortable with."

"Well, I'm not exactly a business major," he replied, "but shouldn't that be good news?" He took a sip of his coffee.

"That's what Jeffrey said, but I just have a strange feeling about it."

"Are you worried about your job?" he asked, now appearing concerned.

"Not really ... I can't quite explain it. I guess I'll just have to wait it out and hope for the best." I looked around for a server. I really needed a drink.

The Craig Keller conversation was imminent, and I was not sure how to start the awkward dialogue. When a waitress appeared, we ordered food and I asked for a glass of wine, hoping it would loosen me up. By the time the food came, and I had had several sips of wine, we had exhausted all the work small talk and I knew it was time to broach the sore subject.

"Derek ... about last night," I started. I looked up and traced my finger around the rim of the wine glass. A group of women near us burst out laughing loudly.

His eyes lowered, and he drew in a breath like he was readying himself for something awful. "I'm listening." He had been cutting his flat iron steak into small pieces, but he put both his knife and fork down to hear me speak.

I rested my fork and knife in the bowl of my baby kale salad. "Well ... you asked me what really happened with ... you know, *that guy*." A bead of sweat had formed on the back of my neck and I felt it rolling down my back underneath my navy DVF sweater dress.

"You mean Craig Keller," he shot back. "You can say his name, Jane. It's not like it's a mystery."

"With Craig," I corrected myself and continued. "You see, it started as a crush ... I mean, I met him at a party ... you were there, remember?"

"Yes, I was there, so you can skip that part. What happened after you met him?" There was a look in

Derek's eyes that made me uncomfortable, like he was cross-examining me, ready for the final judgment, but I kept going.

"He wanted to hire me at his agency," I explained, thinking back to the sordid interview where he toured me through deserted offices, leading me into his private art gallery where he promptly touched me inappropriately and tried to seduce me. "So, at first, it was a professional relationship." I winced slightly.

"You just told me you had a crush on him and now you say you wanted to go work for him?" Derek's tone was incredulous, and he moved his chair a few inches away from me. I noticed the couple at the next table had turned to gawk at us.

I lowered my voice and leaned toward Derek. "Well, I wasn't sure … you know, that it was a crush … I guess I was just impressed by him. He, you know, made the job look very attractive."

Derek narrowed his eyes a bit but didn't say anything.

"Um … so, I interviewed with him and, not long after, I signed a contract to go work there." I was having a flashback to the night I signed the contract with Craig in a suite at Shutters on the Beach in Santa Monica; how he tore my dress apart and had his way with me for hours; how he made sure I was available the rest of the weekend just for his pleasure; and how I let him.

"I had no idea you almost left Warren. Why did you change your mind?" Derek appeared astonished that I had never shared this with him, even though it happened before we officially got together. In fact, as I recalled, Derek and I were not even on speaking terms during that period.

"Well … I found out some things about him that were … um, pretty bad," I confided. "No, really … despicable." My thoughts went to the moment Jeffrey broke the ugly news to me about Craig's indiscriminate pursuit of women. I remembered feeling dizzying nausea after learning he had also slept with my friend Kat … and his secretary, and almost every one of his female employees. I remembered the disgrace and torture bubbling up in my throat to find out that I was one of hundreds of women he had seduced—to find out I was so horribly gullible in the situation—like a lamb being led to slaughter.

"Jane, you're not telling me what happened," Derek interrupted, suddenly impatient. "I know the guy's despicable. I knew it the night I saw you with him. That's not what I want to know. I want to know whether you slept with him, Jane. Did you have *sex* with Craig Keller?"

At that very moment, I saw Craig as plain as day, as heartless, attractive, and manipulative as he always was. My mind became a swirling collage of intimate moments and, as one racy scene after another popped into my head, I began to lose my nerve with Derek. I realized Kat was right. Nothing good would come from telling Derek that I slept with Craig. I could never share it with him. Even if he heard it from someone else, I would deny it. I would take it to my grave. I had to.

"No, Derek," I answered, finally and with confidence. "I never slept with Craig Keller."

Derek pulled in his chin and stared at me blankly, like what I said had not registered. He leaned toward me, so he was only an inch away, almost as though inspecting every detail of my face would help him decide whether I was telling the truth. "Are you sure, Jane?" He questioned. "I mean, you never did *anything* with him? Not even a kiss?"

"Nothing," I lied again, still seeing Craig's face, and feeling the painful, lustful memory of him touching me, kissing me, entering me … his penchant for biting, marking my body from head to toe so he could keep me solely within his grasp. I tried desperately to sweep the images from my mind but, like a stubborn stain, they would not go away. Then I added, knowing this would alleviate Derek's concerns forever, "I would never sleep with a married man, Derek, especially Craig."

When I uttered these last falsehoods, his expression finally softened.

"Jane," he said, obviously relieved. "I'm so happy to hear you didn't. You know I was prepared to hear the story of how you had an affair ... that you liked him or even loved him at one time and ... I have to tell you, Jane, I don't know how I could go on with you ... knowing you'd do something like that."

"Well, now you don't have to worry about any of that, do you?" I asked, feeling like a complete charlatan. But I remembered Jeffrey's words earlier that day ... that it was time I looked out for myself. Well, that was exactly what I was doing. This was about survival. Derek would cast me aside if I had told him what really happened with Craig. That was clear to me now. Kat was right.

I felt Derek's arm around me and the warmth of his body leaning against mine. When I looked in his eyes, he smiled. "I love you, Jane," he said with real emotion. "I love you so much—you have no idea." He kissed me on the lips, and I smelled the faint hint of garlic on his breath—probably from the rosemary potatoes he had been eating.

I was shocked he would kiss me this way in public. Derek shied away from public displays of affection and, over time, had imposed the same set of values on me. The fact that he was kissing me in public meant he fully believed me ... that life would go back to normal and that Craig would no longer be an obstacle to our happiness. I suddenly felt joyous, like I had miraculously saved our relationship ... with one lie ... one major, unadulterated lie.

WHEN DEREK ARRIVED HOME from rehearsal that night, I waited up for him. I had showered and put on the sexiest lingerie I owned. It was a blush-colored sheer body suit that left little to the imagination. But I was on a mission.

When I heard his key in the door, I grabbed a pair of high heels and stole noiselessly toward the kitchen. I peered around the corner into the kitchen and saw him getting a bottle of water from the refrigerator. His back was to me.

I slipped on the heels, snuck up behind him and put my hands over his eyes, startling him slightly. "I have a surprise for you," I said, voice oozing seduction. I could feel his suit rubbing up against my bare legs, the material still cool from the outside air.

"Really? What kind of surprise would that be?" he said, playing my game. Good old Derek was back.

"You can turn around but keep your eyes closed."

He obeyed as I took him by the hand and led him into the bedroom. Once there, I stood about a foot away from him and struck a sexy pose, hands on hips and leaning to one side. "Okay, you can open them now."

When Derek opened his eyes, they widened. "Wow .... what ... do we have here?" he said, approaching me slowly.

"Not much ... but that's the whole point," I answered.

He took off his jacket, unbuttoned his shirt, and gently pushed me on the bed, where we proceeded to make passionate love late into the night. I knew we both had an early morning the next day, but neither of us cared. My mission was accomplished.

Three

TIME WAS FLYING AND I could tell from the clandestine meetings between Jeffrey and Warren and a group of men I didn't recognize that the IPO had to be close to fruition. I think the employees knew it, too, because they nervously hovered in different areas of the office, in groups, swapping gossip and speculating as to who the men were, what was happening, and why. They were acting like children in the middle of their parents' marital crisis, where they sensed something was about to go down, but they didn't know what or how it would affect them. Even as a VP, I could relate.

One Friday morning in early March, Veronica, Warren's administrative assistant, summoned me to his office. When I got there, his door was shut.

"Just go on in, Jane, he's expecting you," she said, like there was a secret she couldn't share. Veronica had worked for Warren for more than seventeen years. An attractive, slender African American woman in her late fifties, Veronica was the one who originally took a chance on hiring me. She knew I had no experience except waitressing and that I had just acquired a degree in psychology before applying to answer phones at the front office. And while I never felt particularly close to Veronica based on her arms-length relations, I had grown to like and respect both her blind devotion to Warren and her dogged professionalism.

I knocked on Warren's door and opened it. He was sitting on the red velvet couch with Jeffrey. "Come in, Jane," Warren invited. I eyed the same pictures hanging on Warren's wall—ones which had been there since the day I started. There was one of JFK on one wall, Steve Jobs was opposite and one of David Ogilvy was right behind Warren's desk. Ogilvy was one of Warren's mentors—a fact that awe-inspired L.A.'s advertising community.

I entered, and my eyes met Jeffrey's. His face was expressionless.

"Jane," Warren began as I sat down across from them in one of the leather chairs, "we have some news to share but, for now, it can't leave this office."

He then proceeded to tell me about the IPO, carefully reassuring me that my job was safe and that the benefits of going public far outweighed the risks. Jeffrey just sat back and observed me, like he wanted to make sure I did not give up that he had divulged the news to me months earlier.

Warren leaned forward and placed his hands flat on his desk. "I want to talk to you privately before I make a formal company announcement. Do you have any questions?"

"When will it be official?" I asked, acting appropriately surprised at the news so Jeffrey would not be compromised.

"Within the next few months. We've just filed the S-1 form for the first SEC review, so the process has officially started and is now public information. There are a lot of factors which could delay it, so I can't commit to a time when we'll begin public trading."

"How will it affect my contract?" I asked. This seemed like an arduous process and I caught myself wondering if Jeffrey was up for it. He had always been a creative director, no matter how grown up or important his partnership had become. "Will you draw up a new one for me to sign?"

"That's a good question," he said running his hands through his thick greying hair. I studied Warren as he spoke, thinking he was still an attractive man, but he seemed to have aged quickly over the past few months. The fine lines on his face had somehow become deeper and his eyes weary. He couldn't be comfortable with this new arrangement. That was all there was to it.

"You see, Jane, there's something called a two-year earnout and that means if you stay here through that period, after the IPO, you'll do very well financially," Warren explained. "So, I hope you aren't thinking of leaving the agency … especially during this exciting time."

I looked from Warren to Jeffrey and back. I noticed Jeffrey was absent-mindedly rapping his pen against a file on his lap—almost to the level of annoyance.

"We have some very hard work in front of us and … well, we need your talent," Warren continued. "You've made us a lot of money by keeping our clients happy and delivering excellent service. We want that to continue, Jane."

I uncrossed my legs and crossed them with the opposite leg.

Jeffrey finally spoke: "And I'll be here just as I've always been to guide the creative team … I think our best work is ahead of us. You definitely want to be a part of it, Jane."

Was it my imagination or were they being overly optimistic? *Why was I feeling like they wanted to sell me on something they didn't believe in themselves?* I had no idea, but one thing was certain, neither one of them seemed sure of the outcome.

"Thanks for sharing the news with me," I said. "It's nice to know I'm appreciated. And speaking of our best work being ahead of us, I'd better get back to it."

Warren and Jeffrey nodded and exchanged glances before I rose to leave. I returned to my office heavy-hearted, feeling like everything was suddenly unfamiliar. I also felt woefully unprepared for the changes ahead.

I CALLED KAT ON my way home. Surely, with her business background, she would be able to shed some light on the situation.

"Kat," I said when she answered. "Where are you?"

"Still in the office," she replied. "What's going on with you? You sound anxious."

"Our company's going public and I thought perhaps you could help me with some of the details—you know, to prepare me for what's ahead."

"Wow … I didn't see that coming," Kat remarked. "Did you?"

"Only because Jeffrey shared it with me months ago. I am sworn to secrecy until Warren tells the employees, which will be Monday."

"Do you want to meet up? We can talk about it at my house where there's privacy. Or do you and Derek have a hot date?"

I knew Derek would not be home until after 10 p.m. "I can meet you," I answered, making a U-turn to get on the I-10 East freeway. We met at Kat's home in Laurel Canyon. The house was Tudor-style, the type of mansion that abundantly speckled L.A.'s most affluent neighborhoods. It resembled a medieval cottage, with its steeply pitched roof, decorative half timbering and embellished doorway. It always reminded me of a story book—I half-expected Hansel and Gretel to greet me at the door.

After she divorced her husband Jack, Kat had contemplated selling the house and downsizing but, given her booming business, she decided to stay. As far as I knew, Kat was not dating but I had a feeling there was someone in her life because she was always coy when I questioned her.

"How's everything?" I asked when she ushered me into her home. Kat was as striking as ever: She wore a rich yellow velvet dress with princess seams defining the bodice, a flattering style for her tall, slim figure. Her long blonde hair was swept up into a messy bun, which somehow, on Kat, still looked neat and well-groomed, yet effortless.

"Fabulous," she said, kicking off her nude patent pumps and slinking gingerly, barefoot along dark, hardwood floors into the kitchen to feed Joyce, her Irish Setter. I watched her flit around with exuberance— the profound energy that was the essence of Kat, yet there was something about her that seemed different. I couldn't put my finger on it, but Kat appeared to be having the time of her life. *Was it the new role? Or was it something else?* She came bounding out of the kitchen with a bottle of champagne and two flutes.

"What are we celebrating?" I asked, smiling, as Kat popped open the champagne and began pouring it into the flutes. I looked around for a place to sit—the house was elegant and decorated fluently, with a combination of rustic warmth and modern style. There was an oversized red shag rug and distressed black leather chairs in the living room.

"Do we need an occasion?" she asked with a coquettish grin. Even though I had known Kat for years, I was always struck by her beauty. I was amazed she wasn't dating some wealthy celebrity by now; she was such a catch.

"Okay … give it up, Kat. What has you so tickled

these days?" I asked, accepting the full flute of champagne she handed to me. I settled onto one of her overstuffed black leather chairs, anticipating some sort of a story.

Kat eyed me as though she were about to share something, but she simply held her flute out to me. "*Salut*," she said as we clinked glasses. "If I tell you something," she said, "you have to promise you won't tell anyone—not even Derek." She set her flute on the coffee table and hopped up on the chair across from me, tucking her feet underneath her.

"Of course, I won't," I promised. "Girl talk is always off-limits to the men in our lives. Everyone knows that."

She leaned over to pick up her flute and took a sip. "What if I told you I was dating someone much younger than me?" she asked, watching my expression carefully.

"Who is he?" I inquired with interest. "How much younger?"

"Well … as you know, I'm about to turn forty. He's twenty-five," she announced, pausing for my reaction.

"Why, Katherine Blakely, you cougar," I exclaimed, letting out a high-pitched laugh. "You know you're old enough to be his … aunt. For shame."

Kat laughed but her expression turned serious. "There's one small problem other than his age," she said. "He works for me."

I couldn't believe what I was hearing. Kat was a Harvard-educated, upper-crust New England woman. She was one of the most successful businesswomen I had ever met, and she had built an impeccable reputation over many years as a professional. There was no way she would throw it all away because of a crush on some boy-toy … one who was also her direct report.

"Kat," I began slowly, being careful how I worded things. "I'll bet he's amazing … he has to be if you're into him … and I have no problem with the age difference but … don't you think you're taking a dangerous risk?"

Kat put her hand up to stop me. "I know, I know— it's elementary HR—you don't date your employees."

"Then why would you pursue this?" I asked, now concerned.

"I just want him, Jane. You know what that's like."

I assumed she was referring to our mutual bedfellow, Craig Keller. "Yeah, I know—but you're smarter than I am," I responded, wondering immediately if she really was smarter than me. "You've learned. Haven't we both learned a valuable lesson?"

"I'm not talking about business ethics, Jane— I'm aware of the risks. I'm talking about pure sexual satisfaction."

"I don't know, Kat. I think there are some places you don't want to go and that's one of them. Does he know you like him?" I shifted my legs uncomfortably on her couch, noticing the latest issue of *Cosmopolitan* lying on her coffee table. One of the headlines read, 'Quick and Hot Sex Tips' with the subhead, 'Get in and out … in 10 minutes or less.' *Cosmopolitan* was a magazine we all eschewed because of its reliance on male/female stereotypes and silly promises of a charmed sex life. I was shocked Kat was reading it. She used to read nothing but *The New Yorker*.

"He's coming over in an hour, Jane … so, yes." Her blue eyes sparkled with excitement.

"Does he have a name?" I asked, thinking I was going to get nowhere with her on this one. It's like her mind was made up and there was no changing it.

"Caleb," she answered.

"How biblical," I commented without thinking. "Well, I just hope you're discreet. That's a scandal that could potentially ruin your life and, at the end of the day, will it be worth it?" As I said this, my thoughts drifted back to my lie to Derek, which Kat had suggested in the first place. Was it my imagination or was Kat becoming

37

a little reckless? Maybe it was a mid-life crisis. Or maybe she was one of those people who went through phases of promiscuity. After all, she slept with Craig Keller while she was married to Jack. I thought that was one isolated mistake, but maybe I didn't know Kat as well as I thought. Maybe she was more like Craig than I ever thought.

"Thanks for your support, Jane," she returned with sarcasm. "And, by the way, did you ever talk to Derek?"

"Yes," I answered, before taking another sip of champagne. "I took your advice and lied."

"Good girl," Kat replied, smiling roguishly. She pulled several pins out of her hair and I watched it fall past her shoulders in chunks.

"I'm not so sure that was the best thing I could have done." I suddenly felt somber.

Kat paused a moment to sip her champagne. "Why, because I disappointed you with my dating news?"

"Maybe we should talk about something else ... like the IPO," I interjected, thinking it was tough to watch Kat make such a horrendous mistake that could potentially cost her everything.

The way Kat explained it, the IPO was exactly what Jeffrey said and there was upside and downside. But she felt that it could be an incredible financial boon—a life-changer.

"Remember when you told me you'd never be in my league?" Kat asked after some discussion. "Well, you're very close to being right here with me," she stated excitedly. "All you have to do is stick it out for a while, work hard, and you'll start making some real money."

"I'm going to have to sign a new contract, you know," I said, recalling a time when I signed a contract with Craig Keller, who made sure it included stipulations about stealing clients from other agencies.

"Yes, and you should hire your own lawyer to look it over before you sign anything," she answered. "You have leverage there and Warren loves you, but his lawyers will be looking out for his best interests, not yours. And once a board of directors and shareholders come in with their own agenda, you never know how that'll play out over time."

I made a face. "That all sounds so complicated. Do you have a lawyer to recommend?"

"Of course," Kat replied. "I'll forward her contact information. And I'll help you anyway I can."

Regardless of my impending new financial status, I went home that night feeling sad. The Kat I knew always did the right thing ... at least that's what I thought. I felt like I didn't know her anymore, and it bothered me. *I mean who was this Caleb, anyway?* And, at twenty-five, why did he deserve Kat's exclusive attention? After all, she was no ordinary woman—she was Kat.

L

FOR THE FIRST TIME in months, Derek was in the apartment waiting for me when I walked in the door. Derek was an excellent cook and had made a fancy dinner as a surprise. It was beef tenderloin with a port, bacon, and shallot sauce, green beans, carrots, and gratin potatoes with oyster mushrooms and gruyère cheese. It was the kind of meal reserved for special occasions, like New Year's or Valentine's Day but it was only a Friday night on a not-so-special week.

The apartment smelled like heaven and Derek was stirring the port wine reduction. A mix tape I made for Derek when we first got together was playing on our sound system. It was a couple of years old and I cringed at the sappiness of the songs I had selected for Derek.

"What's all this?" I asked. Derek appeared smartly domesticated in his dark blue chef's apron, I thought, as he set his spoon down and grabbed my hand, pulling me in for a kiss.

"It's just because," he replied. "I requested the night off and decided we needed a nice dinner. I hope you're hungry."

"I am hungry," I declared, opening pots, and smelling the aromas of various dishes on the stove. My cell phone rang, and we both knew it was my grandparents because I gave them their own ringtone—*Surrender* by Cheap Trick. I groaned as the lyrics, *Mommy's all right, daddy's all right, they just seem a little weird,* blasted through the kitchen. "Do you mind if I take this?" I asked Derek.

He grinned. "Please do."

Derek had gotten used to my grandparents calling at odd times and he rarely complained. He knew they had raised me in the absence of my parents and that they were the only parents I knew. My grandparents loved Derek, although now, instead of badgering me to find a boyfriend, they badgered me about when we were going to get married as opposed to "shacking up," as Grandma called it. "A man won't buy the whole cow if he can get the milk through the fence," was another of her inappropriate and endlessly irritating comments.

"Hello?"

"Jane, honey, what are you doing?"

"Getting ready to eat, Grandma. Derek made us a fancy dinner." I hoped she would get the hint that I didn't want to be on the phone long.

"This late?" She inquired in an obnoxiously loud tone. "I don't understand you kids these days … why don't you eat at a proper hour? It's almost bedtime."

I rolled my eyes at Derek. "Grandma, we both have jobs that keep us working late and this is the only time we have to eat dinner. Plus, I'm lucky to have such a wonderful boyfriend, who has the cooking skills of a professional chef." As I said this, I leaned over and gave Derek a peck on the cheek.

"That's very nice, pigeon. I called to see if you and

your professional chef want to come over for brunch on Sunday. Rabbi Lenny is coming over and I thought it would be a nice time for us to spend together."

"Really, Grandma? Rabbi Lenny, huh?" I knew where this was headed. "Are you planning a wedding, or did someone die?"

"No, smarty pants … I just thought it would be nice for all of us to be together."

"I'll ask Derek and get back to you," I responded, watching Derek light the taper candles on our dining room table. He had put out our best black placemats and matching cloth napkins. I really had no interest in seeing Rabbi Lenny but was not sure how to get out of it. Derek and I had not seen my grandparents for weeks and it was time we visit.

"Can you ask him now?" she badgered.

I sighed. "Hold on."

"Derek, do you want to have brunch this Sunday with my grandparents and their rabbi?" I asked, purposely without covering the phone.

"Do they want to convert me? I don't think I'm ready for that," he laughed, wiping his hands on his apron.

"I won't let them. Yes or no."

"Tell them I look forward to seeing them." Derek was one of the most family-oriented men I'd ever met, and he made it a point to be solicitous of my grandparents. I had met Derek's family in Seattle several times during our courtship and, while they weren't thrilled either that we were 'living in sin', his parents genuinely liked me—especially his father—and were kindhearted and encouraging about our relationship.

I remembered meeting his parents for the first time—David and Patricia Lowell. David was a successful dentist and Patricia a loving housewife. Their home was the most all-American home you could possibly imagine, a two-story tract model in an incredibly well-manicured and maintained development. It was so suburban, so agonizingly normal, that I immediately felt out of place. How would a family who lived in this neighborhood accept their son's Jewish girlfriend who grew up in a non-traditional family in Southern California and had a job selling ideas to businesses? I was so nervous at our first lunch that I spilled my iced tea all over his mother's antique tablecloth. Then, out of the blue, my period started and bled through my white shorts while we were out on his parents' boat, sailing on Puget Sound. His mother was so understanding about everything. I remember her kindness in seeking out tampons for me—finding a box in the bathroom on the boat. They had been left behind by Derek's sister Carey. Of course, I was happy to accept the items, though mortified that so many things had gone wrong while I was trying to make a good first impression. She gave me her sweater to tie around my waist and hide the blood stains until I could get to dry land and change my clothes.

I wasn't too sure of his sister Carey, who was older than Derek and overly protective of him. She was married to a straight-faced accountant named Brandon and they had two young boys, Lindsey and Ethan. At first, I thought Carey was turned off by my profession because she never treated me with warmth, only distrust. I hoped the relationship would improve over time because I knew how much Derek loved and respected Carey. I simply had to make her my friend.

I got back on the phone. "Grandma, we'll see you Sunday," I confirmed.

"Great, pigeon, 12:30 and … can you do me a favor and dress modestly … you know, it's the rabbi and all."

"I'll be sure to show up in a turtleneck and long skirt," I replied, smiling princess-style into the receiver before hanging up. In truth, that was the right outfit to wear in the presence of a man like Lenny, whose real name was

Rabbi Leonard Wolf. Grandma insisted on calling him Lenny and *Boychik* much to Grandpa's chagrin. And the Rabbi's surname was appropriate. He had done my Bat Mitzvah, and all I could remember while refining my Hebrew was the lecherous way in which he eyed me as a pre-pubescent teen. He had a history of opioid addiction from a motorcycle accident when he was in his twenties, and he had become sober through Narcotics Anonymous. But, somehow, he replaced one addiction with another, and turned his obsessive personality toward sex. Now that I was grown up, he stared freely at my breasts and planted wet kisses on my lips every time he saw me, which made my stomach lurch.

During dinner, I noticed Derek watching me intently as I ate. "This is really delicious, honey," I remarked. "You've outdone yourself."

Derek said nothing but continued to watch me eat. He almost seemed apprehensive as he picked up his wine glass and put it down again without drinking.

"Is there anything wrong?" I asked.

"No … why?" he stammered, looking embarrassed.

I set down my silverware and looked him right in the eye. "Because you're looking at me funny."

"Maybe it's because there's something I want to tell you," he said cryptically.

"That I'm the most beautiful girl you've ever met and that you will love me forever?" I picked up my glass of Bordeaux and took a generous sip.

"How did you guess?" he said, chuckling nervously. Something was obviously bothering him.

"No, really, Derek. You seem nervous or something … tell me … what is it?"

Instead of answering me, he got up and disappeared into the bedroom.

"Derek," I called after him. "Where are you going?"

"Wait there," I heard him say. "I'll be right back."

We had finished dinner, so I began clearing the plates, rinsing, and putting them into the dishwasher. When Derek returned, he had his hands behind his back and was regarding me strangely again.

"Derek, what's gotten into you? What did I do now?" I asked, suddenly wondering if he had somehow found out I lied about sleeping with Craig Keller and was upset with me again.

"You've definitely done something, Jane," he replied. "You …" his voice trailed off as he moved his hands from behind his back, revealing a small box.

I put the dishes down and stared at the box. "I … what?"

"You made me fall in love with you," he uttered as he opened the box. From where I was standing, it appeared to be a sparkling diamond, and, upon closer inspection, it was princess cut and encased in an elegantly simple platinum setting.

I gasped. "Are you … what are you saying, Derek?"

"I want to marry you, Jane Mercer," he stated, eyes misting slightly. "Will you make me the happiest man on the planet and be my wife?"

My mind was careening as I stared at Derek in shock. This was why he wanted to know what really happened with Craig Keller. He must have bought the ring and had this planned. He wanted to make sure I was marriage material. I didn't know whether to burst out crying from the guilt of having lied or let the tears of joy flow down my face. It was such an unexpected moment and I had no idea how to react. Yes, this is what I wanted my whole life—to meet a man like Derek and live happily ever after. He was, of course, my prince, my knight in shining armor, but I had lied—lied to save myself, and he had believed me. Would I be able to accept his proposal, or would the same awful subject destroy the happiness that was being put before me now?

"Jane," Derek said cocking his head to one side, still holding the box open. "Did you hear me? How come you're not saying anything?"

It occurred to me that I had been silent a little too long and Derek must be worried that I was getting ready to reject him. "I—I don't know what to say," I said, eyes welling up with tears. "I mean, just a couple of months ago, I thought you were going to break up with me."

"That's all over now. I'll never bring it up again," Derek said, brows furrowing slightly at my reaction, which he obviously didn't expect. "I love you, Jane. And I want to be with you forever."

I stood there, as if frozen, staring at him, thinking about what was really happening. I was twenty-eight and Derek was thirty. We had been dating for more than two years, living together for a year plus. We had everything in common and were famously compatible. Our families approved, and we had our whole lives ahead of us. There was absolutely no reason why we should not get married. Still, something was gnawing at me, something making me feel as though the timing was off ... or wasn't it? I was terribly conflicted.

"Jane, if your answer is no, please just tell me," he said delicately. "Because, honestly, I don't know why you're just standing there not saying anything." Derek's hazel eyes were tinged with sadness and I had an epiphany that there was nothing wrong and that, in fact, everything was quite right. That's what scared the hell out of me.

"Derek," I sputtered out finally. "I'm sorry ... I just ..."

"You just what?" He looked as if I were about to crush him without mercy.

"I ... yes," I managed to let drop. "Yes, I want to get married ... to be your wife ... yes, Derek."

Derek breathed a huge sigh of relief, grabbed me and

threw his arms around me. He held me close for what seemed like an eternity. When he finally loosened his grip, he gently removed the ring from the box and took my left hand.

He peered deep into my eyes with a look that melted me, and he slid the ring on my finger while my hand trembled. Then we kissed … we kissed right there in the kitchen among all the pots and pans and cooking utensils … in the place where we lived every day together, eating and talking and sleeping and breathing. We were going to be husband and wife. This was it.

Four

ECSTATIC ABOUT OUR ENGAGEMENT, I wanted to call everyone at once and announce the news. I called my grandparents first.

"What's wrong, pigeon?" Grandma demanded when she answered. "There must be something wrong for you to be calling this late. I thought you two love birds were having a fancy dinner?"

"Well ... Grandma, I'm calling because I thought you should know that Derek and I are ... engaged to be married!"

"What?" she exclaimed in a mock surprised manner. I realized Derek must have done the gentlemanly thing and requested my hand in marriage before asking. "Bruce, pick up," she yelled without shielding the phone from her deafeningly loud voice, which sounded like a wounded hyena, and caused a ringing in my ear. "Bruce ... pick up the phone this instant. Jane and Derek are getting married!"

When Grandpa got on the extension, he was already excited. "Janie, you're getting married to Derek! We couldn't be happier for you, love."

"Have you set a date?" Grandma asked. "Will you have

a Jewish wedding? Should we talk with Rabbi Lenny on Sunday?" Grandma was eager to sew up the details.

"Grandma," I said, eyeing Derek, who was smiling and squirting dish detergent into the sink. He always insisted on washing the dishes the old-fashioned way rather than rinsing them and loading them into the dishwasher. "We aren't rushing things—no date yet and we haven't discussed the wedding at all. So, please, be cool with the Rabbi ... okay? Just for now. I wanted you to be the first ones to know, that's all."

"And the ring ... did he give you a ring? What does it look like? Is it a big rock?" she pushed.

Oy, did she ever stop? "Yes, Grandma. It's beautiful," I said glancing down at the glittering ring on my finger. "You'll see it Sunday. Bye now."

Derek was busy cleaning the rest of the dishes.

"Are you going to tell your family?" I asked, carefully setting our wine glasses on the counter. Derek did not allow me to wash the impossibly thin stemware we used on special occasions. He imposed that rule the day I broke two at the same time.

"I already did," he answered calmly, wiping a bowl, and setting it to the side of the sink. "I told them I was going to ask you tonight—so they know. I'll call and give them details tomorrow."

"Did you tell Carey?" I asked, trying to sound casual. Derek knew I was sensitive about her opinion.

"Of course," he said. "She couldn't be happier for us."

Sometimes Derek was oblivious to the nuances of his sister Carey's attitude. He never understood why I thought she didn't like me. Girls just always know these things better than men.

After we finished cleaning the kitchen together, we went to bed and made love. But when I went to sleep, I had a crazy dream ... about Craig Keller. I was marrying Craig, not Derek, and we were walking down the aisle of a Catholic church, having an elaborate ceremony. He looked gorgeous in a black tuxedo with long tails. I wore an angelic white dress, and a priest was officiating the wedding. As soon as we were pronounced man and wife, I looked up at his handsome face and into those irresistible green eyes and we kissed. Suddenly, he disappeared down the aisle. I tried to keep up but felt myself losing sight of him. Every step became slower and heavier until I knew I had lost him for good in a crowd of people who were barely acquaintances. My angelic dress had transformed into rags and I was suddenly out in the cold, dirty and lost ... I didn't have a phone, so I couldn't call for help. I just wandered down an unfamiliar street in a dreary neighborhood looking for someone I knew— someone, anyone who could help me find my way. I woke myself up in terror, my eyes immediately darting at the clock ... 2:30 a.m. I felt Derek next to me, breathing heavily, in deep slumber. I slid my foot under his warm leg to ensure we would never be separated, even in sleep. I was so grateful Derek was there and that it had only been a bad dream—a nightmare.

ƛ

IT WAS SATURDAY MORNING and I awakened at 10:30 to the sweet aroma of French toast cooking. I yawned and slowly rose, wandered to the kitchen where Derek was busily cooking breakfast. He looked up as I entered the kitchen.

"Good morning, sleepyhead," he greeted me. "You were out like a light. I'm glad you slept. How do you feel?"

"Good," I replied, suddenly remembering the nightmare about Craig Keller, and feeling frightened. *How is it that I could have such a dream?* I twisted my new diamond engagement ring around my finger to ensure it was still in place. "Did you sleep well?"

"Great," he answered, flipping over the French toast

in the pan and getting two plates from the cupboard.

I advanced toward him and circled my arms around his waist from behind as he cooked, smelling his scent through the back of his shirt. My eyes fixed on an ornament hanging from one of our kitchen cabinet knobs. It was a wreath of small clay starfish, assorted shells and pale blue pebbles overlapping with each other. A little sign on it read, "The Beach is Calling." I recalled the day we went to Catalina Island and found that ornament in a local shop. Derek celebrated Christmas so he was excited to start a collection for our own tree. We had only been living together for two months.

He spun around and gave me a kiss, running his fingers through my tangled bed hair and commenting, "You need a good brushing, girl."

"Yeah?" I said. "That's what I usually say to Weez."

He laughed. "Just so you know, Weez has been fed," he informed me. "I've decided if we're going to be married, I need to officially adopt him as my fur son."

"Does that mean you'll love him like he's your own?" I asked. "Maybe I should have a little talk with him and see how he feels about you as his daddy."

Derek shimmied the spatula underneath a piece of French toast and flipped it. "I think you'll need some caffeine before that conversation," Derek said before handing me a cup and gesturing toward the coffee pot.

Again, I felt like the luckiest girl on earth. I knew it was just a matter of time before we would be planning our wedding: thinking about a date, guest list, wedding songs, décor, and food. I was beyond excited and couldn't wait to tell Marisa and Kat. They would be surprised, there was no doubt.

L

LATER, ON SATURDAY, I called an emergency lunch with the girls to officially make my announcement. They had no idea, other than I had big news for them.

We decided to meet at Fred Segal on Sunset for some shopping and then have lunch at the café, where it was common to spot celebrities. The truth was, I felt like a celebrity—no, I felt like a princess, getting ready to break the news to my best friends about finally marrying my prince.

I entered the store, which was right off Sunset Boulevard, and I touched things here and there. I was in the mood for shopping—fashion, pampering—everything that a bride would do before her wedding. I lingered near a Proenza Schouler slip dress with a green and black gingham print, thinking it would make a great honeymoon dress. I daydreamed about Derek and I vacationing in Hawaii—me in the gingham dress wearing a white orchid lay around my neck. I had never felt such pure joy in my life.

I spotted Marisa and Kat in the café, seated at a sterile white table, and I beamed. I could not wait to share my engagement.

It turned out, I didn't need to say anything, because Marisa the hawk noticed my ring right after we ordered our iced teas. "Oh my God—Jane—is that what I think it is?" she exclaimed, grabbing my hand, and holding it as she stared down at my finger.

"What?" Kat chimed in. "Is our Jane getting *married*?" she said, smiling with her mouth wide open. She wore a black racerback tank without a bra, and I could see her nipples poking out from behind the fabric. Kat always wore a bra. My mind immediately went to Caleb, thinking that he must have been the inspiration for Kat's decision to go braless in public.

"Yes," I announced, trying to avert my eyes from Kat's nipples—they were standing at attention and seemed to be staring right at me. "It's official. Derek asked me last night."

"Were you expecting it?" Marisa asked, unwilling to let go of my hand. She was continuing to examine my ring. "I mean, did he act like he was going to propose?"

I shook my head and took a sip of my tea. "Not in the slightest. I actually thought he was going to break up with me only a couple of months ago." I caught Kat's eye at that moment and her smile disappeared.

Marisa looked puzzled and let go of my hand. "Why would you think that? He's totally into you, Jane. Everyone knows that."

Kat's eyes met mine again and this time, she shook her head and mouthed the word, "don't." I swallowed hard and decided it was best if Marisa remained ignorant of the Craig conversation and subsequent lie, as well as Kat's exploits of late. It would ruin the occasion, I thought, ruefully.

The waitress approached our table to take our orders, which was a welcome break in the awkward dialogue about how Derek could have broken up with me as opposed to asking me to tie the knot.

"Have you two set a date?" Marisa asked as soon as the waitress had left. She was now eager for details.

"Not yet ... but you'll both be the first to know," I said, smiling again. "I still can't believe it. It's like a dream that finally came true." As I said this, I couldn't help but be reminded of the dream I had—about Craig and I getting married. I tried to shake it off but couldn't get the images out of my mind.

"You deserve this, Jane," Kat commented wistfully. "You and Derek deserve happiness."

"We want to help you plan every detail," Marisa declared. "You don't have a sister, or a mother, so consider us your official wedding planners. I'm imagining a beach wedding," she offered sighing. "If I'm still with Ewan, maybe he can perform at your reception. Wouldn't that be cool?"

"That's a great idea, Marisa," I responded, laughing. "But I doubt we can afford Brave Harlots."

"You never know," she said mischievously, shifting in her chair to lean toward me. "I suppose I'd better stay with him."

"Have you thought about the dress yet?" Kat asked with bright eyes, tossing her blonde hair to one side, nipples still protruding out of her top. "I'm picturing something simple—something strapless."

Of course, you are. The more exposed skin, the better.

"Are you going to wear white?" Marisa asked, innocently. Kat and I exchanged mortified glances and she shook her head as if to say, 'don't go there, Jane.'

"I haven't decided yet; but I want you both to go shopping with me to find the perfect dress—once we have a date, that is." Marisa's white dress question really had me confused. I wondered whether I should wear a white dress at all, given my past.

ON SUNDAY, DEREK AND I drove to my grandparents' house in Los Alamitos, which was in the Long Beach area. Derek had been several times already and always got a kick out of going into my childhood bedroom.

"There's so much purple," he would always say. "It's hard to imagine you so girlie."

When we arrived, Grandma was already waiting outside in the front yard, puffing away on a Salem Light. Her blonde-grey beehive was neatly piled atop her head, and she had taken extra time to strategically place curlicues of hair around her face and neck. She wore a fuchsia maxi dress with a ruffled bodice, and a snare of matching tangled beads hung around her neck and on both wrists. Clearly, she had dressed up for the occasion. When she spotted Derek's car, she threw her cigarette on the ground and stomped it out with her silver kitten-heeled mules.

"Here comes my grandson-in-law," she squawked as we got out of the car. She ambled over to the driver's side, beads clanking a discordant symphony, as Derek emerged. "Come over here, my handsome boy, and give me a big hug."

"Hi Barbara," he greeted her shyly. I watched as Grandma proceeded to give Derek a bear hug and didn't appear to want to let him go.

"Grandma let the man breathe," I protested. "He wants to live long enough to get married."

"Pshaw," Grandma retorted before letting Derek go and turning her attention to me. "And, you—let me see that ring, pigeon."

Before I could react, she grabbed my left hand and bent over so she could inspect my ring. "*Oy vey*, it's a huge rock," she exclaimed. "How long did you have to save for that, Derek? I didn't think you musicians made *bupkis*."

"Grandma, you're embarrassing us," I chastised. "Now, let's go in and say hi to Grandpa. He's probably wondering where we are." Derek caught my eye and we both smiled while corralling Grandma into the house. The house, an old 1970s rancher, had pretty much stayed the same since my childhood. The shag carpet was dark brown, or the Crayola equivalent—Burnt Sienna—and deeply worn. The furniture was a mixture of earth tones and heavy dark wood. Grandma always kept it dimly lit so, regardless of the horrendous décor, it always felt sort of cozy.

Grandpa was busy stocking the bar with booze and mixers when we walked in. He stopped immediately when he saw us. "Derek," he called out heartily, walking over and holding his hand out to Derek. "Congratulations, I hear we're going to be family." Grandpa was in his Sunday best: a blue short-sleeved button down tucked into black pants. His white Einstein-like hair stuck out in every direction.

"That's right, sir," Derek answered, taking Grandpa's hand, and shaking it. "I'm looking forward to it."

"And Janie," Grandpa added, giving me a hug and kiss. "You must be very happy."

"Bruce, get a load of Jane's ring. It's the most beautiful diamond I've ever seen," Grandma said. "How many carats is that, Derek?"

"It's a little over two and a quarter," Derek replied. I could tell he was still not entirely at ease with Grandma's brashness and complete absence of tact. Derek was raised not to talk about business or money in public, so he must have been uncomfortable with Grandma's boorish behavior.

"Never mind, Grandma. Do you need help with anything? Where's Rabbi Wolf?"

"Our *boychik* will be here soon," Grandma answered with a wink. Rabbi Wolf was in his fifties, but Grandma perceived him as young. "You know how much Lenny likes you, Jane. He'll be happy to know you're marrying such a wonderful man."

Sure. He will be more overjoyed that he can ogle my ass again. I didn't bother warning Derek about Rabbi 'Lenny'—I didn't think he would react well to his lascivious reputation.

"Would you two lovebirds like a mimosa?" Grandma asked.

"Mimosa?" I repeated. "You mean you have champagne and orange juice?" I couldn't help but be surprised at Grandma's sudden sophistication. She only drank pink wine out of a box, so I shuddered to think of what her version of a 'mimosa' might be.

"Don't act so hoity-toity, pigeon," she said glaring at me. "Who doesn't know what a mimosa is?"

And with that, she disappeared through the wooden saloon doors into the kitchen, promptly emerging with a cheap bottle of sparkling wine and a family size bottle of Orange Crush.

"Bruce," she yelled across the room at a thunderous decibel level. "We need some glasses."

Grandpa promptly delivered four juice glasses, ones that had not been replaced since my childhood, and then I watched, in horror, as Grandma proceeded to mix four of her special concoctions, smiling and chattering about how lovely it was to have mimosas for Sunday brunch.

I bit my lip and shot a glance at Derek, who was evidently amused at the spectacle before him. I patted his arm and said, "See what you're marrying into, honey? You still have time to change your mind."

"I heard that, Jane," Grandma scolded as she handed each of us a neon-orange-colored drink. "Now let's have a toast."

"To Jane and Derek," she pronounced cheerfully. "May you have happiness and joy throughout your lives together. *Mazel Tov!*"

We all clicked glasses and I felt a wave of emotion. Despite the bickering Grandma and I did most of the time, I knew she was happy for us and I realized at that moment that I was not going to have my grandparents forever. The mere thought saddened me.

Derek and I settled on their blue crushed velvet La-Z-Boy couch and barely sipped Grandma's creations, they tasted so horrific. I heard the doorbell ring and Grandma bolted to the door and flung it open, ushering in Rabbi Wolf.

"Lenny," she exclaimed. "Come in, come in ... I'm so glad you could make it."

Rabbi Wolf entered the house. He wore khaki pants with a blue and pink argyle sweater. He always wore loafers without socks. He was of medium height and mostly bald. What was left of his hair was salt and pepper. He wore mirrored aviators and didn't take them off right away when he walked inside. I knew what he was doing. It was easier to gawk at me when I couldn't see where his eyes were looking. I sighed. This was going to be a long brunch. I felt Derek put his arm around me, which was unusually comforting at that moment.

"Jane," Grandma bellowed as though we were at a loud rock concert. "Come say hi to Rabbi Lenny and introduce Derek." Then she turned to Rabbi Wolf and said, "Jane has some big news."

I stood up, smiled princess-style and approached Rabbi Wolf with Derek. "Hello, Rabbi. It's nice to see you."

"Ah, Jane, you look lovely today," he said, smiling widely, mirrored glasses still firmly in place. We hugged, a little too closely, and I knew he could feel my breasts cushioned against his chest. Then, he tried to plant the inevitable wet kiss on my lips, but I quickly turned my face to the side, so he got my cheek instead.

"Let me introduce you to my fiancé, Derek," I announced serenely, gesturing to Derek.

"Nice to meet you," Derek offered, holding his hand out to Rabbi Wolf, who inspected him without smiling.

"Your *fiancé?*" he asked, accepting Derek's hand. "Well, how about that? Little Janie Mercer has a fiancé. Now isn't that nice. What business you in, Darrin?"

"It's actually Derek," he corrected politely. "I play violin for the L.A. Philharmonic."

"Oh, you're a musician!" he exclaimed and then turned to me. "You know what they say about living with a musician, don't you? It's the same as being homeless."

I felt my cheeks flush. "Rabbi, being in the L.A. Philharmonic is the real deal—it's not like he's some broke lounge singer." I was trying to keep the anger out of my voice. *How dare he say that?*

Rabbi Wolf had already returned his focus to Derek. "You're Jewish, right?"

Of course, he had to go there.

"No, I'm not," Derek answered, not volunteering more information.

"Then, what are you?" he interrogated, mirrored aviators still in place.

"I was raised Episcopalian," Derek responded.

"Oh, you mean Catholic-light," the rabbi joked. "Half the guilt."

"Oh, please, Lenny," Grandma cackled, elbowing him in the ribs. "Talk about guilt. We Jews are the worst when it comes to that and you know it."

I was utterly cringing at the hideously inappropriate conversation and silently apologizing to Derek for being under the scrutiny of Rabbi Lech. I never should have agreed to this brunch, but there was nothing we could do now except smile and act semi-cordial.

"Would you excuse us for a moment?" I said, taking Derek's hand. "We're going to step out for some fresh air." I led Derek out through the kitchen and into the backyard. My old rusty swing set still sat in the corner of the yard. The firepit, which was the patio's centerpiece was surrounded by mismatched lawn chairs and the odd folding end table. I inhaled the cloyingly sweet scent of Grandpa's gardenias. He loved to garden and spent his retirement planting, weeding and manicuring the lawn.

"I'm sorry," I said immediately to Derek. "I owe you on this one."

"What are you so worried about?" he responded looking down at me and putting his arms around my waist.

"Don't tell me you're having a good time," I answered, shaking my head in disdain. "I mean, first she starts with that disgusting drink … that color is not even found in nature, let alone in a proper mimosa—and then the rabbi comes in and starts in with all that stuff. I'm mortified."

"Jane, this is your family. And I'm honored to be a

part of it," he replied, smiling encouragingly. "But, do you think your Grandma will be insulted if I don't drink that thing she made?"

We both started laughing and then we couldn't stop. It was all so surreal and hilarious at the same time. When we finally calmed ourselves, I threw my arms around Derek's neck and kissed him on the lips. He kissed me back and soon we were making out in my grandparents' yard. Our hot and heavy session was soon interrupted by Grandma's booming voice.

"Hey, you two ... will you stop necking long enough to get some brunch? We have bagels and lox, all kinds of *schmear*, whitefish salad and herring, fruit, you name it. Now come on in. There will be plenty of time for that stuff once you're married."

Derek looked horrified that Grandma had caught us making out and he just stood there, motionless.

"Come on, honey ... let's go in," I said quickly to Derek. "Don't worry. She really didn't see anything."

Grandma held the door open for us and, as we walked past her, she eyed Derek and said, "come on in, lover boy," and to me, "get in here, hot pants."

There was simply no end to the humiliation.

When the brunch was thankfully over, and we could make a swift getaway, we took the opportunity to leave.

I thanked Grandma and Grandpa, hugged and kissed them. Derek did the same and we got back into the car and drove toward Santa Monica. Whew, I thought, we got through it.

Five

MONDAY ARRIVED, AND I entered the office in a rare state of enthusiasm, something it usually took me until Wednesday to achieve. I felt like a different person—a beautiful woman engaged to Derek and soon to become Mrs. Jane Lowell. It had a nice sound to it. I considered whether I might keep my old name. Mrs. Jane Mercer Lowell. I liked that, too. I immediately began practicing my signature on a notepad and contemplating which was best.

Jeffrey barged into my office, temporarily bursting my pre-marital bliss bubble.

"You free?" he asked impatiently. "I need your help with something."

"Of course," I replied, smiling with my newly found peaceful confidence. "Anything you need."

"What's with you, anyway?" he demanded, eyeing me with suspicion.

"What do you mean?" I asked disingenuously.

"I don't know," he said. "You're usually in a crap mood on Mondays, that's all. Today you seem to be floating or something."

"Maybe it's because I just got engaged, Jeffrey," I

announced, holding out my left hand to him so he could see my ring.

He broke into a huge smile. "Wow—look at you—congratulations," he exclaimed, examining my ring. "Derek sure opened the purse strings for that beauty," he added. "He's a good man, Jane. I've always liked him. Good for you."

"Thanks, Jeffrey." My voice was filled with happiness.

"Now, can we get to work?" he said, turning right back into business mode and taking a seat across from my desk. "There's a potential new client coming in later today and I need you to run the meeting. Warren and I are going to be busy with this IPO for the next few months."

"Of course," I replied. "Who's the client?"

"For once, it's not entertainment," he said crossing his legs and leaning back in his chair. "It's fashion—women's fashion, which is why you'll be perfect."

"Now you have my attention," I responded eagerly, instinctively scanning my outfit to ensure it was impressive enough for a meeting. "What kind of fashion? Do you have photos? A website?"

"There's all of that," he answered. "They're based in London and want to get their brand out in the U.S. They need an enhanced website, national media plan, and completely new assets, which includes a photo shoot."

I was beyond excited. This was right up my alley. "What's the brand?" I asked, now almost salivating at the idea of representing a fashion client.

"The designer's name is Noel Marques and his brand is simply 'Noel'. He's the hottest up-and-coming designer, and he took the lead at London's Fashion Week this year. They would like to have their new campaign ready to go within the next couple of months, so they can capitalize on some of the momentum with their launch in the States."

I was half-listening to Jeffrey as I did an internet search on Noel Marques and began sorting through his website. It was amateurish at best and the models were mannish and not very attractive. But the clothes were magnificent. Noel's line had only been in existence for five years and he had a talent for deconstructed jackets and unpredictable hemlines, but he also did something I personally loved ... he mixed masculine with feminine. I saw a full-length grey pinstriped light wool slip dress with a raw edge and chain straps. It was unlined and had a long slit up the side—the kind of item I would die to wear. But one thing was certain from their website—they really needed a slicker brand and I was just the woman to help them with it.

"Who am I meeting? I asked, turning my attention back to Jeffrey. "Will Noel be here?"

"Yes, along with his marketing person," Jeffrey replied. "Three o'clock in the small conference room."

"You got it," I responded. "Anything else?"

"Yes, I need you to attend a charity dinner Friday night at the Ritz Carlton, Marina Del Rey," Jeffrey explained leaning forward, elbows on his knees. "It's for Shelter Partnership Inc., benefitting the homeless. Both Warren and I will be out of town, so you're the next in line."

"Of course—I've heard of Shelter Partnership—it's a great cause," I answered.

"Warren bought only one ticket so, unfortunately, you can't bring your new fiancé this time. He thought he'd be the only one attending. It's a black-tie event and you'll be representing the agency."

"In other words, don't look like a *schlump*," I said with a smile. Jeffrey had grown to appreciate my Yiddish.

"You could never look like a *schlump*, Jane, but it's an important event so feel free to uncover some hidden treasure from your closet." He gave me a wink. "Call me if you need anything. I'll be out of pocket, but I'll get back to you when I have a free moment."

"Good luck, Jeffrey," I said, bursting with pride that I was being put in charge of the agency while the partners were out of town.

ꭝ

PROMPTLY AT 3 P.M., Veronica called me. "Jane, your three o'clock is here," she announced. "I'll show them to the small conference room."

"Thanks, Veronica," I replied, grabbing my notepad and pen, and making my way to the meeting.

Noel Marques was a tall, thin man with high cheekbones, shoulder-length red hair, and freckles … a true ginger. He spoke with a strong British accent, but I could tell it was the Queen's English, extremely proper. He wore a white long-sleeved button-down shirt of a soft fabric that almost billowed like a small parachute when he moved. He wore black jeans and boots and smelled faintly of expensive cologne. His marketing director was a woman, also British, with short blonde hair and an androgynous look. She wore a black pantsuit with skinny pants tucked into combat boots. The only makeup she wore was red lipstick.

"I'm Jane Mercer," I introduced myself, smiling and holding out my hand to Noel.

"Noel Marques," he replied shaking my hand. "This is Meredith Sheen," he added, gesturing to the blonde, who shook my hand as well.

"It's a rare occasion when Warren and Jeffrey are out of the office at the same time," I began. "But they felt this account is an excellent fit for me, given my own love of fashion."

As I said those last words, I noted both Noel and Meredith eye my outfit, which was a Gucci cream-colored knit dress with black collar and cuffs, and a red leather belt. The whole look was simple and smart, and it seemed to pass muster with Noel and Meredith.

"I'm very excited to discuss the creation of your U.S. brand," I offered, urging them to take seats at the conference table, which was round and wooden, taking up most of the room. Warren always wanted everyone to be on equal footing in meetings, so he never had tables that were rectangular, requiring someone to sit at each head. He didn't like his team jockeying for position and even encouraged us to sit in different seats at every meeting so we didn't fall into a hierarchal rut.

Once seated, we began to discuss the Noel brand in detail. It seemed that Noel had a vision of his brand but was unhappy with the way it was executed in their advertising.

"We just haven't found our marketing niche," he admitted, sighing. "It's as though our clothes are diminished by the murky photography and clumsy website design."

"Well, you're in the right place," I responded. "We can take your brand to the next level. We're a full-service agency, so we offer everything from research to creative development, copywriting, photo shoot production, and campaign deployment. And you already have the amazing product ... we just need to capture it in a unique way and get it in front of the target audience."

I gave an overview of the agency and discussed how we operated with clients. I also told him I felt that his brand had a ton of potential in the U.S. Noel talked a lot about having frequent photo shoots to update the website and asked me if I had any thoughts on the style of photography and the setting.

"While I think it's premature to talk about photography without a creative brief, I'm envisioning images that highlight the diverse fabrics and structure of your pieces," I responded, being purposely vague, knowing the creative department would strangle me if I stepped on their toes and started jabbering about art. "Tell me about your current collection and what's coming up for spring and summer."

"We showed a lot of tweeds and velvets for the winter months, lots of big sleeves and pencil skirts," Noel said. "But for spring and summer, we are moving into more shimmering dresses with a lot of the lighter wools and damask silks. Have you seen our collections?"

"I did a bit of research," I responded. "I'll be honest, I'm already a huge fan of your clothes."

"Which collection did you see?" Meredith inquired with interest.

"Everything that's on your current website ... I especially fell in love with one particular dress," I said. "It's the grey pinstriped wool dress with the chain straps and slit ..." I stopped myself because I was starting to drool.

Noel appeared to be delighted by my enthusiasm. "I know just the dress," he announced, and picked up his phone to scroll through his photos, searching for the dress. Once he located the photo, he held the phone for me to see.

"That's it," I exclaimed, grinning. "That's the dress ... I love it."

Noel and Meredith exchanged a prideful glance.

"Jane, it looks like we'll get along just fine," Meredith said, smiling. "What are our next steps in hiring your agency?"

"I'll generate a scope of work and budget, based on everything we've discussed today, and submit it to you both for approval," I said. "Once it's been approved, we'll draw up an agreement for you to sign and then we'll move the creative process forward."

I gave each of them my business card. "I'll be your main contact and you'll be involved in every step of the process," I said. "Only with your approval will we execute against the creative brief."

Noel and Meredith left the office with smiles on their faces and I felt great, having held a successful first client meeting without Warren or Jeffrey being present.

ᠺ

ON WEDNESDAY, I RECEIVED a thank you note from Noel, along with a box that I lay on my desk. It was rather large and, when I opened it, there was a lot of tissue paper covering something. Once I dug through it, I pulled out a hanger with the dress that I had singled out to Noel and Meredith. It was a British size six, which equated to a U.S. size two. I breathed deeply, realizing that they had offered me the dress as a kick-off to our new marketing relationship. I thought about the upcoming charity event in Marina Del Rey that Jeffrey had instructed me to attend. It was perfect ... a blend of late winter and spring for a March evening in Southern California. I loved this dress with all my heart and couldn't wait to wear it. I just wished Derek could be by my side when I did. I remembered Jeffrey telling me to aim high with this event, given I was representing the agency. The dress was perfection. I was all set.

Six

I SAT IN MY OFFICE on Friday anticipating the evening's charity event with enthusiasm. I ran my fingers over the invitation, which had been elegantly printed with gold foil against a midnight blue background. Even though the invitation was originally intended for Warren, and I would be going stag, I had the gorgeous Noel Marques dress to debut. I had selected metallic strappy heels that matched the chain straps of the dress and had planned to wear minimal jewelry—just diamond stud earrings and, of course, my diamond engagement ring. I never took it off—even when I went to bed.

The Ritz Carlton Marina Del Rey valet was packed with cars when I pulled my silver BMW up and was promptly greeted by the valet attendants. I had my hair blown out for the occasion, so I looked perfectly coiffed and preened from head to toe. I had no idea what to expect or who I'd be mingling with but, with my original menswear-inspired gown with the thigh-high slit from the hottest new designer in London, I sashayed into the hotel oozing grace and confidence.

As I approached the check-in area, the place was

bustling with beautiful people, all clamoring to get their seat assignment and proceed to the silent auction. When I finally advanced to the front of the line, a pleasant-looking woman with reddish hair greeted me.

"Hello," I said. "Jane Mercer, from Warren Mitchell and Partners."

"Yes, of course, Ms. Mercer," she said, scanning her tablet. "I have your name and will check you in. Would you like to leave a credit card number for the auctions? There are both a silent and live one."

Knowing these types of events, it was unlikely I would be able to afford anything at the auction, but I gave her my credit card to scan anyway, in the doubtful event I wanted to bid on something.

The ballroom was lit in soft pink-gold and a swirl of tuxedo-clad men and women in cocktail dresses milled about. A band on a high central stage platform was doing a Frank Sinatra number. A man with a tray of champagne flutes approached me and offered one, which I was happy to accept. I sidled from one auction item to the next, all displayed on the skirted tables that lined the ballroom. There was everything from designer handbags to jewelry, and spa packages, sports memorabilia and original art. I lingered at a display with a Prada bag. It was one I had long since wanted for my collection but could never afford. It was a smart, medium-sized satchel, color blocked navy, red and cream. Although the organizers made it clear that customers were not supposed to touch the goods, I couldn't help but wrap my fingers around the handle, just to see how it felt. The opening bid was set at $2,000, but the bag itself retailed for at least $4,000, I knew. It would likely end up being a $10,000 bag by the end of the evening.

After loitering a little too long by the bag, I moved on to the next table and froze when I saw him: *Craig Keller*, dressed to the hilt in a black tuxedo. My heart skipped a beat and I quickly retreated to the opposite corner of the room, praying he didn't see me as I got lost in the swarm of people. When I found a corner of the room safe from Craig Keller's view, I set my champagne glass down on an empty table. My hands trembled. *After everything that happened, why do I still get that rush when I see him?*

Another man with a champagne tray was approaching and I beat him to it by grabbing a flute and proceeding to gulp it quickly, the bubbles burning my throat like acid. I pulled my phone out of my bag and sent a text to Derek: 'Sorry you're not here. Hope your Friday night is great."

He texted right back: 'See you when you get home. Have fun.'

I took another sip of champagne and the lights dimmed several times to signal that it was time for the dinner and presentation. I quickly located my table, which was close to the front of the room where the presenters would be. Of course, Warren had one of the best tables—after all, I reminded myself, the ticket had been for him, not me. I found my name card and sat in the correct seat. I picked up the menu and event brochure which were underneath the plate charger and began to browse through them. It looked like a full program. I occasionally lifted my gaze to survey the room but there was no sign of Craig. I breathed a sigh of relief. *Maybe I could get through the night and sneak out without running into him.*

A few people began to settle at my table, and I made sure to introduce myself to each. It looked like only couples, which felt awkward. I struck up a conversation with the wife of some producer from Warner Brothers, who took the seat to my right. We were chatting so intently, I almost failed to notice someone standing near, getting ready to take the empty chair to my left. When I finally glanced in that direction, I almost gasped out loud. It was Craig.

Fuck! Of all the people I had to be seated next to. I wondered how the seating arrangements ended up this way, but realized we had to be two of the only people to attend the event without a guest. I was stuck spending the next few hours with the guy who almost, unknowingly, wrecked my engagement. I was simply not sure what to do. My mind drifted to Warren and how he would have felt being perched right next to his mortal enemy for an entire evening. He probably would have left the event.

Craig was the first to speak. "Ms. Mercer," he said, eyes lighting up at the sight of me as he pulled the chair out and lowered himself into the seat. "What an unexpected pleasure. And here I thought this evening was going to be tedious." He gave me the most glamorous of smiles with those teeth. His tux, upon closer inspection was really a very dark navy, which shone exquisitely whenever the house lights hit his jacket. His bowtie was a rich black velvet. I was reminded of the dream in which I was marrying Craig in his tuxedo and had a creepy moment of revelation that the dream could have been a premonition of some kind.

"I … I'm not sure how this happened," I stammered. "This was originally Warren's ticket. I'm just here representing the agency."

"Well, I much prefer your company, anyway. You're a lot easier on the eyes, too," he averred, lowering his glance to my exposed thigh. I instinctively shifted in my chair, pulling my body closer to the table so the long black tablecloth covered my leg.

"That's a nice dress, Ms. Mercer. Did you come into some money?" As he said this, he gave me an all-knowing wink, like he somehow knew who the designer was and how much the dress must have cost.

I glared at him, saying nothing.

"We might as well make the best of it, don't you think?" he asked playfully, signaling to one of the waitstaff. "What's your pleasure?" he asked me as a young man approached. "Oh, how could I forget. Champagne, right?"

I didn't respond, just quietly observed him. Craig Keller was undoubtedly the best-looking man at the event … and the dastardliest. He turned to the young man and said, "I'd like a bottle of Dom, please," while pulling his wallet out of his pocket and handing the kid a few hundred-dollar bills. He returned to me and said under his breath, "Only the best for you, my dear."

I was beyond uncomfortable—first at his grand gesture and secondly at his ability to pretend like nothing ever transpired between us. My mind went back to the days when he had an uncanny control over me—when I would have done anything he asked. It was painful to recall, but what frightened me most was, even though he used me, abused me, and threw me away, I was still deeply attracted to him. *What was wrong with me?*

When the waiter returned with the bottle, he held it out to Craig, who examined the label and nodded. The waiter popped the cork, put two flutes in front of us, and filled them with champagne. "Just keep our glasses full," Craig commanded.

"Yes, sir," the waiter responded before marching away with the bottle in hand.

Craig held up his glass in a toast. "To the most gorgeous woman in the room." I tentatively rose my glass and clinked it against his. We both took a sip. That's when Craig must have noticed my diamond.

"What's that on your hand, Ms. Mercer?" he asked, eyes fixed on my ring finger.

"What do you *think* it is?" I threw back, a little defiantly.

He gave me a half-smile. "It's obviously an engagement ring. Who's the lucky guy? Anyone I know?"

"Absolutely not," I affirmed, not wanting to discuss Derek with Craig. I didn't want to sully our relationship by reducing it to dinner conversation with this rogue.

"I can't believe it," he said, taking another sip of his champagne. "Jane Mercer is going to enter holy matrimony." Then he paused before looking me in the eye with amusement. "Are you sure you know what you're getting into?"

"What's that supposed to mean?" I demanded in a shrill voice, giving a sideways glance around the table to make sure no one could hear us. The other guests seemed to be engrossed in their own conversations.

"I'm just saying. Marriage is not all it's cracked up to be," he remarked, leaning back in his chair, crossing his legs.

"Coming from someone who cheated the entire length of his marriage with different women, I suppose you're not an ideal consultant on the topic." Again, I looked around the table to ensure I was not attracting attention.

Craig did not respond. He instead leaned over and whispered in my ear. He was so close I smelled the familiar soapy scent that I had found impossible to resist two years earlier. "Neither of us is married right now." He backed away to gauge my reaction, which could not at all have been what he expected.

I felt my cheeks getting hot. "Please excuse me," I mumbled, grabbing my bag, and getting up, feeling the weight of his scrutiny as my eyes darted around the room for the nearest exit. Once in the hallway, I picked up my gown and ran in my heels to the closest bathroom.

In the ladies' room, I took a deep breath. *How could this be happening?* I glimpsed the mirror and caught a disconsolate look on my face. I was once again being seduced by Craig Keller and, unlike before, I had something real to lose. I didn't trust myself with him; that was the bottom line. I could stay and tough it out or I could leave now and be home when Derek arrived. I considered it for a minute. Jeffrey might be pissed but, under the circumstances, he wouldn't blame me.

Just then, I received a text from CK, a contact I somehow could not bring myself to delete from my phone, which read: 'Come back. I promise to be good.' Suddenly, I laughed out loud. *What was I afraid of?* I was the one in control. It was just a dinner and there were so many people around us, what could possibly happen? I was being overly sensitive. That's when I decided to return to the dinner and sit with Craig. I was not about to let him win.

The event went by like a flash of light and Craig behaved himself. In fact, he remained a perfect gentleman throughout the evening as we continued to sip champagne. As Craig had requested, our glasses were never empty, and I didn't think the one bottle of Dom would have lasted so long. But the more I drank, the more I loosened up and started to have a great time with Craig. I had forgotten how charming and quick-witted he was. I started to view him through the old lens, and he appeared as magnificent as ever. He alternated asking me questions about work and Warren, which seemed a little intrusive, but I answered as best I could without directly compromising agency information. And he soon had me laughing hysterically at his sarcastic asides and funny observations. He was always so polished in public. In fact, everyone else at the table ceased to exist and it felt like Craig and I were alone, on a date.

At certain times, I felt Craig's long leg rub up against mine under the table and I would look up at him, trying to figure out if he were doing it on purpose. He was about six foot five, so there was the likelihood that the chair was uncomfortable, and he did not know what to do with his legs. Still, whenever I felt the warmth of his strong leg, I stirred with desire—something I hated to acknowledge.

At one point in the evening, I caught the Warner Brothers' executive's wife observing Craig and me with a curious smile. When our eyes met, she leaned in and made a disturbing comment. "You and your husband make a gorgeous couple," she said. "I've been admiring you both all evening … but you must get that all the time."

"Oh, but he's not—we're not," I started to say, feeling awkward that she assumed Craig and I were *married*. The idea was impossible to imagine. But it did wake me up to the reality that I was allowing myself to fall under his intoxicating spell once again. A Florence and the Machine song was playing in the background. I smirked at the ironically appropriate lyrics while eyeing my extraordinary table mate: *How could anything bad ever happen to you? You make a fool of death with your beauty and, for a moment, I forget to worry.*

When the program was almost over, Craig suggested we leave early to avoid the crowd. "Come on, Jane—they won't even know we're gone," he persuaded. "You leave first, and I'll meet you right outside the door in two minutes." He gestured towards the exit.

I obeyed and stole out at the right time so that no one noticed. I waited by the door and felt myself wondering vaguely what I was doing. I nervously rummaged through my bag for my phone. I grabbed it and saw there were several text notifications and two missed calls from Derek. Before I could check the messages, Craig appeared at my side and took my hand, pulling me through the hotel.

"Where are we going?" I asked as he gripped my wrist and pulled me along. "Valet's in the opposite direction." I heard myself slur a little. My free hand was still gripping the phone.

"For a walk," he answered mysteriously. He looked so dashing in his navy tux, taking long strides like he was on an important mission. I breathed deeply and just let myself get pulled along. I was tipsy from the champagne and didn't feel like I could drive quite yet, so it was probably a good idea we get some fresh air before I got behind the wheel.

Once we were outside on the hotel's back veranda, Craig held my hand and pulled me over to a place where there was a tall column. The only lights were from tiki torches and large pillar candles. No one else was around. He peered around the column and then turned back to me. "If you stand right where I am, you'll see the full moon."

I advanced to where he was standing. He gently took the phone out of my hand and dropped it into my bag for me. "You won't be needing this," he said and stood aside so I could take his place and see the moon. There it was in all its blazing lemon-yellow glory, hanging low and bright like a huge ball of fire. After a few minutes of moon-gazing, I turned to find Craig so close behind me that I almost smashed my body into his. I bit my lower lip and stared up at him. Gently, he put his arms around my waist and moved me toward the column until I was pinned against it.

"Jane, you're so hot—you know that, right?" he whispered as he pressed his body against mine. I was so high from the champagne, suddenly everything was blurry. My petite frame weakened under the strength of Craig. He was holding me up with his body. I let my bag fall to the ground underneath with a soft thud.

"Tell me," he began, taking each of my wrists and pulling them above my head, fixing them against the column as though I were in bondage. "Did you really think you could tease me all evening in that dress and not expect me to go after you?" He slowly lowered his face to mine and ran his tongue along my lower lip, from one side to the other, before backing away slightly to look me in the eye. I could smell his breath, which always reminded me of cherry-flavored candies, mingling with the soapy scent of his body—the scent reminiscent of freshly washed cotton towels.

I closed my eyes and felt his lips on mine, the penetration of his tongue in my mouth, and I did not fight him. I let him kiss me with intensity, all the while holding my wrists above my head. At some point, he let go of one of my wrists and I felt his hand wander to my leg where the slit in my dress started. From there, he slid his hand under my bare thigh and pulled it upward, wrapping my leg around his body so my stiletto dug into the back of his leg. His hand was climbing up my dress and I felt his fingers crawl underneath my panties. I moaned slightly at his touch.

He paused kissing me to intone, "You've wanted this all night, haven't you?"

The thought that I went this far with Craig Keller right there on the veranda resonated in my mind like a loud clap of thunder and I put my free hand up to stop him. "Please, don't," I protested, placing my palm on his jacket lapel, and pushing against his chest. "I—can't do this. I'm drunk."

He withdrew his fingers and released my other arm, taking a small step back so I could lower my leg. Once my foot was on the ground again, I pulled my dress down and wiped my mouth with the back of my hand. I looked around wildly but there still seemed to be no one else there.

Craig was not easily deterred, and he backed me against the column, this time, with the full weight of his body. He shoved up against me, so I could feel, in no uncertain terms, what he was ready to do. "Craig ... please stop," I pleaded. "This is crazy ... we're in public." I felt even dizzier from the champagne.

"We don't have to be. Let's go to my apartment." He backed about a foot away and gave me his seductive slow blink.

"I'm engaged to be married and ... I love my fiancé. He's the only person who matters to me."

"He'll never know," Craig returned, eyes on mine.

I backed up to the column and squared my shoulders against it to steady myself. "He hates your guts."

"Me? How does he even know me?" Craig looked surprised and then amused.

"He suspects we were together—okay? He suspects it but doesn't know for sure because I lied. I denied it. So now, I'm not only a liar, I'm also a slut." My voice trailed off and my eyes filled with tears. "If Derek found out about what happened tonight—about what happened before—he would never, *ever* forgive me." My kneecaps liquified, and I could no longer stand. I felt the cold cement underneath me as I sank onto it like a pile of gelatin.

"You're definitely no slut, Jane," Craig responded, looking down at me and casually putting his hands in his pants pockets. "I can vouch for that. And you were right to lie. Never cop to anything, even if there are pictures."

"I don't know what's more pathetic," I declared, staring up at him with bleary eyes. "The fact that I've gotten myself into this situation or that I'm getting relationship advice from *you*."

Craig shifted his weight, watching me in silence. Then, he held his hand out to me lazily. "Come on, Jane. Let's go. You're in no shape to drive."

I just stared at his hand.

"Jane, come with me. I'll take care of you tonight. You don't have to worry about anything. We can go to my apartment and you can stay there."

I glared at him in disbelief. "Go home? With *you*?"

He shrugged. "If you'd rather not go home in your condition," he said, "you can stay with me until you feel better."

"You planned this," I suddenly blurted out, slurring again. "You meant for this to happen, didn't you? Tell me, Craig Keller, why is it that you set out to ruin my life?"

Craig looked behind him to make sure no one else was around to hear my drunken diatribe and then turned to me, appearing genuinely wounded. "What?" he said. "I don't know what you're talking about—I don't want to ruin your life. I *like* you."

"Oh, please," I retorted. "You almost ruined my life before and now you're trying to do it again. You ordered more than one bottle of champagne, didn't you? That's why my glass was never empty."

"Jane," Craig replied calmly, adjusting his tuxedo jacket by the lapels. "You're being dramatic. It's going to be okay. Just let me get you out of here."

I scoured the ground for my bag and lamely allowed him to pull me to my feet. He led me, on wobbly legs, across the lawn toward the hotel. I had to walk on tiptoes to avoid my stilettos getting stuck in the moist earth. The smell of freshly cut grass permeated my nostrils as I shivered in the night air and hugged my arms to my body. On cue, Craig removed his tuxedo jacket, which I noticed had a Tom Ford label in it, and he placed it around my shoulders, then took my hand to guide me forward. I hopelessly inhaled his soapy essence. We walked, in silence, toward the valet and Craig ordered his car. I saw him tip the valet guy generously, so his vehicle would be a priority. When a new black Bentley Grand convertible pulled up, I knew it had to be Craig's. He always drove a black Bentley convertible, but had upgraded it since the last time I saw him.

Craig opened the door for me, and I attempted to seat myself with grace, hazily aware that the valet service was full, and people were gaping at me—mostly women inquisitive as to who the mystery girl was who had captured Craig's attention for the evening. He was now the most eligible bachelor in L.A., with his stunning good looks and endless stream of revenue. I breathed new car scent and felt my champagne buzz fading, confusion setting in. *How did I end up here again?*

Craig drove away from the hotel and we fell silent until he pulled over onto a side street and put the car in park. "Jane, I feel terrible about this," he confessed, sounding genuinely contrite. "I only ordered the champagne because we were having such a good time. I didn't mean to get you drunk. I forgot what a lightweight you are."

I lowered my eyes for a minute in shame, and then leaned back to examine Craig. If it were possible, he was the most handsome I had ever seen him. Maybe it was because there seemed to be a barely perceptible level of compassion shining through his deep-set green eyes, or maybe it was just that I felt like I had no one else. I was suddenly exhausted but edgy about seeing Derek. Maybe he would already be asleep, and I wouldn't have to worry about lying to him again.

"Do you want me to take you home? Or would you rather come to my apartment?" he asked again. "Because, Ms. Mercer, I'm not finished with you yet."

That last line was a familiar mantra—he had used it with me before—until he was literally *finished with me.* "I have to go home," I insisted, ignoring his last comment. *He already knew I was easily lured into doing something naughty in a public place, so he assumed going to his apartment was the logical next menu item.*

"Come on, Jane," he coaxed. "You're not married yet,

and just think of all the fun we'll have. Don't tell me you don't want this because *that* I know *is* a lie." As he said this, he lay his hand on my thigh and slid it under my dress again.

I grabbed his hand and pushed it away. "Stop it! Please stop touching me," I cried. I was thoroughly humiliated at having fallen for his advances so easily.

He put his hand on the steering wheel and abruptly looked in his rearview mirror, as though he were reminded of something, and then he leaned back and sighed. "Okay," he finally said. "I'll stop."

"Also, do me a favor and pretend this never happened," I added.

"Fine. It never happened," he said to placate me. "But if I'm going to take you home, darling, then I need your address." I reluctantly gave him the address and he promptly typed it into his phone app. I used his car mirror to fix my face and lipstick so that I wouldn't look ravaged by another man by the time I got home. When Craig's car pulled up to our apartment, I saw the lights piercing through the upstairs window. *Derek's still up.*

"Would you like me to wait a few minutes?" Craig asked.

"No, thank you," I responded wearily, eyeing the lighted window, and twisting the chain straps on my dress.

He got out of the car, walked around, and opened the door for me. When I stepped out, he took my hand and touched my face, brushing the hair away from my eyes. "You have my number. Call me if you need anything."

I shrugged and shook my head, turned my back on him, and entered the building. I took a deep breath before pressing the elevator button. *What was I going to say? How would the conversation go?*

Derek was in our bedroom pulling clothes out of his closet when I walked in. His open suitcase lay on the bed, half-full. He looked up and frowned as I entered the room.

I glanced at the suitcase quizzically. "Where are you going?"

"I've been texting and calling you. Why the *hell* haven't you been answering? I have to go to Seattle in the morning." His tone was a combination of anger and sadness. "My dad had a heart attack and is in the hospital. They aren't sure what needs to be done yet, but I have to get there as quickly as possible."

"Oh my God, Derek," I said moving toward him, feeling the immediate sting of guilt, and trying like hell to put Craig Keller and our nefarious activities out of my mind. "Are you okay?"

He just shrugged with an impudent look on his face and continued packing. I sat near the edge of the bed and just watched him, helplessly, in silence. I still felt the effects of the champagne and didn't want to say too much. After about ten minutes, he closed the suitcase and I stared at a sticker on it that read, 'Common Sense is My Superpower' printed in a comic-book-like candy apple red font. I finally had the nerve to speak. "Derek—please sit down for a minute and talk to me."

He finally stopped what he was doing and stood in front of me. His face was pained and his lips were pressed together as though he were trying not to explode. When Derek was angry, it looked almost as though he was chewing tobacco—getting ready to spit.

"Honey please don't shut me out—I'm here for you. We're a team. I'll come with you," I offered, glancing at the sticker again, the feeling of Craig's hands still tingling all over my body.

He shook his head. "No, Jane. I know you're filling in for your bosses right now. I don't want to interrupt your work schedule unless it's an emergency."

"But this *is* an emergency. I'm your fiancée—we're

going to be family. I want to be with you while you deal with this." I stood and hugged Derek's stiff body, trying to break him down by holding him close. He didn't relent. I withdrew to look at his face. His eyes were serious and his demeanor grave. "Derek, please let me be there."

"Man, you reek of alcohol." He pushed me away. "How much did you have to drink tonight?"

I recoiled and put my hand over my mouth. "I guess I had too much champagne," I replied. There was a sheepish quality to my tone.

"And you drove like that? You should have called me to come pick you up." Derek eyed me reproachfully, as though he were an actual cop.

"I didn't drive—I got a ride from a female colleague." I couldn't believe how easily the lies just escaped my lips now. And I did not understand why he was interrogating me like this, when his father should be the focus. "Look, Derek," I said to redirect the conversation. "I can get some things together and come with you in the morning. I'm sure the flight isn't sold out."

Derek shook his head. "No, Jane. I'll call you every day and, if I need you there, I'll let you know."

I had no choice but to respect his decision. I showered, brushed my teeth, changed into my pajamas, and was soon joining Derek in bed. My thoughts were racing. *What had I done?* I know I was tipsy but that could not have been the only reason. Craig Keller had gotten to me again. I thought about how I felt when he touched me and how all my values flew out the window like a wanton flock of birds. After two years, and almost losing everything, it appalled me that I could still act this way.

I felt Derek in bed and put my hand on his shoulder, pulling him over so that he was on his side, facing me. I ran my hand down his arm to his wrist and then touched his stomach, which felt taut. I lowered my hand further and he responded—which surprised me. He pulled me toward him and put his mouth on mine. We made love in the dark as images of Craig flashed before me. I carried on with fervor, desperately trying to block the fantasy that Derek was really Craig—the fantasy that I had chosen a different path, gone home with Craig and was right now fulfilling the passionate, frenetic desire he ignited in me behind the Ritz Carlton. It was as though Derek and I had never made love before, and it lasted for what seemed like hours. I felt like I was making love to him for my life that night.

Seven

WHEN DEREK BROUGHT MY coffee the next morning, he sat on the side of the bed and stroked my hair until I opened my eyes. He looked so cute sitting there in his sweater and jeans. His hair was still damp from the shower; it lay in uneven clumps along the sides of his face.

"That was some night," he said with a smile—not just an ordinary Derek smile—it was the one he gave me when we were about to talk about sex—the corners of his mouth turned up ever-so-slightly with just a tiny swatch of front teeth showing. "I don't know what got into you, but that had to have been one of the best ..." his voice trailed off.

I blinked sleepily and smiled back, thinking of exactly what had gotten into me. Derek just had no idea. The same feelings of guilt and shame filled my soul. In my head, I justified that letting loose on Derek sexually was a lot better than what could have happened had I said yes to Craig's invitation.

"You really gave me something to take to Seattle," he said softly, leaning over to kiss me on the lips. It killed me that Derek so readily believed me. *Well, he's still a guy.*

"Do you have to leave this early?" I asked, hoisting myself up on my elbows and lifting the coffee cup he set on the nightstand, taking a sip.

"I'm afraid so, baby," he replied. "I'll call you as soon as I land."

"I'll miss you, Derek," I vowed with an element of sadness in my voice, like he was leaving me forever. "Please give my love to your family and especially your dad."

"I will," he responded, kissing me one more time and then standing. He picked up his suitcase and carried it to the door. When I heard the door lock behind him, I lay down on our bed and thought about my predicament.

The hole I was digging was now cratering. It was a coincidence that I ended up seated next to Craig last night ... *or was it, really?* There were certain things I knew about Craig Keller and one was that he never let himself be surprised by anything. Could he have orchestrated the seating last night? And why was he asking so many questions about Warren Mitchell & Partners? Whatever the truth, I had to prepare myself for the eventuality that I would see him again. That was all there was to it. I could not risk my relationship by being alone with him ever again. I just wished I felt more confident about it.

AFTER TAKING AN UBER to retrieve my car, I went home to the burn of loneliness upon entering the empty apartment. Since Derek was out of town, I called Kat to see if she could meet up for dinner. Miraculously, with her heavy schedule, she was available.

After showering for the evening out, I heard our apartment intercom buzz. Apparently, there was something being delivered. I quickly pulled on jeans and a T-shirt and answered the subsequent knock on the door. I signed for a rather large box and asked the delivery man about its origins. He had an inordinately large face and thin eyebrows, permanently affixed upwards, as though he were eternally surprised. He explained that he worked on behalf of the charity and was delivering silent auction items that were not claimed the night before.

"But there must be a mistake," I protested, now confused. "I didn't bid on anything."

The delivery man shrugged and replied, "Well, it has your name and address on it, so you'll have to take it up with the charity."

I sighed and accepted the box, placing it in the hallway before opening it. Inside was a black box with the gold Prada logo on it. I gingerly pulled the lid off the box and inside was a dust bag. My heart pounded when I realized what it was. I slid the dust cover off and there it was ... the Prada bag I had admired so profoundly the night before.

I could not figure out how my name got attached to the bag and then I realized it must have been charged to my credit card by accident. I pulled up my account online to check and there was no trace of a charge. I searched the bag and found, along with the Prada certificate of authenticity, another card. It was Craig Keller's business card. I turned it over and there, in his bold handwriting, it read: 'For you, beautiful.'

At that moment, my cell phone rang. I jumped, thinking it was Derek but, instead, the initials CK flashed on the screen. "Hello," I answered cautiously, still holding the bag by its handles.

"Where ... *are* you?" he said in his familiar seductive tone. That was how he always greeted me on the phone—in our past life as lovers.

"At home," I responded, unsure of how to react to his generosity, which sliced through me like a proverbial double-edged sword. On the one hand, I was impressed by his incredible wealth and ease at providing me with something I so blatantly desired and, on the other, I resented him for so cavalierly giving it to me.

"Did you get my gift?" he asked with a smile in his voice.

"Just now," I answered with anxiety. "What are you trying to do, anyway?"

"A simple 'thank you' would be fine," he said, clearly amused.

"How did you know I wanted that bag?" I demanded, suddenly feeling vulnerable, setting the bag down on the couch to somehow separate myself from it.

"I must be psychic," he answered. "How did everything go last night? I mean, with your boyfriend."

"You mean my fiancé," I corrected him. "It went great."

"That's good to hear," he commented tentatively, as though he didn't expect that response. "Is he there now?"

"No, and it's a good thing because then I'd have to explain the bag to him," I said, thinking about that scenario and feeling relieved to have intercepted the gift while alone.

"You bought it for yourself," Craig responded. "That's what you tell him."

"You mean lie again," I said. "You should keep your sordid advice to yourself."

"Lighten up, Jane," he replied casually. I could tell he was driving because I heard his turn signal ticking with a steady pulse.

I gripped the ends of my hair and wound them around my hand in frustration. "Craig, I'm serious. You can't buy me things. I'm getting married soon."

"Like I said last night, Ms. Mercer, you're not married yet."

"Yeah, not if you have anything to do with it," I said wearily. "Craig, please listen to me. These overtures—what happened last night …."

"Yes," he interrupted in a playful tone. "Let's talk

about last night, Jane. There's no question in my mind what you wanted."

"You need to forget all that, okay?" I responded, feeling terrified, like he was intentionally taunting me.

"Don't tell me what I need, Jane. I know all about that. And so, do you." His voice deepened as he uttered those last words.

Why was he doing this to me? What was in it for him? The one thing I learned about Craig Keller is that there was always something in it for him. I was silent, trying to think of what to say to deter him. It was no use. The images flashing before me of him in that navy tux were too overpowering.

"Are you still there, Jane?" he asked.

"I am."

"What are you doing tonight?"

"I'm meeting my girlfriend for dinner. I … my fiancé went out of town." *Damn, why did I tell him that? That's the last thing he needs to know.*

"Call me for a nightcap," he suggested, again with the smooth voice. "I'll send a car for you—wherever you are."

"I can't do that, Craig. I have to go." I hung up on him.

I studied the bag again and sighed. *How did I get myself into this mess?* He was pursuing me with a vengeance, and I had no idea why. It could be because he was single but there had to be more to it. The man could have any woman he wanted, anywhere he wanted. I clutched the Prada bag around the handles and swung it gently, remembering what happened when he gave me money two years ago. He ended up trying to sue me for it. There was no question—I had to beware.

⚓

KAT HAD JUST COME from a tryst with Caleb and was fresh-faced and high-spirited when we met at Olvera

Street, an historical landmark in downtown L.A. "You wouldn't believe how good he is, Jane," she remarked excitedly. "I won't give details but let me just say he's attentive."

"I suppose that's very nice," I mused as we passed a shop hawking Aztec striped wool ponchos and hand-painted wooden maracas. A marionette puppet with big red lips dangled in front of me, grotesquely, as we sauntered by.

I considered Kat's comment and decided that Derek was also an attentive man—a stark contrast to the way Craig approached women—like a wild race car with no brakes—headed off a cliff. We settled on dinner at La Colondrina Café, and the hostess seated us outside. where we could people-watch and absorb the exquisite tackiness of the pink, tangerine, and turquoise décor. The predictable assault of a strolling mariachi band blasted from the restaurant's interior.

"He's so gorgeous," Kat went on as soon as we were seated and given menus. "He has the most beautiful eyes and long dark hair. You'll die when you see him. He looks like a movie star."

"Oh, I believe you," I remarked. If Kat was going out on a limb to sleep with her twenty-five-year-old employee, he must be something else. Besides, Kat had better taste than anyone I knew. After all, she hooked up with Craig once upon a time—before she found out what he was really like.

The waitress had just placed a big bowl of chips and a side of salsa between us and took our drink orders. I reached for a chip immediately, realizing I hadn't eaten much all day. They were still warm from the oven.

"You know Derek's in Seattle," I told Kat after crunching into a chip. "His father's ill. I'm praying he gets better, but they aren't sure how serious it is yet."

"Oh no! I'm so sorry, Jane. Is Derek okay?" she asked,

with a look of concern.

The waitress set margaritas in front of Kat and me. "It's so hard to tell with him," I answered, remembering how he was, both last night and this morning. "I think he's okay. It's just the waiting part. He's worried, you know. I tried to go with him, but he didn't want to tear me away from work right now."

"That man is considerate and you're lucky," she commented, grabbing her margarita and taking a sip. "I hope Caleb turns out to be just like Derek."

I felt my shoulders tense up. "Oh, Kat. Are you seriously considering Caleb long-term?" There was judgment in my tone. My thoughts went back to Craig and what we did the night before and a feeling of dread filled my stomach. *How could I judge Kat in the face of my own misadventures?*

"I told you, it's purely sexual," Kat replied, dipping her chip deeply into the salsa. "But he's also a nice companion."

Then I realized that Kat was exactly the person I needed at this moment. It's like we had a perverse new bond based on forbidden fruit and relationship taboos. "Kat," I said before taking a sip of my margarita. "If I tell you something, will you promise not to judge?"

"I would never judge you," she said quickly. "I mean, look at everything we've been through together."

I scanned the room to make sure no one could hear our conversation. With the mariachi music, it's a wonder Kat and I could hear our own conversation. I leaned toward her conspiratorially. "Do you swear not to judge me, even if I tell you about something I've done that is so stupid, you won't believe it?" I asked.

"Of course. What is it?" She took another sip of her margarita, staring at me expectantly.

"It's the worst thing you can imagine," I admitted, eyeing her for reaction.

"Uh oh. It's him, isn't it?" Kat guessed, mouth dropping open. "It's Craig Keller. What about him, now?"

"I can't control myself with him," I blurted, feeling pitiful as the words came out. I then proceeded to recount the night's details, including how the evening ended. The only thing I left out was the Prada bag, which she was about to see because I had carried it to the restaurant. Deep-rooted materialism outweighed morality in my accepting such a gift from His Highness.

Kat stayed silent a minute, as though she were assessing the damage. "Jane, honey," she began gently, "you have everything you want right now and you're just going to sabotage it. And for what? For a night in bed with him? You already know what that's like."

"What about you?" I asked. "You're doing the same thing with Caleb—you could lose your job and hurt your reputation—over some *kid.*"

"He's decent and harmless, Jane, and I happen to be unattached at the moment, unlike you," she retorted. "Caleb's nothing like the man you're toying with—that's like having a ferocious tiger by the tail—did you forget all the rotten things he did to you?"

"No, Kat, but I was drunk, and he was … well, he was aggressive. We had such a great time during dinner. It was like I was with him for the first time and nothing had ever gone wrong between us. Then … I just let things happen. I mean, not all the way but … things got pretty hot and heavy." I pulled the Prada bag from where it was hanging on a hook under the table. "Look at this," I said, holding it up for Kat to see.

"When did you get that? It's beautiful," she said, temporarily distracted from the Craig conversation, attention now on the magnificent bag.

"Guess."

"*He* bought you that?" she asked, in a sober tone, while sitting up straight in her turquoise wooden chair.

It was dark outside now, and the waitress placed a lit candle between us. I watched the fire dance in different directions as waitstaff milled around our table. "It was on silent auction last night, which means he probably paid triple what it's worth."

Kat fixed her blue eyes on mine with concern. "Jane—you have to stop this—stop it now. Derek will find out and you'll lose him."

"Don't you think I know that, Kat?" I said, anxious. "I told you I can't help myself. I'm like a drug addict with a load of heroin sitting in front of me—just begging for me to shoot up. I just can't stop." I placed my head in both hands with my elbows on the table.

"You have to. Stop answering your phone when he calls—or better yet, block his number."

I shook my head at that suggestion. "No. I can't bring myself to even delete his number, Kat. There's something about him—he's still a part of my life—I know that sounds awful."

Kat sighed. "If you insist on keeping him in your life, then you're going to have to control yourself. Don't return calls, texts and don't accept gifts," she said, gesturing toward the Prada bag. "Leave the premises when you see him somewhere. You simply must." She studied me carefully me for a minute, like she was still thinking. "You've got to see him for who he is, Jane. I know he's sexy, but he's also the guy that screwed you around two years ago. Remember that? He nearly crushed you."

"Of course, I remember," I said, now depressed about the whole situation. He had promised me a high-level job but gave it to another woman at the last minute without telling me, all while constantly seducing and controlling me. "You know him, Kat. Why do you think he's doing this?"

Kat shrugged. "I don't pretend to know what goes on in that man's head. But I do know what'll happen if you don't stop. Let me ask you this: do you *want* to lose Derek?"

"Oh my God, no, Kat. I *love* Derek. I don't love Craig. I barely even like him. But there's something about him I can't resist." I touched my cheeks with both hands, and they felt warm.

"Then the answer's simple. Don't be around him." Kat was now leaning back in her chair.

"But what about last night?" I argued. "There's no way I could keep from being with him. Our seats were next to each other. Warren ordered me to go. There was no avoiding him." I felt like I was testifying before a judge and jury, frantically trying to convince them of the logic to my abhorrent behavior.

Kat leaned forward again. "You could have said no to the champagne and no to the moonlight walk. I mean, come on, Jane, that's the oldest trick in the book. I can't believe you fell for it." Kat shook her head, her long blonde locks twisting from side to side.

I sighed and looked down. I knew she was right, and I felt like a fool.

ON MY DRIVE HOME, Derek called. "Hi, honey," I said, genuinely grateful to hear his voice. I was stuck in a sea of traffic lights heading back to Santa Monica.

"Hi," he said.

"How's your dad?"

"He's not great, Jane. They think he's going to need a triple bypass."

"Oh no ... when?" I clutched the steering wheel like I might veer off the road at any second.

"In the morning," he answered.

"Do you need me there?" I asked, silently praying he would say yes, so I would have a reason to leave town.

"Not right now," he replied, and my heart sank. "Are

you doing okay? You sound kind of ... I don't know ... down."

"Oh Derek, it's because I miss you and I've been worried. I just need you right now. I know you want me to stay here but I feel like I need to be with you." Although I wanted desperately to be with Derek in his time of need, in the back of my mind was Craig Keller and the thought that physically removing myself from the situation might make it disappear, at least temporarily.

"It's only going to be a lot of waiting around, baby," he said "And Mom and Carey are here with me so ..."

"So, I'd only be in the way?" I burst out, feeling hurt that his clan did not consider me immediate family. I also had the distinct impression it was Carey who didn't want me there.

"Please don't take it the wrong way. Let me call you tomorrow after the surgery. I love you, Jane."

"I love you, too," I responded, feeling my eyes tearing.

When I arrived home, a text from CK was waiting. He gave me the address of his apartment in Brentwood and told me that I had been granted permanent access to his building entrance. All I had to do was show my ID at the guard gate. He was not giving up.

On Sunday afternoon, I received word that Derek's dad made it through the surgery and was recovering nicely. Derek was going to stay another week until his dad was released to go home. Although I was disappointed that it would be another full week until I would see Derek, I was grateful the absence was not going to be longer—especially with Craig Keller lurking in the background, waiting for an opportunity to pounce. He made me nervous. He was brazenly unpredictable with his impromptu gifts and spontaneous phone calls—it's like Craig represented a volatile earthquake's fault line right down the middle of my heart—ready at any second to shake up my stability.

Eight

THE FOLLOWING WEEK WAS spent managing the office and the employees by day and going straight home every night. In the back of my mind, I rationalized that a strict lifestyle while Derek was absent might negate my transgressions at the charity event the previous Friday night.

Without Derek, there was no one to cook, and so I got takeout from Lee's every night—the same Chinese chicken salad—on the way home from work. I would pick at the salad with chopsticks on the uncomfortable grey couch, while binge watching *Sex and the City* reruns until I was sleepy enough to go to bed. I would do my beauty routine, which consisted of scrubbing my face with a motorized brush and some expensive cleansing gel from Paris. Once cleansed, I would apply my various creams and emollients. Derek called them 'plotions'—a cross between lotions and potions.

Slowly, the guilt started to dissolve, and I began to feel strong again. Craig had not texted nor called since Saturday night, which generated both relief and suspicion. I had a hunch he was up to something.

Late in the day on Wednesday, Jeffrey called to check

on me. "How's it going, Jane?" he greeted me when I answered the phone.

"It's going tremendously well," I replied, feeling genuinely proud that I had managed to keep the balloons up in the air without a major screw-up. I gazed out the window at the thick foggy marine layer shrouding downtown Santa Monica. "How's it going with you?"

"Everything's falling into place." Jeffrey dropped a triumphant little laugh into the phone. "I swear, this is a marathon, but we may have everything wrapped up and ready to go on the road show soon. The process is exhausting but it's working out great, Jane. I really think we're going to pull this off."

"I do have some good news," I teased.

"Tell me."

"I was able to seal the business deal with Noel Marques. The meeting went well and they're signing on with us for a one-year contract with a monthly retainer. I have everything for you to review when you return." I sprang up from my swivel chair with a little cheerleader hop, genuinely pleased with myself.

"That's great. I knew you could do it. By the way, how was the charity event last Friday?"

The thought of the charity event made my stomach erupt. I wasn't sure whether to tell Jeffrey who I had to sit next to throughout the dinner or just keep it to myself. I chose the latter. There was no need for Jeffrey's thoughts to be clouded with that gossip right now—especially when he was spending every waking hour with Warren. "All good," I answered. "It was a very high end and well-attended event."

"That's awesome. I have to say, you're handling everything just fine without us ... sounds like a partner-in-the-making," he said. "I'll let Warren know."

I smiled into the phone. "Is there anything else you need from me now?"

"No, Jane. I'll see you Monday."

We hung up. *A partner-in-the-making?* I couldn't help but envision what really happened at the charity event and the image of me outside on the veranda fooling around with Warren's biggest rival. A long shudder rolled down my spine. No, there was no way I could tell anyone other than Kat what had really happened. I caught a glimpse of the desk photo of Derek and me. I picked it up gently and gazed at the photo, sighing. *Oh Derek, please come home soon.*

My phone was ringing, and a smile tugged at the corners of my mouth thinking it might be Derek. But it was Marisa. I replaced the photo on the desk and eyed the phone screen warily. I never shared the Craig situation with Marisa but that was on purpose. She would go ballistic on me if I told her the truth about Friday. "Hey, Marisa," I answered the phone with aggressive cheerfulness.

"Jane," she sounded distraught. "Where are you?"

"In my office," I answered, glancing at the open office door, and somehow wishing it were closed. "Why?"

"Um … have you seen the latest issue of *LA Insider Magazine?*"

"No, I haven't," I answered, wondering why Marisa sounded panicked.

"Then you don't know what's in it?" she asked.

"Um, no Marisa—what's going on?" Marisa never cared what was in that rag.

"You need to get a copy immediately. There's a picture of you … with *Craig Keller,*" she exclaimed.

"What?" I stood up from my desk, feeling light-headed. "What do you mean? What picture?"

"It's a picture of you walking with him to his car, with his jacket around your shoulders."

Fuck! This couldn't be happening. I felt my heart pounding in my chest. There must be a copy of the magazine in the office somewhere—probably near Veronica's desk at the agency entrance.

"Marisa, let me get a copy of it and call you back," I said, breathlessly. I was already running down the hall-way. I passed many open offices and heard the clicking of fingers on keyboards, and a couple of account executives on conference calls, arguing with their clients.

When I got to Veronica, I tried to calm myself and regain at least a veneer of self-control. "Veronica," I said, slightly out of breath. The air was thickly perfumed with her favorite candle fragrance, which was usually calming, but, at the moment, was making me queasy. "Did we get this week's issue of *LA Insider Magazine?*"

She barely looked up from her computer screen, bored, and only gestured toward the reception area. "It should be over there," she said in her monotone. I quickly advanced to where she was pointing and spied a stack of magazines sitting on the gleaming mahogany guest coffee table near the lobby couch. I flipped through them and found the copy, which I stashed under my arm before making my way back to the office, where I shut and locked the door behind me.

When I got to the pages where they recap charitable events and high-profile parties, I felt my heart sink. Marisa was right. There was a prominent photo on the upper right-hand side of the center spread. There I was walking with Craig leading me by the hand. I was looking down, but you could still tell it was me in my Noel Marques dress. I had Craig's tuxedo jacket around my shoulders and the black Bentley was in front of us. The caption read: 'Craig Keller, managing partner, Keller Whitman Group, and Jane Mercer, Vice President of Accounts, Warren Mitchell & Partners, attending Shelter Partnership Gala'. From the picture, it sure looked, like I was there with Craig—like he was my date for the evening. I slowly sank into my office chair and put my head down on the desk. Hands trembling, I picked up my cell phone and dialed Marisa.

"Did you see it?" she asked.

"Yes," was all I could mutter in my distress.

"Well? What the hell were you thinking?" she asked, incredulous. "Were you there with him?"

"No, Marisa," I said, voice now shaking. "I was not there *with* him … listen, it was all a mistake," I explained. "He was there and … somehow we were seated together. I … um, drank too much and he offered me a ride home. I left my car there."

"Oh my God, Jane—you know that guy has paparazzi all over his ass day and night. His life is fodder for the tabloids. It's just not smart to be seen in public with him."

"Well, I wasn't thinking clearly at the time. I didn't see any cameras." I realized right then that there could have been cameras out on the veranda, too, and I broke out in a cold sweat thinking that those photos might surface at some point.

"There are cameras everywhere at those events—and especially anywhere Craig Keller is," Marisa scolded. "Has Derek seen it?"

My thoughts went to Derek. He would be furious if he saw the picture, especially given I lied to him about getting a ride home from a female colleague. "Derek's out of town," I answered. "His dad's ill and he's going to be gone at least until next week."

"Lucky for you. What about Warren?" she asked.

"He and Jeffrey don't get back into the office until Monday morning," I said anxiously. "What should I do?"

"If I were you, Jane, I'd be proactive. Go directly to Warren and Jeffrey as soon as they're in the office. Show them the picture and tell them you took an Uber to the event and happened to be seated next to Craig. Then he offered you a lift home. Don't act like it was a big deal or anything."

"What about his jacket and the fact that he's holding my hand? I mean, that looks a bit suspicious, don't you think?" I asked, staring at the picture again. There was something about the body language between Craig and me—something that belied the flimsy story that we were only colleagues sharing a ride, especially with Craig's reputation.

Marisa sighed into the phone. "It does. But everyone knows what a womanizer Craig is. It wouldn't be out of character for him to have given you his jacket. The hand-holding is another issue altogether." She stopped and was silent for a minute. "Jane—what about the digital version? I get it emailed to me every week. Oh, and all the social media they do surrounding those events."

I put my palm against my forehead and slumped down in my chair, wishing I could sink into the floor and disappear. "Oh no—I forgot about that."

"Yeah, and that means if someone searches your image, that photo is will always come up—it'll come up every time someone searches Craig, too. Oh, Jane—how do you get yourself into these things?"

"I don't know, Marisa, but I'm really worried about Derek," I said, now barely able to hold back tears.

"Come on, Jane—don't fall apart now. You need to stay strong and confident. If I were you, I'd just hope Derek is out of town long enough to miss this week's issue. You don't get it at your apartment, do you?"

"No," I answered. "But you never know where he might see it—it could be at his work or on a newsstand, for all I know. He's already edgy about Craig and this will push him *over* the edge."

"You'd better hope he doesn't hear about it some other way," Marisa warned.

When I hung up with Marisa, my office line began to ring. I picked up the phone. "Jane Mercer."

"Jane—is this a good time?" a man's voice said.

I quickly recognized the British accent. It was Noel Marques.

"Hello, Noel, of course it is. How are you?" I was doing my best to sound professional under the circumstances.

"Well, I'm very impressed by you," he said in a gracious tone.

"Impressed?" I asked, clueless as to why he would say something like that so soon in our work relationship. I hadn't done anything yet to impress him. Nothing that I knew of.

"We've barely signed a contract with your agency and you've already given us brilliant publicity," he gushed.

"Oh?" I said, still trying to figure out what he meant.

"The dress—you wore it to an event and it's in *LA Insider Magazine*. Did you see it yet?" he asked. "I'm so glad I took a bit of a mini-break in Los Angeles, so I was able to pick up some copies of it. I'm looking forward to showing them to my colleagues in London."

I placed my hand to my forehead again and shook my head. "Oh yes," I answered, trying not to groan aloud. "I'm so glad it worked out that way."

"I don't mean to be presumptuous, Jane, but your date is one good-looking chap, indeed. It seems you have amazing taste in both men and clothes."

This conversation was coming as a huge slap in the face for making such a stupid mistake leaving the event with Craig. I just wished Noel would stop going on about it—he was just making matters worse. I didn't even have the energy to argue that Craig was not, in fact, my date, just a drunken partner with whom I had engaged in dirty hijinks on the veranda before being carted off to his car like a wayward child.

"I'm happy to let Warren know what a great job you're doing right out of the gate, Jane," Noel gushed.

I felt my heart stop at this suggestion. "Noel, that's not necessary at all—it was my pleasure to wear your dress to such a high-profile event." I prayed he would leave the subject immediately.

By the time I had accepted enough gratitude from Noel about my publicity coup and got off the phone, it was already after 6 p.m. I sat at my desk for a few more minutes with the magazine open. Yes, the image was incriminating but it could have been much worse. *What if someone had snapped a photo of us on the veranda?* That would have been both a career and relationship buster for me. I put the magazine in my messenger bag and got my things to leave for the evening.

On the way to the parking lot, I passed several people from the art department and felt that they were looking at me funny. I wondered whether any of them had seen the photo. Marisa was right. I needed to get to Warren and Jeffrey and nip this in the bud as soon as they were back from their trip. With Derek, I just hoped and prayed he would never, ever see the photo.

AT HOME THAT NIGHT, I did something I hadn't done for a while. I immediately reached for a bottle of wine in the fridge—an ice-cold Napa Valley Chardonnay was going to be my friend for the evening. I uncorked it and poured a glass. What a day it had been. I lay down on the couch, taking long sips of wine in a short time, trying to relax and calm myself. Weezer jumped up next to me and stretched his legs.

"Oh Weez," I said to him softly. "You always know when Mommy's in trouble, don't you? I've done something terrible and it might shake up our whole world." I put my hand on his back and smoothed his silvery stripes—his coat felt like soft velvet. "You're so lucky to be a cat. I wish we could trade places right now. I know you're smarter than me—you wouldn't give Craig Keller the time of day, would you?"

The more I talked to Weez about my plight, the more agitated I became. And soon, I was petting him with short, impatient jerks, which displeased him greatly. He jumped down and skittered away indignantly. My phone began ringing. *Oh no—it's Grandma.*

"Jane Mercer, I need to talk to you," she said, in a disciplinarian tone.

"Hello, Grandma, how are you?" I said, thinking this would be the topper for my shitty day.

"Not very good after seeing your picture in one of the papers. Tell me, young lady, who is that guy you were with? And why on earth would you wear a dress slit that high?"

I groaned aloud. Of course, Grandma had seen the picture. *She only reads trash magazines.* She considered them hard news. "Grandma, I honestly don't want to talk about it right now," I said, taking a large gulp of wine and shutting my eyes.

"Well, we're *going* to talk about it," she demanded. "Where's Derek, anyway?"

Then it hit me that I hadn't even told my grandparents about Derek's dad. "Don't kill me, Grandma—but Derek left over a week ago. His dad had a heart attack and had to have a triple bypass. He's fine and Derek's still in Seattle with him while he recovers. He's helping his mom and sister."

"What? A heart-attack? And you wait until *now* to tell me? Shame on you, Jane!" Her tone then changed from anger at me to compassion for Derek. "Oy what sad news," she commented. "Poor Derek—and how come you're not there with him?"

Back to knocking me. "Because he didn't want me there," I threw back in a shrill voice, now wishing I had never answered the phone.

"He's your fiancé, Jane. When you're married, you be with your husband's family when something like this happens. Didn't we teach you anything? And the one thing you don't do is go out in a dress that's cut all the way up to your *tuchus* and be seen with another man. I didn't bring you up to be a shameless hussy!"

Grandma was now worked up into a frenzy. I could hear her cigarette lighter flicking in the background. "Grandma, please stop. I can't deal with this right now. I feel miserable as it is."

"You still haven't told me who that man is—the tall *goy* in the picture. It says his name is Craig—*Craig Keller*. Who is that?"

Hearing Grandma say his name made me feel even more perverse. I had somehow placed Craig in a compartment that had nothing to do with my real life. He was a fantasy that never materialized in my familial world—until now. "He's just a guy I know who works in advertising," I answered, putting my hand on my abdomen in agony. "He was giving me a ride home."

"But you were wearing his jacket, Jane."

"Because I was cold," I spat out sharply.

"Don't you use that tone with me, missy," she retorted. "You were cold because you were half-naked."

"Grandma, this conversation is over and I'm hanging up now. And, for once, please keep your mouth shut about this the next time you see Derek—he's not your son-in-law yet. He has enough to worry about right now with his father being sick anyway." I hung up the phone and poured another glass of wine, shooting it down in one big gulp. This magazine mishap was becoming my biggest nightmare. I drifted to my bedroom, collapsing on the bed in alcohol-induced exhaustion.

Nine

EVERY FRIDAY, I HELD a staff meeting for my direct reports. I had five directors in all. We used the time to update each other on clients and I would share pertinent company information. Of course, everyone knew about the impending IPO, so there was not much to say these days. I was on edge, anyway, knowing Jeffrey and Warren were returning Monday.

When everyone had gathered in the small conference room, I shut the door and sat at the head of the table. "How's everyone?" I asked as they settled into their chairs and pulled out their tablets and files. I had three women (Nichol, Elli, and Ashley) and two men (Harlan and Kevin) on my team, and they were a diverse group. However, they had one thing in common: they had my back. It was one of the things I required of my employees—and it was a quality I valued far beyond anything else. The way I saw things, a job skill could be improved upon, but if there was no loyalty, it would never work.

They were normally a talkative group but, for some reason, they all seemed uncomfortable. Tension filled the room like an unpleasant odor, and no one wanted to say anything first. "Let's go around the room for updates," I announced to start off the meeting. "Nichol, why don't you go first."

Nichol wore horn-rimmed glasses and her dark hair was long and wavy. She cleared her throat and started to go through her list. The others just sat passively and listened, and I started to wonder what was going on. They were never this placid in meetings. In fact, most of the time, I had to act as referee and get them to compose themselves when discussing clients as a group.

Nichol finished. After I asked her a few questions, I finally had to say something to the group. They were fidgeting nervously in their chairs now. "Okay, what's up?" I asked. "You guys are acting weird."

They exchanged glances uncomfortably and then Harlan spoke. "Jane, um, have you seen the latest issue of *LA Insider Magazine*?" he asked, lower lip stretched against his teeth.

Great. My entire staff knew about the Craig photo debacle. I should not be surprised because I put it in their job descriptions that they must keep up on everything that went on in town, especially monitoring the local rags for gossip about competitors. "I have," I answered with a forced air of calmness. "What about it?"

Harlan eyed his cohorts for help and Elli was next to chime in. "There's a picture of you in it," she said.

"Yes, I know all about it," I responded with confidence. *No use letting them know how damaging that image really was.* "Warren sent me to the event and my seat happened to be next to Craig Keller. He gave me a lift home. Why do you ask?"

"How do you know *him*?" Harlan asked, with awe in his voice. "I mean, what's he like?"

Harlan was gay, so I suspected some sort of a boy crush on Craig. I wasn't sure how to respond to his question. *I'm glad you asked, Harlan, because I do know him, but mostly in the Biblical sense. What's he like? He's gorgeous*

and charming until he bites you, literally and figuratively.
"We met a long time ago," I said in a tone that indicated
I'd like to shut down the conversation.

Harlan was not ready to let it go. He sat up straight
in his chair. "Look at Jane—hanging out with a power
player—you have to tell us—does he look that good up
close or is he just super photogenic?"

"Guys, we really need to get through this list of
action items," I said, ignoring Harlan's question.

They exchanged intrigued glances again before
Kevin piped up. "We just wanted to make you aware of
it—you know, so in case anyone ..."

"Consider me *made aware*," I interrupted him before
moving on to Ashley, who was sitting next to Nichol.
"Ashley, let's get to your updates."

For the rest of the meeting, I could not focus. If any
one of my direct reports asked me to recap what was
said, I would have nothing to offer, other than Craig
Keller had been brought up in the inquisition. I was so
preoccupied that I could think of nothing else. I had to
admit, I was appreciative that my team was trying to
protect me from negative gossip; however, the way they
reacted felt like a precursor to what I would experience
when Jeffrey and Warren returned to the office.

OVER THE WEEKEND, DEREK called and announced
that he was flying home Sunday. The only odd thing
was that he was bringing his sister Carey with him. "You
don't mind if she stays with us for a little while?" Derek
inquired on the phone Saturday. "She just needs to get
away after the whole ordeal with Dad. Brandon's going to
look after the boys. She's also looking forward to spending some quality time with you. Are you okay with that?"

I thought about it and, what could I really say? I
wasn't a huge fan of Carey's and I was pretty sure the

feeling was mutual; however, I wanted to please Derek and, if it were true and Carey really wanted to spend time with me, I should embrace it. "Of course, darling," I answered. "I'd love to see Carey. She can stay in the spare bedroom. I'll get everything fixed up before you both get here."

"Jane, you're the best ... do you know that?" Derek said.

"I just want you back, sweetheart—please hurry," I said, voice reeking of vulnerability.

"I'll see you tomorrow night," he confirmed. "I can't wait to have you in my arms again. I love you, baby."

When I hung up, I thought again about how lucky I was and how I needed to fight relentlessly to preserve what Derek and I had. It was imperative I do everything in my power to make Carey comfortable and to impress upon her that I was the right woman to be marrying her precious little brother.

L

I SPENT ALL DAY Saturday and part of Sunday fixing up Carey's room, washing the bedsheets and towels and sprucing up the guest bathroom with soaps and elegant products so she would be pleased.

I went to Ralph's and stocked up on food and snacks for the week, not knowing how long Carey would be staying with us. And, even though I was not at all a cook, I decided it would be a great move if I tried to make dinner and have it waiting when they got home.

I picked something that could not be easily ruined: pan-seared salmon, baked sweet potatoes, and broccoli. I would start with a mixed green salad with balsamic dressing. Derek always made his own dressing but that was a little beyond my capabilities, so I settled for the store-bought variety.

Later, while I was prepping for dinner, my cell phone

rang. I glanced at the screen and saw the initials "CK" flashing. I sighed. *What did he want with me now?* My mind went back to the dreaded *LA Insider Magazine*, which would be replaced on the racks within a few days. I remembered what Kat told me the prior week and how I should never again answer Craig's calls. It was tough. A part of me was dying to hear his voice and another part wanted him to disappear from the planet. I took a deep breath and let the phone ring. After five rings, it went to voice mail. I wondered whether he would leave a message.

It was already 6 p.m. and Derek was due home any minute. I checked myself in the mirror, making sure I was not wearing too much makeup. I wanted Carey to think me conservative. I also made sure I was wearing a modest outfit: a baggy sweater and loose, boyfriend jeans cuffed at the hem. I wore white sneakers and no jewelry, except for the diamond engagement ring. When I heard the door unlock, I was in the kitchen putting the salmon in a heated pan.

"Jane?" Derek called.

I wiped my hands on a dishtowel and ran to the front door to greet him. He threw his arms around me, kissing my cheek and hugging me close. Carey was right behind him and she smiled and held her hand out to shake mine. I instead attempted to give her a hug, which she awkwardly rejected before giving in to an anemic effort. I guessed even though I was going to be her sister-in-law, she just wasn't interested in that type of warmth.

Carey was a tall woman, easily five foot eight, and was slightly big boned. Her sandy blonde hair was shoulder-length and cut in a smart style. She had Derek's hazel eyes and easy smile. Carey dressed casually, wearing only sweaters, jeans, and flat shoes. I'd never seen Carey in heels or dressed up in any way. She would likely be turned off at my excessive and indulgent clothing and shoe collection, which took up all three closets in the apartment, plus a couple of large dressers and shelving for my handbag collection. Poor Derek had a corner of our walk-in for his own clothes, which he never seemed to mind.

"Come in, both of you," I urged right away. "I'll have dinner ready shortly."

"Dinner?" Derek asked observing me suspiciously. "Have you *met* you?"

"Now, now," I responded with a grin. "I picked something fool-proof … even for me."

"I take it you're not much of a cook, then," Carey remarked in a snide tone as she eyed the décor in our apartment. When Derek and I moved in together, we got rid of all but a few pieces of his furniture, which was mostly bachelor-style Ikea. I was the one with the antique Eames-era gems. Her gaze stopped on a molded plywood lounge chair sitting in a corner.

"I guess that remains to be seen," I said. "May I show you to your room?"

She tore her eyes away from the chair, shrugged and picked up her suitcase. "Sure."

As I led Carey to the guest room and showed her around, I heard Derek lug his suitcase to our bedroom to unpack. After I finished showing Carey where everything was, the smell of something burning wafted into the room.

"Oh no," I cried, immediately excusing myself and hurtling to the kitchen, where the three salmon fillets were flaming in the pan, plumes of smoke billowing up to the ceiling, tripping the smoke detector. Mortified, I twisted the stove button into the off position, and began opening the kitchen windows to dispel some of the smoke. The alarm was both deafening and relentless.

Derek appeared with a concerned look on his face and began helping me with the mess. Apparently, I had used too much olive oil and the pan had sparked and spat hot oil onto every surface, including the floor, which had become greased up and slippery. Derek fiddled with the smoke detector to quell the noise and, once he was able to shut it off, he just stared at me, befuddled as to how I could have done something so stupid.

I heard Carey's voice from the living room. "Is everything okay in there?" she called.

"Got it handled," Derek shouted back. "Just relax, we'll be out in a second."

"Oh, Derek," I said, eyes filling with tears. "I'm so sorry. I just wanted to make a good impression on Carey and look what I've done now."

"Don't worry about it, honey." He put his arms around my shoulders to console me. "I know you can't cook … and now Carey does, too." He chuckled when he delivered that last line.

I pulled away from him. "It's not funny. I can barely boil water. What kind of a wife will I be, anyway? Carey's going to think I'm a total moron."

"You want to know the good news?" Derek offered, taking my hand. "I'm not marrying you for your culinary skills—I'm marrying you for the wonderful, brilliant, and beautiful woman you are. Now, let's clean this mess and I'll take my two best girls out for a nice dinner."

I gave him a sheepish look and then nodded. "Okay. Sorry about this."

"Don't apologize," he said. "Just please never come near the kitchen again unless you have the fire extinguisher handy." We both laughed and began the process of de-greasing the kitchen.

CAREY WAS SURPRISINGLY UNDERSTANDING about the dinner mishap, but she still did not warm up to me throughout the evening. Once we retired to our respective bedrooms, I went into the bathroom to wash my face and put on my pajamas. My phone was sitting on the edge of the bathtub where I had left it earlier. I noticed there was a voice mail message waiting so I picked up the phone and dialed in to listen.

The familiar deep seductive voice oozed from the phone: "Ms. Mercer, where ... *are* you? Call me." I looked up instinctively, as though Derek could overhear the message, and took a deep breath. *Why was he calling me?* I tried hard to remember Kat's warning that it was up to me to stop this liaison with Craig Keller—that Derek would find out and I would lose him for good. I quickly deleted the message and brushed my teeth. When I came out of the bathroom, Derek was already in bed reading a paperback. Derek loved mystery novels.

"You know, Derek," I started, sitting on the edge of the bed, and studying him thoughtfully. "I don't think Carey likes me much."

Derek sighed, slapped the book down and glanced at me. "And why do you think that?"

"I can just tell," I answered glumly. The mattress springs creaked underneath my weight.

"I think you need to get to know her before you come to that conclusion," he said. "Is it possible maybe she's shy around you? She really doesn't know you and that's why she's here. She told me she wanted to get to know you before we get married. That's all. You need to give her a chance. She's an amazing person and I think you'll become good friends."

I pulled my legs up onto the bed and heard the mattress creak again. "What if we don't?" I asked, thinking that would be a nightmare because Derek idolized Carey. She was, after all, his big sister—his only sister.

"You will. Now, can we end this conversation and move on to something more important?" he said, leaning over and tossing his book on the nightstand. He turned to me, took my hand, and pulled me toward him.

"And what do you consider more important?" I slid under the covers and tangled my legs with his.

"Hmm …" he said before planting a lingering kiss on my lips. "I've been away for a long time and I just can't get that night before I went to Seattle out of my mind."

"Is that right?" I said putting my arms around his neck. I touched his sandy hair and it felt a little unruly—like wool.

"Some of those things we did—well, I was sort of surprised—pleasantly surprised."

"You know we'll have to be very quiet—we do have a guest right down the hall." I gestured toward Carey's room and made a face. "Plus, this mattress is noisy—maybe we should think about getting a new one."

"I think that's a splendid idea," he replied. "Let's buy a whole new bed—as a wedding present for ourselves."

I beamed at him. "That sounds great." I was reminded of our upcoming nuptials. "But, until then, we'll have to be extra careful when guests are visiting."

"Oh, I'll be quiet, Jane. The question is, will you be able to stifle that little moan you always make right before …."

"Right before what?" I asked, now giggling as Derek climbed on top of me. We made love noiselessly, being careful to stay on the side of the bed where the creaking was less obnoxious, and fell right to sleep, completely at peace to be reunited at last.

Ten

WHEN I HEARD JEFFREY enter his office the next morning, I thought about the dreaded magazine and whether he or Warren had seen it. I considered the situation, and, for some reason, I began to lose my nerve to be proactive, as Marisa had advised. I still had the magazine in my messenger bag, but I had accidentally left the bag at home. Maybe I would just let things be and see if either of them said anything. They were so busy with the IPO that they likely had no clue nor cared what was in the magazine, which would be obsolete in two days when the next issue hit the shelves. I decided to take my chances.

At around 10 a.m., Veronica summoned me to see Warren. I assumed he wanted updates, so I gathered files and notes for the most important clients and then stopped by Jeffrey's office to say hello. He was just finishing up a phone call when I popped my head in.

"Welcome back," I greeted him with a cheerful smile. "We missed you."

Jeffrey had an irritated look on his face and his hair was sticking up in front—in a more extreme than usual fashion. "Are you headed in to see Warren?"

"I am. Do you know why he wants to see me?"

"I have no idea, but he didn't sound happy when I spoke to him last night. He wants me in there with you, so let's go."

As Jeffrey and I trudged down the hallway to Warren's office, I couldn't help but feel anxious. I wondered what Jeffrey meant about Warren not sounding happy on the phone. My mind briefly went to the magazine photo and I was hit with a sudden fright that perhaps he had seen or heard about it. I tried to stay calm.

When we entered Warren's office, he was sitting at his desk signing what looked like legal documents. He lifted his gaze when we walked in. His expression was one I could hardly describe. He looked downtrodden as he got up and walked silently to the red velvet couch and gestured for us to sit down. Warren gently shut his office door. Once he was seated across from us in one of the black leather high-back chairs, he finally spoke.

"Jeffrey, Jane, I have some news for you and it's going to come as a big surprise, but I want you to know that I've considered the situation from every angle and have concluded that I have no other choice in the matter."

He paused and looked from Jeffrey to me and back. I focused my eyes on Warren's face, trying to read him. *What was this all about? Why was he acting so serious?*

"You see," he continued, "we've had a major change in direction, and I want to talk to both of you before it goes public." Jeffrey and I exchanged quick worried glimpses and then sat expectantly, trying to assess what he was about to lay on us. This just wasn't like Warren at all. "You know about the IPO, especially you, Jeffrey, since you've been a fully engaged partner every step of the way. But, as you both know, once we filed the S-1 form, the news that we were about to go public traveled fast and, well, there are some businesses who had their eyes on us."

He paused and then added, "One in particular. You're

familiar with Keller Whitman Group, right?"

I felt my mouth drop and stole a glance at Jeffrey, who looked just as dumbfounded.

"Mr. Keller and I have quite a history and I'm sure you've heard it's not all good." Warren shifted uncomfortably in his chair. "He's come to me with an offer to buy out our company and I've no choice but to accept."

I felt my heart racing and my eyes widening. "But ... why?" I blurted out.

"You see, the agency's undergone some financial distress and that's one of the reasons I'm motivated. Keller offered me a premium on the shares, so that we would have a deal before any of it went through."

I thought about the charity dinner and how Craig had been asking strategic questions about agency business. I then wracked my brain to think of what I had said. There's no telling after I'd drank so much champagne. Then the sickening thought that Craig had orchestrated the whole night, using me so he could get intel on Warren's agency, hit me like a lightning bolt. *That's why he was pursuing me.* He got me drunk and tried to get me to his apartment with the hope that I might tell him exactly what he needed to move in on Warren's agency. Pillow talk, so to speak. *What had I done?*

Jeffrey finally spoke out. "After the hard work all these years to build our agency, this guy just gets to come in here and take it all over? I can't believe you'd accept that from him. I mean, I know your relationship with Keller. I was there, *remember*? I was creative director when he left the company and took all the executives and clients with him. That *bastard!*" Jeffrey was angrier than I'd ever seen him in Warren's presence.

"Now, calm down, Jeffrey," Warren said, palms facing him for emphasis. "Part of the deal was that Keller needs to keep all the employees at our agency for two full years."

"What about you?" I asked, wringing my hands. "What happens to you?"

"He asked me to stay on but that's one thing I can't do. It just wouldn't work. I'm leaving the company and retiring—I haven't decided what I'm going to do yet, but I'm ready to leave the industry. I've done everything there is to do with this business and it's time to move on." He paused for a moment and licked his lips. "Jeffrey," Warren continued, "you'll remain a partner, but you'll join the other partners at Keller Whitman Group. He'll probably keep you far away from the art department there, especially since their creative director is one of the most infamous prima donnas in town."

"So, I get swallowed up in Keller's monolith—that's just great," Jeffrey sparked angrily. His face turned scarlet as he must have been imagining not only working for a man whom he respected so little, but also having the creative function completely ripped from his purview. He shook his head, eyelids now squeezed together.

"Jane," Warren said. "I urged Keller to keep you in the position you're in, but I'm forewarning you—he already has someone in the same position at his agency. I don't think he's decided how he's going to handle that. I, of course, gave you the highest recommendation and let him know I had planned to make you a full partner within the next year."

I simply could not believe what I was hearing. I was potentially losing a partnership and having to go work for Craig Keller. He was going to be my boss. Warren was *leaving*. It was all so unfathomable. I suddenly felt a sharp pain tear through my stomach.

"I know this information is upsetting to you both," Warren said. "But there are times in life when you just need to accept things as they are and take a step forward."

"Oh, come on, Warren, that's a company line if I've ever heard one," Jeffrey snapped bitterly. "These are our lives you're talking about—we didn't get into this business to work for someone like Craig Keller—he's an underhanded, cut-throat power-monger and you're telling us to move *forward* with him? You know him better than any of us, and that's why *you're* leaving."

Warren sighed and cast his eyes down for a minute, letting his hands drop limply in his lap. "Jeffrey, what do you want me to say? That I'm devastated? I think you know me well enough to guess how I feel about this. I wish I had an alternative, but I don't. I know all about Keller—you don't need to remind me. But as you said, this is about your lives and, for right now, this is your livelihood." He crossed his legs before continuing. "I have nothing to say about where you go from here—whether you want to leave for another agency or, hell, maybe start your own. I do care for you both and will never forget all the hard work and creativity you've brought me over the years. Don't squander it because of one man—your jobs have been salvaged—so none of this is necessary."

I sat quietly, just thinking. I had never seen Warren so raw before—so beaten down and honest—so bereft of the aloofness that made him the boss he always was with such unwavering consistency. This was a major blow and we all knew it. Despite what Jeffrey was saying, I knew Warren had no choice. He had done the best he could for us and that's all we could expect. He was a good man and I would miss him terribly. My thoughts went to Craig Keller. *Could I work for him after everything that had gone on between us?* I now wondered why he had called the night before—maybe to pre-warn me of what was going down today? *Whose side was he on, anyway?* Nothing made sense anymore.

"Jane," Warren said gently. "You've been quiet. How are you feeling right now about all this?"

My eyes dashed up to meet Warren's and I shrugged. Unlike Jeffrey, Warren was aware of my involvement with Craig a couple of years earlier. It was understood between us but never discussed. "I guess I'm just in shock right now," I replied. "I need to digest this whole thing. Can you at least tell me when the merger will take effect? I mean, like when will we be moving to the Keller Whitman Group offices and operating as one?"

"Within the next month or so," he responded. "We need to shore up a lot of legalities first."

ᴌ

I DROVE HOME THAT night in a fog from the terrible news. I realized my assumption that Craig was trying to break up my engagement was ridiculous. It was all about business. That's all he cared about—that's all he ever cared about—and I was just a pawn, yet again. I gritted my teeth.

ᴌ

I WANDERED INTO THE apartment so absorbed in thought that I almost zipped right by Carey, who was plopped on the sofa watching television. I heard a familiar voice stemming from the TV and realized Marisa's show was on. The apartment still smelled faintly of last night's salmon incident.

"Hi, Jane," she greeted me. "How was your day?"

"Um, fine, I guess," I absentmindedly responded, still distracted by the turmoil at work. I sat down on the sofa next to Carey and breathed deeply, desperately trying to decompress.

"You seem upset, Jane," she said, flipping her sandy blonde bob to the side. "Is anything wrong?"

"I—just, well, it's been a crazy day at work. I found out something and—um, it was not what I wanted to hear." I hardly felt comfortable talking to Carey about what happened. I just wanted to call Kat but, with Carey in the house, there was no place to have a private conversation regarding Craig Keller.

"Oh no, do you want to talk about it?" she asked. There was something in her voice that I couldn't put my finger on—there was a tone—*was it sarcasm?*

"I found out my company was bought today by a competitor. I know you aren't familiar with ad agencies in L.A., but this agency, Keller Whitman Group ..." my voice faded off while the pain of what had occurred in Warren's office only hours earlier rang loud and clear in the form of nausea.

"I've actually heard that name," Carey said slyly, like she knew something I didn't. She then pulled a magazine from the coffee table that was open to a certain page. She handed it to me before saying, "Is that who you're talking about?"

I quickly glanced at the magazine page and, there it was, the photo of me with Craig Keller, holding hands and walking toward his car. My jaw dropped, and I glared at her. "Where did you get this?" I demanded.

"You left your bag here and it tumbled off the couch. That magazine fell out and, since I'm from out of town, I thought *LA Insider Magazine* might be interesting. Turns out, it's more interesting than I'd ever dreamed." Her tone had become accusatory. "Tell me, Jane, when was this photo taken? Was it before or after my little brother left town to take care of our ailing father?" Now she was being plain nasty. I had always suspected she was capable of this behavior but was sure of it now.

"What do you want from me?" I asked, leveling with her. She obviously wanted to play hardball.

"Me? It really doesn't matter what I want, now does it? The only thing that matters is what Derek wants and, quite frankly, I don't think he'll be very impressed to find a photo of his fiancée, plastered all over a gossip magazine, holding hands with another man and wearing his jacket." She let out a snarky laugh. "I mean, you know him well by now … what do you think his reaction will be?" Her glare followed me coldly.

I felt my eyes burning with anger—anger at having left the magazine where Carey could find it and anger at her for using it against me in such a calculated manner. If it was never fully clear that Carey hated my guts, it certainly was smacking me right in the face now. I just sat and stared at her because there were no words. She had all the cards and was ready to play them.

"Are you going to tell him?" I asked.

"Oh no, Jane," she said matter-of-factly. "That's your job. But if you don't tell him right away, and that means tonight, I *will* tell him. He's my brother, and he deserves to know everything about the woman he's about to marry."

I ducked my eyes to my watch. It was close to 7 and Derek would be home any minute. "I'll tell him tonight. But please do me a favor and make yourself scarce. The conversation needs to be private and that means you need to leave. Go somewhere—there's a movie theater around the block." I pointed to the door.

She got up quickly and grabbed her purse, which was a shapeless purple fabric sack with a green peace sign embroidered on it. I felt a sliver of satisfaction that she had such hideous fashion sense.

"I'm happy to go," she said, casting a bitchy look at me, "but know that I'll be close by and have my phone turned on in case my little brother needs me." She marched out the front of the apartment and slammed the door behind her.

My hands shook violently. I was going to have to come clean with Derek about Craig. And this time, I just knew he would not be understanding. I folded my body on the couch with my head between my knees. I never wanted any of this to happen … to be in a situation where I had lied to Derek. And now, I was about to break the news to him that the woman he was engaged to marry had been untrue.

For another fifteen minutes, I just sat motionless and stared at the clock as it ticked neurotically, waiting for the proverbial other shoe to fall. Finally, I heard footsteps in the hallway and the key in the door. This was it. I got up from the couch, heart pounding in my chest, as Derek entered the room.

"Hey baby," he said smiling and walking over to where I stood. "How was your day?" When he leaned over to kiss me, I lost it. Huge sobs wracked my body. I held on to Derek tightly, hugging him close like I was never going to feel him again. "Honey, what's happened? Why are you crying? Tell me, please." I just continued to weep as he held me with a confused, concerned look on his face. "Jane, please tell me what's happened to make you like this … is it your grandparents?"

I finally caught my breath between sobs. "No, Derek. It's me—it's something I've done."

"Baby, sit down here, and we'll talk about it. There's nothing you and I can't handle together. Please sit and calm yourself, Jane." His tone was so tender and caring, it made me cry even harder. I let Derek pull me onto the couch next to him. I could barely breathe. He put his arms around me, and I felt his strength and warmth. *How would I tell him?*

"I'll get you some water," he said and got up to go into the kitchen. When he returned with a glass of water, he said, "By the way, where's Carey?"

"She went out," I answered softly. "I asked her to."

"But … why?" he asked, standing in front of me, holding the glass awkwardly.

"Because we need privacy. I have some things to tell you." I looked up at Derek and his brows were furrowed. He looked like a little boy lost in a maze or in a world he didn't understand. I felt sick to my stomach again.

Derek sat down next to me and set the water on the coffee table. "I'm here, Jane. You can tell me anything. Please, honey ... *please* just tell me."

I looked him in the eye and then said, "You're not going to like it, but here goes." I picked up the magazine, opened it to the page with the photo of Craig and me, and handed it to him. He accepted it and took a long look at its contents. His eyes didn't stray from the photo for what seemed like an eternity. He was silent. Suddenly, he placed the magazine between us and looked me in the eye.

"I remember that night," he said. "That was the night you went to the charity event and I got the news that my dad had a heart attack." He spoke slowly, like he was trying to process the information.

I closed my eyes and nodded but didn't say anything. I was waiting for Derek to piece it together for himself.

"You were drunk," he said like it was all coming back to him. He brushed his hand over his forehead. "You said you got a ride home from a colleague—a woman— but it was him, right? *He* took you home." As he said this, his eyes blazed through mine.

Again, I nodded but didn't reply.

"You didn't say anything about seeing him there." He picked up the magazine and studied the photo again. "You're wearing his jacket, Jane—holding his hand?" His tone wasn't angry or incredulous. It was disappointed. It was hurt beyond belief. "I just need to hear the truth. Please don't lie to me. I need to know." Derek's voice was almost pleading.

"It's all true," I responded. "I sat next to him at the charity event—that wasn't by choice. I had Warren's ticket, so I was stuck there. I almost left." I paused to look at Derek, who went back to studying the photo, like he was trying to interpret it.

"I drank too much champagne," I continued. "I didn't

realize Craig was ordering multiple bottles and my glass was never empty. I didn't intend to drink so much, but I did. And, after the event, we went for a walk behind the hotel and—well, I was barely able to stand. Derek, he kissed me and, well, I kissed him back and … I let him touch me."

I couldn't believe I was telling him everything, but it's like I had to expel it from my soul. I had held it there for so long, I just wanted to rid myself of this horrible secret, open it up like a moldy box of rotting fruit and bring it into the light.

Derek blinked and stared at me, like he was unsure who was sitting next to him—like I had somehow turned into someone else. He sat waiting for the next painful, ugly truth to be revealed.

I continued. "At some point, I realized I was drunk and didn't want to be there—with him. He offered to drive me home. I was so messed up, I just allowed him to lead me to his car. That's when the picture was taken."

Derek studied the photo again, like he was trying to imagine what had really happened. "What about before? You told me you never slept with him. Was that also a lie?"

"Yes," I said robotically, the truth pouring out of me like computer data. "I slept with him several times before you and I got together. It was while he was married. He totally used me. I thought it was completely over but … when I was at the event, I let myself go there, I mean not all the way, but I did what I did. And there's no one to blame but me. I'm at fault. And what's worse is today, I found out that he bought out Warren's agency. I am going to have to work for him now—see him every day."

Derek's eyes widened and then he looked disgusted. "Why did you lie to me?"

My eyes again filled with tears. "Why did I lie to you? Because of the way you're looking at me now—because I knew it would ruin us and I didn't want to lose you. Now I know I'm going to—because I know you. You can't live with this. You want to know why I lied to you? Because I know this is how it ends."

Derek looked down a moment as though he were considering my words. By the time he was able to glance back up at me, his eyes were watery. He nodded. "You're right," he said, almost in a whisper. "You know me too well."

With that, he rose from the sofa and walked stoically into our bedroom. I followed him passively, not knowing what to say or do. He wheeled his suitcase from the closet and opened it on our bed, began making trips to the closet, mechanically folding clothes and placing them in his suitcase. His expression was blank, as though he had fully tuned me out ... like his mind left his body.

"Derek," I murmured softly after about five minutes of silence. "I understand you're upset. But are you just going to leave? I mean, can't we talk more about this?"

Derek didn't answer for more than a minute; he just kept making trips to the closet. Finally, he sighed and faced me squarely. "Jane, you had an affair with a married man, you lied about it, and then you were unfaithful to me while we were engaged. There's nothing more to discuss. I refuse to live in this guy's shadow. And even if I could get around the cheating part, it's the lying—that's what kills me. You never even considered how I might have felt while you were out playing around with that guy. You kissed him? Let him touch you? Have you *any* idea how that makes me feel?"

The words that stood out to me: "*were* engaged." That meant we were over. "So that's it? We're no longer engaged?" My voice was heightened with emotion.

Derek shook his head. "How can I marry you now? You're not the woman I thought you were—you're not the woman I proposed to."

The reality hit me with a terrible force, and I found the ring on my finger, removed it, my green eyes focused on his hazel ones. I handed him the ring and he promptly placed it in his pants pocket, as he methodically continued packing clothes into his suitcase. I felt my heart seize. "Where will you go?" I asked, tearfully, wringing my hands.

"I don't know. I just know I can't stay here with you." He shot another sickened look my way.

"You know, Derek, nothing really happened between us at that event. I mean, it didn't happen like that. I stopped it because I was thinking about you." I was now standing right in his path so he could not make another trip to the closet.

He eyed me coldly. "Jane let's be real. I was the last person on your mind that night. That's perfectly clear. Now if you'll excuse me, I'd like to continue packing without interruptions."

"Fine," I said, turning on my heel and leaving him there. I knew the minute he was out the door he would call Carey for a recon. I was sure she would be happy to commiserate with Derek on what a poor choice he made in getting engaged to a two-timing jezebel like me. There was no question.

By the time Derek was ready to walk out the door, it was past 9 p.m. He didn't even look in my direction as he passed me with his suitcase. He closed and locked the door behind him and that was it. He was gone.

Eleven

*T*HE HISTORY BOOKS TEACH you that events repeat themselves, no matter how much one has learned. Such was the case with Craig Keller, who would now be my boss. I recalled the time I was voluntarily going to work for him. Now, it was no longer up to me. With Derek gone and out of my life, I had to support myself and that meant sucking it up and going through the merger with Craig's agency. I was going to have to make it work or face unemployment.

I arrived at the office early the next morning, mostly because I couldn't sleep after Derek's departure. I had had the displeasure of seeing Carey at the front door about an hour after Derek left. She was there to gather her things. There were no pleasantries between us, no words at all. I numbly stood aside and let her in. I could hear the floorboards groaning as she nudged around packing things up in the next room while I stared blankly at the television. She was gone within fifteen minutes and I locked the door after her. My mind was still jumbled with everything that had occurred within the last twelve hours. I hadn't even called my friends. I had no words left and felt completely drained of life.

This morning was another story. I knew I looked like hell after crying so much. My face wore the puffiness and bloat of a sleepless night and, no matter how many tea bags and cucumber slices I placed around my eyes, they were still swollen and red with sadness. Nevertheless, I showed up at the office, powered up the computer and tried to go through emails like everything was normal. I had this habit of looking at my phone every five minutes, as though there might be a text from Derek ... maybe telling me he was okay ... that he found a hotel or somewhere to stay ... anything. I desperately longed to hear from him. I thought about calling, but every time I picked up my phone, I put it down again in torment, knowing he didn't want to hear from me. I also realized that, with Carey in the picture, he was less likely to weaken and call me—she would be heavy-handed in keeping him on track in the process of cutting me out of his life for good.

When Jeffrey arrived at the agency, he immediately entered my office with a much calmer demeanor than the one I'd seen the day before. He settled in a chair across from my desk and leaned forward, resting his elbows on his knees in his familiar stance.

"Hey," he said. "You okay? I was going to call you last night, but something told me to wait."

"You must be clairvoyant," I uttered in a zombie-like stupor. "Last night was not a good time for me."

"What happened other than the obvious?" he queried, blinking at me with curiosity.

"Just personal stuff," I replied vaguely. "How was your night? Are you still seething about having to work for Craig Keller?"

Jeffrey leaned back in his chair. "Nah ... I mean, yes, I'm still disgusted. But I have a motto: 'You can only be mad for twenty-four hours when something doesn't go your way at work.' Then you just have to swallow it."

"That's some motto. Maybe I should try it," I said

without enthusiasm. "When's Warren going to tell the employees?"

"Probably soon … although I'm sure Keller will want to be a part of that discussion, you know, to show everyone he's boss now."

I thought about the employees getting a glimpse of Craig for the first time and realized that the females were in for the thrill of a lifetime. They would be falling all over themselves for attention from him. I sighed heavily, revolted at the thought of his head getting even bigger than it already was—if that were possible.

"You really think you can swing working with him?" I asked, fidgeting in my office chair.

Jeffrey shrugged. "I don't know, Jane. I knew him in a different life, and he wasn't exactly my cup of tea. I guess I'll find out soon enough. How about you?"

I thought about my history with Craig, which was quite a bit different from Jeffrey's but somehow related. "Well, I'm not independently wealthy, so I really have no choice other than to make it work." As I said this, I glanced at the photo of Derek and I on my desk, recalling with agony those days when we were so carefree—so blithely unfamiliar with each other's fallibility.

"But you're getting married soon—do you think Derek would support you while you look for something else?"

I swallowed hard, instinctively putting my hand over my now ringless finger. "Derek…." I started to say, but my voice shook and then straggled off. Jeffrey eyed me curiously again. After several deep breaths, I began again in a somber tone, "Derek is no longer a factor … as of last night."

Jeffrey's expression changed to one of shock. "What? Oh no, Jane, what happened? Did you guys break it off?"

I felt my eyes filling with tears, and Jeffrey immediately got to his feet and shut my office door. He sat back down across from me, now regarding me with apprehension.

"I wasn't ready to tell anyone," I whispered, grabbing a tissue from the box on my desk and blowing my nose loudly. "So, I'd appreciate if you don't repeat this."

"You know I won't, Jane," he replied quickly. "But tell me this—is it totally over or is there a chance you may reconcile?"

I shook my head, tears still flowing down my cheeks. "No—there'll be no reconciliation."

"Damn—I thought you two were the perfect couple." Jeffrey looked genuinely saddened at my news. "Did he do something to hurt you?"

"No, Jeffrey. It was something I did. And I really don't want to share anything else."

Jeffrey now rose from his chair and moved around my desk to where I sat. He took my hand, lifted me up and pulled me in for a hug. I felt his chin rest on my head as he held me close. I could smell his aftershave—which reminded me of a wheat field. "I'm so sorry, Jane," he murmured. "Let me know if there's anything I can do."

"You can keep people out of my office today," I requested, withdrawing from the embrace with a wry smile and wet eyes.

"Maybe you should take the rest of the day off," Jeffrey suggested. "I'll cover for you."

"Thanks, but I would just sit at home depressed. I'll be okay. It would be great if you could just cover for me in a few meetings, so I don't have to show up looking like a lost refugee from the island of despair."

Jeffrey half-smiled. "Of course. I've got you." And he exited my office, shutting the door behind him.

LATER THAT AFTERNOON, I stole to the ladies' room to freshen up. I looked in the mirror and saw that most of the swelling had gone down and that I looked present-able. I added eye makeup and touched up my lipstick. I stood back and viewed myself in the full-length mir-ror. Even in my destroyed emotional state of disrepair, I had chosen a smart outfit. It was a white pantsuit, ele-gantly tailored, with a lacy blouse underneath that tied at my throat with a secretary bow. The blouse was sheer, but you couldn't see anything because I kept my dou-ble-breasted jacket buttoned all the way up. The whole look was classic, yet slightly sexy—maybe a bit too sexy for the office, but I didn't care. The fact that I made it to the office that day at all was a major feat.

When I exited the ladies' room, I almost ran right into Warren who was walking with … *Craig Keller*. I froze for a minute, not knowing what to say. They were both gazing in my direction.

Craig was the first to speak. "Ms. Mercer—it's nice to see you." He approached me and held out his hand to shake mine.

"Hello, Mr. Keller," I replied, shaking his hand un-comfortably.

"I hear you're going to be my new best friend," he announced, giving me his lazy grin, along with a once-over. He wore a dark blue checked wool suit that draped perfectly over his tall, lean frame. I realized then that he was much taller than Warren, who was around five feet eleven inches. This could not have made Warren happy.

"Oh?" I responded doing my best to keep a princess smile on my face and recalling that 'princess smile' was a term coined by Marisa and me long ago. It was a way of smiling like a princess in the face of controversy or misery. I was in the middle of both. "Yes, I suppose so."

I caught Warren studying me, but he remained silent.

"I'll be in touch with you soon," Craig said to me.

Then the two proceeded to walk past me toward Warren's office.

I immediately returned to my office and continued working. I guessed I had to get used to seeing Craig, since he was taking over Warren Mitchell & Partners. It was just a matter of time. I couldn't help but think of how attractive he always was … there was never a time I saw him look like anything other than an icon. He just had that way about him. I found my messenger bag and pulled out the magazine, laying it carefully on my desk, opened to the incriminating page. This was what broke up Derek and me, I thought sadly. If I could just do that night over again … everything would be different. *Or would it?* Derek was always leery about my relationship with Craig and, even though he had initially accepted my lie, he would always be looking for things. Now that the truth was out, there was no way he would ever trust me again. It was over.

Around 7 p.m., I decided it was time to go home, even though the thought of entering the dreary, empty apartment I had shared with Derek only yesterday made me sick with dread. I began gathering things and heard a knock at my office door.

"Come in," I called.

The door opened, and Craig Keller appeared in the doorway.

"It's you," I uttered, somewhat surprised. "What can I do for you?" My voice trilled with forced professionalism.

He entered the office and shut my door, turned and gave me a closed-mouth smile. "I thought we could have a little chat while I was in your neighborhood. May I?" he asked, gesturing to one of the chairs across from my desk.

"Of course," I replied straightening up in my chair. "After all, I think you're technically my boss now, right?"

He sat in one of the chairs and leaned back, crossing his long legs. I noticed he wore funky-colored striped socks underneath his suit—perhaps some statement of independence in the face of corporate minimalism. "And how do you feel about that, Jane?" he challenged, looking me directly in the eye.

I shrugged. *What did he want me to say? That I was devastated he was my boss because my indiscretions with him had led to my engagement being broken and, as far as I was concerned, my life being over? Other than that, I guess I was fine with it.*

"Come on, Jane," he prompted, giving me his seductive slow blink. "We know each other pretty well. Don't you feel comfortable talking to me?"

"Know each other?" I asked in disbelief. "You know *nothing* about me." I put both palms on my desk and leaned toward him as I said this, accidentally knocking over the photo of Derek and me so it was face down.

His eyes drifted to my left hand and then back to my eyes again. "What happened to your engagement ring?" he asked. "Did you conveniently forget to wear it, or did you and Romeo break up?"

I felt the hot blood rush to my face and my eyes begin to burn. "Do *not* call him 'Romeo'," I answered angrily. "And what's it to you, anyway?"

He shrugged. "Just curious. Because if it's over, that had to be the shortest engagement in history," he remarked, looking amused.

That was it—I lost it. "Are you really *this* callous? Do you want to know why we broke up, Craig? Do you really want to know?"

I pulled out the *LA Insider Magazine* and slid it straight across the desk, watching it fly off the surface and promptly tumble into Craig's lap. He picked up the magazine and observed the cover casually, then looked up at me again, unmoved.

"Open it to page forty-six," I ordered, getting more upset by the second. "Then you tell me why I'm no longer engaged." My voice had risen to a shrill pitch, and

I could feel my heart pounding. *This bastard needed to understand how he ruined my life.*

He stared at me coolly before flipping through the pages. He stopped on the page and studied it carefully for a minute. Then he casually tossed it back on my desk. "Well," he commented. "You look beautiful in the picture, that's for sure. But then you always do—like right now." His eyes were lingering on the sheer blouse underneath my suit jacket. I didn't respond. "If you ask me, this guy's a little too tightly wound for you. I mean, it's just a picture. It's one night and nothing happened. I'm happy to talk to him if you think it would help."

"I can't think of a worse idea," I countered, imagining Craig approaching Derek to explain what really happened that night. Derek would probably want to punch him in the face. No good could come of it. "I already told you he hates you anyway. This was just salt on the wound. Plus, it's done—there's no going back now."

Craig sat back, and took a deep breath, eyes on mine. "I know you probably don't believe me, Jane, but I'm very sorry to hear about your engagement," he divulged contritely. "And, I'm even sorrier if I had something to do with it."

"Yeah, I'm sure you're just destroyed over the news," I voiced bitterly, eyes cast down, no longer wanting to discuss the subject with Craig. When I looked up, I caught him ogling my lace blouse again as he shifted in his chair.

"Tell me, Ms. Mercer—is this how you dress every day at the office?" he asked with a devilish grin. "Because if it is, I'm going to have one hell of a time concentrating on work."

"Oh, you love this, don't you?" I was seething inside. I stood and folded my arms in front of my chest. "You love that you're going to be my boss and have me under your thumb from now on."

He silently rose from his chair and walked around

my desk, now looming over me. I remained where I was, peering up at his handsome face and hating myself for still feeling his chemistry. He was using his height to intimidate me, but it wasn't going to work. I just didn't care anymore. "You orchestrated the seating arrangements at that charity event, didn't you, Craig?" I felt my face getting hot and my cheeks burning. "You ordered all that champagne, so I'd get drunk and tell you things, right Craig? When I said 'no' to going home with you, I foiled your master plan, didn't I? You expected me to give you even more details about Warren's agency, so you could ultimately take it over."

Craig's expression didn't change, but his eyes turned a darker shade of green as they locked on mine. I knew from experience that indicated his frustration, even if his demeanor remained cold and calculated. His eyes were sort of like mood rings; one could figure out exactly how he was feeling by tracking the color gradation.

"You're over-estimating your role in all this," he finally expressed, slowly, as though he were choosing his words carefully. "Those plans were made long ago. I had no idea I'd be seated next to you at that event. I'd hoped it would have been Warren, so I could start the negotiation process. But I wasn't at all disappointed when I found out he sent you in his place."

His comments just reinforced that I was an insignificant diversion that night and that Craig did everything based solely on what he would gain from a business standpoint; it had nothing to do with me. It was all about him, as usual. "Why are you here?" I demanded abruptly, looking straight up into his eyes as he towered over me.

"Why didn't you return my call Sunday?" he pressed leaning even closer, so I could smell his soapy skin and cherry breath.

"Why were you calling me on a Sunday?" I snapped,

feeling the heat from his body at such close range.

Craig ran his tongue over his lower lip. "Jane, if we're going to get along together, you really need to change your attitude," he said, as though he were lecturing a child. "Besides, just think of how much fun it will be to work side-by-side."

"Is that what you came here to tell me?" I asked, now taking a small step backward so I was out of his immediate trace.

He gave me the slow blink again. "I came here to welcome you to Keller Whitman Group. Warren says glowing things about you, and I want to assure you that whatever may have happened between us in the past will not affect the way I view you as an employee now."

Oh, I'm sure it won't because you view every female employee as though they are objects kept around solely for your pleasure. I looked down at my feet for a moment and then back up into Craig's eyes. They were now light translucent jade with those long lashes, flashing at me with faux sincerity. Finally, it hit me that this was a no-win situation. I could fight Craig every step of the way, but he would eventually fire me. No, I had to be congenial.

"So that's what you wanted to tell me? Well, that's very kind of you. Thank you, Craig." I forced a smile even though my guts were churning with anger.

He dipped a grin back at me. "That-a-girl, Jane. I knew you'd come around." Then he leaned forward and whispered in my ear, "I have to know. Are you wearing anything under that blouse?"

I recoiled so sharply, my back thudded against the office wall behind my desk, my Cal State Long Beach diploma vibrated as though ready to tumble down, and I glared at him with my mouth open. "What?"

"You heard me," he said gazing down at my breasts provocatively and raising his eyebrows.

"That's none of your business," I retorted.

"You're right—it's none of my business—for now." He cocked his head to the left slightly. "But in a few weeks, it will be and, by gosh, Jane, I'd have to send you home in that outfit."

I swallowed hard and just stared at him, tight-lipped, eyes watering.

"And I might have to accompany you," he added with a lazy grin.

"You're … incorrigible," I muttered, exasperated by his shameless ways. I just wanted him to leave now. "Is this how it's going to be, working for you?" I hissed. "Because there are laws that protect women from sexual harassment in the workplace."

Craig's eyes widened a bit as though he didn't expect the comment. "That's only if it's not consensual," he responded without emotion.

We were interrupted by a knock on my door. "Jane," I heard Jeffrey call before opening the door and poking his head in. He did a double take at the sight of Craig. "Oh … I didn't realize you were in here with someone," he said quickly.

"Jeffrey," Craig took over. "How've you been?" He stepped back around my desk and held his hand out to Jeffrey, who reluctantly shook Craig's. Jeffrey's eyes were fixed on me, his look, one of extreme caution. It was as if he were silently questioning why Craig was standing behind my desk and so close to me. "We were just discussing how great it will be to have you both on my team," Craig acknowledged smoothly, like everything was normal. "I spent most of the day with Warren. He thinks the world of this group."

"Thanks," Jeffrey said stiffly. "I look forward to working with you again."

Craig glanced at his watch. "I actually have to run," he announced. "It was great seeing you, Jane. And, Jeffrey, let's schedule time for you to come by the office next week so I can show you around and you can meet the other partners."

"Fine," Jeffrey agreed dispassionately.

Craig turned and traipsed out of my office, leaving the door open behind him.

"What the hell was that?" Jeffrey asked, once he was certain Craig was gone.

"He was in here to welcome me to Keller Whitman Group," I answered, rolling my eyes.

Jeffrey studied my face to figure out whether I was lying. Then he turned and shut my door so no one could eavesdrop. "Jane," he started. "You're like family to me and I know I've warned you about him in the past but ...." Jeffrey took a deep breath. "That man has a crazy sickness with women. You're beautiful and talented, and I have no doubt he'll go after you."

Oh Jeffrey, you don't know the half of it ... been there, done that. I just listened as he continued.

"And, if he does make unwanted advances toward you, I want you to know you can come to me and we'll go to H.R." Jeffrey's voice had become solemn, like he was truly frightened for me.

Really? What if I have a crazy sickness with him and what if it is, as Craig just mentioned, consensual? I'm not worried about Craig's advances I'm worried more about my inability to control my impulses. I'm worried that I want him even as we're having this conversation—that losing my fiancé and every shred of stability in my life still won't quell my lust for that man.

"Do you understand me, Jane? I'm here to protect you from that type of harassment. You don't have to put up with it." Jeffrey's face and spiky hair looked a little greasy, like he had been out in the heat sweating today. I had a hunch it was more emotional, though.

I sighed. "Oh, Jeffrey. Thank you. It'll be fine. Don't

worry about me. I'll stand up for myself." The truth was, I was not sure how I was going to get through it if Craig was still intent on pursuing me with sexual overtures and unbridled commentary about my outfit selections.

Jeffrey didn't look convinced. Without waiting for a response, I stood up, gathered my things, and flew past him out the door, out of the building, and to my car. I had had enough drama for one day.

Twelve

DRIVING HOME THAT NIGHT, I was immersed in my predicament. I sat in traffic like a rigid automaton, shifting gears and pumping the brakes—completely unaware of which direction I was headed. Somehow, I made it home. When I entered the empty apartment and put my messenger bag down, I felt Derek's presence everywhere. I kicked off my high-heeled pumps and staggered to our closet where some of his clothes were still hanging. I put my arms around them as though they were Derek and hugged them close, burying my face into them, inhaling his scent. I felt a stream of tears flow down my face. I wiped my eyes with one of his shirts and stepped out of the closet, knowing my actions were masochistic but hardly caring. *This is what grief feels like.*

I wandered into the kitchen and realized I had not eaten a thing since Derek left. The nausea enveloping my insides made it impossible to entertain any kind of appetite. I opened the refrigerator and longed to see Derek's leftovers like I did only two weeks earlier—even if I was not in the mood to eat. Just seeing the plastic containers filled with food made with Derek's passion and energy would make me feel hopeful. They would provide something to hold on to—a memory of the days when Derek still loved me and intended for us to be married. I stood staring at the anemic food ingredients I had purchased for Carey's stay—the ingredients that needed Derek's skilled hand to turn into something edible—and I felt vomit bubbling up in my throat.

I ran to the bathroom and put my head in the toilet, heaving with violent peristaltic contractions, but nothing came out except water and bile. Tears flooded out as I just lay there with my head on the toilet seat. I finally picked myself up off the bathroom floor and caught a glimpse of myself in the mirror. My face was covered with mascara. I reached for my phone and caught that there was a voicemail from Marisa. This was the dreadful part of the breakup—the notifying of friends and family, but I knew it was inevitable.

I called Marisa who answered right away. "Hey," she said brightly, "what's up?"

"Marisa, listen to me. Something awful has happened. I ... um, Derek and I ... well, we broke up last night. The engagement's off ... everything's off."

Marisa was silent for a moment, likely processing what I just said. "Oh no, Jane. What happened? Are you okay?" she asked, voice filled with concern.

"No, I'm not really." Tears were trickling down my face again. I wiped my eyes with the back of my hand. Then, I noticed a large nugget of rosin Derek had been using for his violin sitting on his nightstand, and my heart tugged. I picked the rosin up and rolled it between my fingers. Its corners were sharp, like a rock.

"I'm coming over. See you in a bit," Marisa replied before hanging up.

I curled up on the couch in my white pantsuit and closed my eyes, breathing deeply. I must have fallen fast asleep because I was awakened by a loud knock at the door. I managed to get to my feet, still dazed, and hobbled to the door.

When I opened it, Kat and Marisa stood there, with glum looks on their faces.

"How did you guys get in?" My voice resembled an old smoker's. "I didn't hear the buzzer go off."

Marisa held up a key. "You gave this to me a long time ago—way before Derek moved in." I ushered them into the apartment, glancing at the clock and saw that it was past 10 p.m. "I called Kat," Marisa blurted, taking my hand.

"She told me it was an emergency," Kat added.

"Isn't it?" I said with gravity.

"Why are you still in your work clothes?" Marisa asked, eyeing my now wrinkled and disheveled white pantsuit. The lace blouse had come untucked while I was asleep on the couch and there were vomit stains on the secretary bow.

I looked down at myself and shrugged. "I ... I'm not feeling well."

"Of course, you're not," Marisa answered with empathy in her voice. "That's to be expected."

"Let's get you into your pajamas, honey," Kat said softly. "You'll feel much better."

Kat and Marisa led me into the bedroom, helped me out of my work clothes and into my pajamas. Then they sat me on the toilet lid in the bathroom and Kat washed all the dried mascara from my face with a warm soapy washcloth while Marisa brushed my hair. I just sat there staring blankly at a picture on the wall. Derek and I had bought it in Denmark. It was really a paper greeting card with a pale blue sailboat cut out and red threads to depict the sails. I pictured Derek's face when he saw that I had framed and hung the sailboat card in our bathroom. I recalled him smiling and telling me how clever I was—what a creative way it was to memorialize our trip that one summer. I could not even remember what year it was that we made the trip. My whole life seemed like a distant memory now.

Kat dried my face, applied lotion and moisturizing cream under my eyes while Marisa disappeared for several minutes. She returned with a hot cup of tea.

The two helped me into bed and pulled up the covers. When I was properly tucked in, they flanked me on either side of the bed, like it was an impromptu slumber party, absent the gaiety. Marisa handed me the cup of tea.

Kat sighed. "Do you want to talk about it?" she asked gently.

"I don't know what to say, other than everything went horribly wrong," I explained, taking a small sip of the hot tea. It had the pungent taste of grass clippings.

"Did it have anything to do with *him*?" Kat said, gracefully slipping off her pumps and lifting her legs onto the bed, scooting closer to me. Marisa looked up at Kat, immediately understanding to whom she was referring.

I nodded. "It was unavoidable. There was a picture of me with him and—I was so guilt-ridden—I ended up telling Derek all the lurid details, including what happened before we got together."

"Oh my God, Jane—I thought you were going to hide the magazine from him," Marisa exclaimed, wildly gesturing with her hands like she couldn't believe what an unadulterated dope her friend was.

"What magazine?" Kat asked. "Did I miss something?"

I handed the teacup to Marisa, who set it on the nightstand. "*LA Insider Magazine* ran a huge photo of Craig and I from the charity event," I answered. "I was going to hide it from Derek, but I forgot it in a bag and his sister found it while I was at work. She confronted me with it when I got home and left me with no other alternative than confessing my sins to her one and only brother."

"What a bitch." Kat groaned and put her hand to her forehead. "I'm so sorry."

"You didn't have to spill the whole story," Marisa scolded, again eyeing me like I was an imbecile. "I mean, remember what we talked about? You were going to say he just gave you a ride home."

"Oh Marisa, I'm so tired of lying. What kind of a relationship is *that*—to have so many secrets—to be constantly hiding something?"

"It's called marriage," Kat replied, rolling her eyes.

Marisa smirked and put her hand over her mouth. "Sorry, Jane. So, he moved out? Just like that? Was he angry?"

I rubbed my hands together, shivering at the memory of telling the story to Derek. "He was mostly surprised that I lied to him. He didn't get angry. He was more hurt than anything else. Derek doesn't show his emotions when he's going through them ... only after he's processed things."

"Where is he now?" Kat asked.

"No clue," I replied. "He left last night and wouldn't tell me where he was going."

Marisa kicked off her heels and pulled her feet underneath her, facing me. "Jesus, Jane—it's not like you actually cheated on him. I mean, it was only a kiss, right? Why is he being so hard-headed?"

Kat glanced at me. "Well, it was a bit more than a kiss, right, Jane? And Derek probably senses you're still attracted to him—did you tell Marisa that part?"

I shook my head and gestured for Marisa to hand me the teacup. "It doesn't matter now. I lied to him. He's gone. I'm miserable. Nothing's going to change that." I took a sip of tea and remembered my work situation. "And that's not even the worst part of the story," I added.

"It gets worse?" Marisa inquired, shifting so she was sitting cross-legged. The bed springs creaked when she moved. It reminded me that Derek and I were about to purchase a new bed—to celebrate our upcoming marriage.

I closed my eyes and breathed deeply. "Our company was taken over by Keller Whitman Group. Craig is going to be my boss." As I uttered that last line, my voice shook.

Both Marisa and Kat gasped at the same time. "What are you going to do?" Marisa asked first. I handed her the teacup again and she took a sip before setting it down.

"What *can* I do? I need my job. Warren apparently saved it, but there's a woman at Craig's agency with the same job title as me. I have no idea what might happen."

"Do you know who the woman is?" Kat immediately zeroed in on the impending job conflict.

I grabbed the hem of my pajama top and twisted it vigorously. "I don't. But I'll find out soon. Rumor has it we have to move to the Keller Whitman building downtown by the end of the month."

"Have you spoken to Craig since the last—incident?" Kat asked, eyes wide.

"I saw him today, actually," I replied, thinking of the way he mentally undressed me. "He was meeting with Warren and stopped by my office afterward."

"And?" Marisa asked impatiently. "What happened?"

I blinked at her. "The usual."

"He tried to hit on you again, didn't he?" Kat threw out with contempt. She was off the bed now, pacing back and forth in her bare feet, heels faintly resounding on the hard wood floor.

My eyes once again filled with tears as I nodded. "I have no idea what I'm going to do when I have to see him every day."

"You're going to report anything he does that's even

remotely inappropriate," Marisa said angrily. "I swear, does this guy think he's above the law?"

"It's not *him* I'm worried about," I responded doubtfully. "It's *me*. You know how weak I am when it comes to him. That's how I got into this mess in the first place."

"You can do this, Jane," Kat encouraged, yet she gave Marisa a rueful look. Kat slipped on her pumps and retrieved her purse from a chair near my bed.

"We should let you get some sleep," Marisa announced. "Do you think you'll be able to?"

I shrugged and glanced around my Derek-free room. "I'll try."

"Wait," Kat said, digging through the contents of her purse. "I have a sleeping pill somewhere in here." She located a small pill box and removed two white pills, placed them on my nightstand. "Here's two nights' worth. I would take one tonight and another tomorrow. There's no way you're going to sleep well after what you've been through."

Marisa got to her feet and stepped into her heels. Kat leaned down to kiss me on the cheek. "You'll get through this, Jane," Kat reassured. "I promise it'll get better and we'll be right by your side the whole time."

"Thank you," I said, suddenly feeling sleepy.

"And that means you can call at any time, day or night," Marisa added, squeezing my hand.

"Are you sure you want to commit to that?" I asked. The two just smiled and left me there with my own, bleak thoughts.

ᚾ

I DECIDED TO TRY to sleep without a pill and fell out quickly after the girls left, but I woke up promptly at 4 a.m. with a jolt. I instinctively put my hand to the side of the bed to feel for Derek sleeping next to me. It dawned on me what had happened, and all the sad memories came flooding back. I shivered and pulled the covers around my body. Sleep eluded me for the rest of the night and I finally got up and sat in front of the TV, watching the *Sex and the City* movie where Carrie gets jilted at her wedding with Big and goes through the heartbreak that came after it. I almost changed the channel, the content hit so close to home.

I finally fell asleep on the couch and awakened at 8:30 a.m. in a panic because I needed to be at work by 9. I scrambled into the kitchen and made coffee. *There's no way I can go to work the way I feel now.* I decided calling in sick was my best option. I picked up my cell phone and dialed Jeffrey, who answered on the first ring.

"How are you?"

"Awful," I replied. "Listen, Jeffrey, remember how you said you'd cover for me yesterday? Well, I need you to cover for me today. I didn't sleep last night and feel dreadful. I just don't think I should be at work."

"Of course, I'll cover for you," Jeffrey answered without hesitation. "I was shocked you didn't stay home yesterday."

I sighed. "Thanks, Jeffrey. I'll be at home if there's anything you need ... I just can't be there today."

"No problem, Jane. Take care."

I went back to the couch in my pajamas and lay down, turning the channel to the *Today Show* and barely watching it. I heard a key turning in the front door and I jumped. The door opened, and in walked Derek, carrying empty boxes.

He stopped dead in his tracks when he saw me, a profound sadness in his eyes.

"Oh," he muttered awkwardly. "I thought you'd be at work."

"I called in sick. I haven't been sleeping."

Derek just stared at his feet and then looked up at me. "I'm sorry to hear that," he replied. "I'll come back when you're feeling better and back at work."

I walked with a slow, careful gait to where Derek stood. He had a worried look in his eye as he took a small step back, like I had a contagious virus. "I need to talk to you," I stated firmly. I watched Derek shift his weight from one foot to the other, obviously nervous in my presence. He said nothing. "Derek, can we please talk? Please?" I caught a glimpse of my face in a nearby mirror and I looked pale and desperate. I also noticed my hair hung around my face in a tangled web. I hadn't even bothered brushing it. I was an utter mess.

"Jane—honestly, no," he finally said. "I just came to get the rest of my things."

"But you're acting like we're strangers, Derek. We've been together for a long time—doesn't it bother you that we're not even on speaking terms? We should work through this together." My voice was pleading.

Derek set the boxes down for a minute, a distressed look on his face.

"Do you want a cup of coffee?" I asked.

He looked as though he were considering whether he wanted to spend any time with the enemy but, after a full minute, he finally nodded. "Okay. You don't have to get it for me." And he walked into the kitchen while I followed along, feeling like I may have gotten my foot in the door, however feebly. I silently watched as he made coffee for himself. Once he had it prepared, he took a small sip and then looked me in the eye, without a word.

"Can you at least tell me you miss me?" I asked, wanting an emotional response from him—anything that might show he was feeling as miserable as I was.

"What do you want me to say?" His tone was cold.

"I want you to say yes and be telling the truth," I replied, searching his hazel eyes.

"And what good will that do?"

"I don't know—all I'm saying is that I miss you—I

miss you so much it's torturing me."

"Torturing *you*?" he repeated. "I don't suppose you've thought about the fact that you're going to be with your rich boyfriend all the time now, and he can kiss and touch you all he wants. I'm sure he will." I flinched when I heard that last line. "But it's torturing *you*," he muttered before taking another sip of coffee and making a face like it tasted bitter.

"Derek, that's not fair," I burst out. "I had no control over what happened with our agency. It's beyond my pay grade. I'm just a pawn like every other employee and we're all going to have to live with it."

"I'm sure it'll be easy for you—after all, you're his favorite, aren't you?" he taunted.

"Stop it, Derek." I was suddenly angered by Derek's sharp tongue. "That's a cheap shot and you know it."

"You wanted to talk—well, let's have a *chat*, Jane. You want to talk about rejection? You want to talk about being strangers?" Derek's voice had risen, and his eyes were flashing. "I don't even know who you are anymore. Maybe I never did."

I put my hand up. "Lower your voice, Derek. There's no need to shout."

"That's because there's no need for us to talk *at all*. I told you there's nothing more to say and you can't seem to get that through your thick head." When he said this, he tapped his fingers against his skull for emphasis.

It was clear I wasn't going to get anywhere with Derek and that I should just let him get his things and leave. "Fine," I said, relenting. "Just pretend I'm not here and do what you have to do."

At that moment, there was a knock at the door. I walked over and opened it and there stood sister Carey with more boxes. "You didn't tell me this was a family affair," I remarked without a word to Carey, my eyes focused again on Derek.

"That's what we do, Jane. *Families* stick together." With that, he turned his back on me and disappeared into the bedroom.

IT TOOK DEREK AND Carey about two hours to get his things in boxes and take them to his car. I was so uncomfortable with Carey there, I pulled on a pair of jeans and a T-shirt and left the apartment, wandering around Third Street and Promenade, entering, and exiting shops without buying anything. I kept seeing happy couples, holding hands, some kissing and some just deep in conversation—it was almost like I never noticed these couples until now. I never noticed them because I was the one holding Derek's hand—I was the one deep in conversation. I felt like I was now on the outside, looking in with longing.

I wandered the streets until I felt it was safe to go back home. I opened the door of the apartment and found all of Derek's belongings gone. He even took the books that we had merged over the year of living together. I surveyed the scene and no longer felt sad— just numb.

Thirteen

THE TIME CAME WHEN I needed to let my grand-parents know what happened with Derek. It had been almost a week since he moved out, so I decided, on Saturday, to make the drive to Los Alamitos to tell them in person. I spent the entire ride stressing out about the dreaded conversation. *What was I going to say? How was I going to position this, so they wouldn't blame me for the breakup?* When I got to their house, I parked, took a deep breath and slow-walked to the front door, nervously rubbing my hands together as though I were cold.

Grandma answered the door. "Jane!" she exclaimed, pleasantly surprised to find me there. "What are you doing here, pigeon?" She was wearing a white apron printed with little yellow daisies all over it. She hugged and kissed me and steered me into the house. The warm scent of vanilla was wafting from the kitchen. Grandpa was outside working in the garden. Grandma went out back and yelled at Grandpa, "Bruce, Jane's here—come on back inside." She began washing her hands at the sink and wiping them on her daisy apron.

"It smells good in here," I remarked. "What are you baking?"

"Cupcakes," she responded. "They're almost done—you got here at the right time." Grandma smiled cheerfully.

I felt small beads of sweat forming on the back of my neck. This was not going to be an easy conversation I just knew it. I was not sure how I was going to explain everything or how much detail they really needed. Once we were seated at the dining table and Grandma had poured coffee, I finally spoke. "Grandma and Grandpa," I began. "I'm here because I have some rather difficult news to share."

They looked at each other and then at me with puzzled expressions. "Is it Derek's father?" Grandma asked. "Did he recover from the heart attack? Oh Jane, please tell me he's better."

"Grandma, please just listen. Derek's father is fine. It's us. We … we broke off the engagement and Derek moved out." *There, I had said it.*

Grandma immediately looked crestfallen while Grandpa just sat and gaped at me in astonishment. "But Jane," Grandma pleaded, tears now in her eyes. "You love each other. What in the world happened?"

I bit my lower lip and took a deep breath. This was even tougher than I expected. "I'm sorry, Grandma, but it just didn't work out."

"But you were just here—I saw you kissing out back—it didn't look like there was anything wrong to me—in fact, it looked like everything was right," she argued.

Grandpa shook his head, sighing deeply and looking down at the kitchen table, fiddling with the salt and pepper shakers, which were shaped like a pair of doves. The timer went off and Grandma sprung up from her chair. I watched as Grandma donned a pair of yellow potholders and gingerly took the cupcake tin out of the oven, setting it on a counter trivet.

She quickly returned to the table and sat. "Now, Jane—I want to know how this happened. Did it have to do with your job?" Naturally, she assumed I was the cause of the breakup.

"Sort of," I confessed, not wanting to get into the real reason, although I knew she wasn't about to let it go. It was the reason I was frightened to have the conversation in the first place.

"What's all this *mishigas*?" she exclaimed in disgust. "That damned job—why can't you just quit work and go be with Derek? I thought you were going to be husband and wife. Why on God's green earth would you let that job get in the way of your engagement?"

"It's not like that, Grandma." Tears were beginning to well up in my eyes.

"Janie, it's going to be okay." Grandpa finally spoke up, smoothing back his longish grey hair with his hand. "We loved Derek like he was one of our own but if it didn't work out, then so be it. There are other fish in the sea."

I closed my eyes for a moment—trying to prevent myself from bawling at Grandpa's kindness and immediate acceptance. Unfortunately, Grandma was not as accepting.

She raised her eyebrows at me like she had a sudden epiphany. "Bruce," she broke in, not letting her gaze stray from me. "Bruce, please leave Jane and I alone for a few minutes." Grandpa obediently got to his feet, walked over to give me a sympathetic pat on the back and then disappeared through the saloon doors. I heard him go outside, the old screen door screeching shut behind him.

Grandma pulled a cigarette out of her pack and, instead of lighting it right away like she usually did, she offered me one. "Here, Jane," she said, holding the cigarette out to me, which I gladly accepted. She lit my cigarette and then hers. After a few minutes of puffing our smokes in silence, Grandma finally spoke. "It was that magazine photo, wasn't it?" she asked. "He saw it, right?"

I took another long drag. "That was certainly part of it," I replied solemnly while blowing the smoke out through my nostrils, cartoonish white swirls floating toward the ceiling.

"*Oy vey*—I knew it," she declared. "Jane, can I ask what you were doing with that man in the first place?"

"I told you," I answered. "It was just a guy I know from work. A guy who's now going to be my boss."

Grandma just sat and observed me for a moment, still smoking. "Jane," she began tentatively. "Did something go on between you and that man?"

"Why do you ask?" I was silently praying my cheeks weren't turning red, although they were burning.

She shrugged. "I don't know. It's just a feeling I have. He's a certain type of man—I could tell by the way he was dressed in that picture—by the way he looks—gallant—a little too gallant for my liking." She took another drag of her cigarette.

I shook my head and smiled inwardly at her use of such an old-fashioned term: *Gallant—I guess that's one way to describe him.* I was trying to keep myself calm but the disappointment in Grandma's voice made me edgy. "Look, Grandma. There are a lot of reasons Derek and I broke up and some of them are very personal," I explained. "I'll talk more about this at some point, but it can't be right now. I just don't want to get into it."

Grandma sighed, blowing the last bit of smoke out of her mouth, and put out her cigarette butt in the ashtray. "Always so secretive—ever since you were a little girl. You know, you don't have to bear the burden of the world on your shoulders—especially when you should be leaning on your family right now."

I thought about Derek's parting shot regarding family and how we were supposed to stick together—implying

I was family-averse. This comment was especially below the belt because he was intimately familiar with my sad upbringing, abandoned by my drunk, punitive father and non-existent mother. But he was right about one thing—I was not comfortable telling Grandma the real story of what happened. It was all so shameful. She would never understand.

When Grandma finally gave up on getting details of my relationship with 'the man in the photo,' she walked me to the front door in silence. I gave her a hug and then ventured toward my car.

"*Bubala*, are you going to be okay?" I heard Grandma call from the doorway, emotion in her voice. I had never heard her ask me that, so I knew she had to be more than a little concerned about my welfare.

"Yes, Grandma," I answered with my back turned to her so she couldn't see how wet my eyes were. I quickly got in my car and drifted toward the freeway.

THE NEXT FEW WEEKS at work were spent packing up our offices, getting ready for the big move over to Keller Whitman Group. I had not spoken to Craig since the time in my office, but I dreaded the thought of having to report to him. I wondered whether he would have me report to one of the other partners, maybe even Jeffrey, which would make the most sense. I just had no idea what I was dealing with because I knew nothing about Craig beyond our affair. He was an enigma who permeated my life in the most insidious of ways—someone both familiar and mysterious.

The employees were not handling the potential move well, and they were frequently seen clustered in corners of the offices, holding private conferences, likely speculating about life at Keller Whitman Group. As soon as Warren or Jeffrey would happen upon them, they would scatter like ants—bustle back to their respective cubicles.

I kept to myself, except for venting to Jeffrey at least once a day in either of our offices. We kept receiving emails from Craig's assistant, Cassandra, who doled out instructions and guidance for working at Keller Whitman Group. She sent us the human resources employee handbook which clearly outlined everything from whether we could have tattoos showing to how short a woman's hemline could be. I mockingly thought about Craig caring whether a woman's hemline was above her knees. He probably prayed for miniskirts and a lack of underwear. They also had a strange policy about the art gallery, a room chock full of original Chagall paintings Craig had collected over many years. I had toured it when Craig was courting me for a job—a lifetime ago. It's the place where he originally seduced me. Only VPs and above were allowed in the art gallery at all, and only during certain hours. I wondered if it was because Craig liked to keep it for his private use, a place to seduce potential new hires. I shuddered.

At home, I was slowly and painfully getting used to Derek's absence. It still hurt to go to bed at night, where sleep eluded me. I had taken Kat's pills already but really needed a whole bottle. I considered going to the doctor for a prescription. When I did sleep, I kept on my side of the bed, knowing full well Derek was not returning. I often awoke in the early hours of the morning, hopefully reaching my hand over to his side of the bed and, when I felt a cold empty sheet, the sadness would pervade my soul like a persistent fog, lapping at the corners of my private universe.

Unable to sleep, I would comb the apartment in total darkness, using my smartphone flashlight to search for Weez. When I would spot his huddled mass underneath a table or on a couch or chair, I would scoop him up and carry him to the bed. There, I would clutch him like a teddy bear near me so the emptiness would seem less oppressive. He would bolt after about ten minutes.

Some mornings, I would wake up and still call out for Derek, like I used to. When he lived there, he would usually be in the kitchen drinking coffee and reading the news on his laptop. Hearing my voice, he would promptly set a mug of hot coffee on my nightstand and then lean down to give me a kiss and hug. It took a while for me to get used to the fact that he was gone—that the kitchen was now empty and that I was the only one there to make the coffee.

Weekends were the worst. I would wake up on Saturday mornings wondering what I would do with my time off. I dreaded weekends the most because I desperately longed for Derek. We had our routine, but it was the non-routine stuff I missed the most. The times when we would just drive up Pacific Coast Highway and find a place for lunch or put together a picnic of Rubio's fish tacos and take it to the beach. We would eat the tacos, even as sand clung to the tortillas, before running to the ocean to cool our sweaty, sun-warmed bodies. Sometimes, we would stroll to the Santa Monica pier and do something silly, like ride the Ferris wheel and make out when we hit the top. The exhilaration of the cool breeze whipping our hair around while we kissed, the feelings of fear—being that high above the city in a rickety metal bucket battling the feelings of safety—being in each other's arms—those memories would never fade. I missed the spontaneous dancing we would do in the living room of our apartment to a playlist we had just created together. And I missed the times we just lay next to each other on the floor, letting the music reverberate through our souls as we absorbed meaningful lyrics and gorgeous melodies, singing them aloud here and there when something spoke to us emotionally.

There were so many times when I would pick up my

phone and write a text to Derek, only to delete it and put the phone down again. Or there were times when I would sit in the kitchen on a bar stool and think about calling him. I agonized over what I'd say, rehearsing it over and over until I was so conflicted, I'd lose my nerve. There was never a simple answer with Derek. I just couldn't get past the shameful memories of Craig Keller and the fact that I cheated on Derek wearing his engagement ring. Derek was right about one thing—there were no more words.

IT WAS FINALLY TIME for Warren Mitchell & Partners to close-up shop, and Warren's big going-away party was scheduled for Friday night. Jeffrey and I were still feeling melancholy over the loss of our beloved leader, and apprehensive about the unknown at Keller Whitman Group.

By the time Friday rolled around, we were still downtrodden, but had reached a place where we just wanted to be happy for Warren—that he would finally be able to do what he wanted with his life.

There were about fifteen of us directors and VPs plus Jeffrey, Warren, and Veronica. Veronica was the only employee not going to Keller's agency. She had instead been hired by Warren to be his personal assistant. Craig Keller was, of course, not invited to the party. We met at Dialogue on 3rd Street Promenade in Santa Monica, where Warren reserved the private dining room for dinner and cocktails. The executive chef was a close friend of Warren's and had created a special menu to make the night memorable.

Warren sat at the head of the long, high top table while Jeffrey and I sat on either side of him. The menu was a little dainty for Warren's taste—the dishes resembled little impressionist paintings—like they were not meant to be disturbed by an eager fork and knife. I had never once had a drink in Warren's presence but, tonight, our relationships felt somehow different. We started with cocktails and progressed to wine. At a certain point, I noticed Warren, someone who was normally spectacularly detached, loosening up and talking to us candidly about his feelings. "You know, I'd like to keep in touch with you two," he said to Jeffrey and me. "I don't want to interfere with anything that goes on at Keller Whitman Group; I'd just like to know how you're doing."

"Of course," I replied, trying to be positive, even though I was still depressed at the thought that Warren would never again be my boss. "Have you decided what you're going to do first? You know, in your retirement?"

Warren sat back and sipped his Cabernet, like he was considering it. "I'll probably spend some time with my wife and kids—I feel like I never do enough of that. Although the boys are teenagers, so they probably won't care much for it." I knew Warren and his wife, Caroline, had two sons, Gavin and Zeke.

Jeffrey laughed. "I know how you feel. As soon as the girls turned thirteen, they wanted nothing to do with Beth and me." Jeffrey and his wife had twin daughters, Mandy and Ariel. It dawned on me at that moment that everyone was married with children except me, which underscored my feelings of being an abject outcast.

"Oh, I'll probably do some traveling, too," Warren added. "You know, I have a lot of friends who've invited me to visit them, some still in business, some who've retired. It's time for me to explore opportunities I've never had the time to pursue."

"Send us a picture here and there so we can all be jealous," I requested wistfully, thinking how much more fun it would be to have Warren's life, rather than mine or Jeffrey's.

"Sure will," he replied with an odd smile.

I thought about the upcoming Monday, when we would move into our new offices and felt a pang of dread. I wondered what the first day would be like. *Would I meet with Craig or one of the other partners? How would I act in Craig's presence, with all the baggage that weighed down our relationship from the first time I met him? Would he be true to his word about treating me equally?* It was the unknown that made me nervous.

I observed Warren there, sipping his wine and talking with Jeffrey and realized I didn't know when I'd ever see him again. "Warren," I interrupted suddenly. "Do you have any advice for us in our new positions?"

"You probably don't want to hear my advice," he claimed, pursing his lips before taking another sip of wine.

"Oh, come on—what do you have to lose now?" I asked. "You can be straight with us."

Jeffrey nodded in agreement. "Yeah, Warren—tell us what you think."

He sat deep in thought for a full minute and then spoke. "It's difficult for me, because I don't want to poison the well before you even get there. But I will give you a piece of advice. Don't trust anything Craig says."

"But he's going to be our boss," Jeffrey protested frowning. "How's that going to work?"

"You asked me what I thought," Warren responded, "and I'm telling you. He has a way of twisting the truth and he's good at it. He's a master manipulator but you can stay a step ahead of him if you cover your asses."

"Cover our asses?" I repeated. "You mean keep good documentation?"

"I mean that, and always have witnesses when you're with him—especially you, Jane." He gave me a protective look, like I was his daughter who was getting thrown to the wolves. "I genuinely worry about you over there. Stay close to Jeffrey," he warned. "He's the only one who'll have your back."

I glanced at Jeffrey, who nodded. "I told you that, Jane."

I drove home that night and noticed my hands trembling on the steering wheel. *What was Warren so worried about?* I mean, I knew Craig Keller was a relentless womanizer and a Machiavellian businessman, but there was something else ... something worse that I sensed Warren was trying to tell me. Whatever it was, I would soon find out.

Fourteen

MONDAY MORNING, I TOOK a long look in the
mirror. This was going to be my first day
at Keller Whitman Group and I was more
than a little anxious. Even though I'd been to the offices
on several occasions, there was a strange foreboding that
something was amiss. I couldn't explain it.

I wore a glen plaid pencil skirt with a Stella McCart-
ney black wool mock turtleneck and tall black Louboutin pumps. It was high fashion without being too out
there, smart but not too sexy. I had decided that I needed
to tone down my style, considering the last conversation with Craig in my office in which he blatantly commented on what I was wearing. I wanted it to be the last
thing he was thinking about when he saw me.

I knew Jeffrey was to report to the agency early to
meet with the partners, and the rest of Warren's ex-
employees were instructed to report to Craig's front
office at staggered times.

Upon arrival, I immediately surveyed the lobby. It was
excruciatingly modern and slightly different from what
I remembered a few years back. Craig must have had
the décor updated. I remembered the hard, white leather

couches and multi-colored throw pillows. I recalled the first time I went to meet Craig, waiting on those leather couches, apprehensive and fidgeting because I had no idea what I was getting myself into—and still didn't. I also recognized the tall glass vases filled with fresh white calla lilies on every surface and some larger vases on the floor. The whole place felt decadent yet stiffly controlled.

Cassandra greeted everyone and then grouped us by department. After that, she led each team to check in with the Human Resources department, undoubtedly, to fill out the mounds of paperwork that came with every new job. It was surprisingly well-organized, almost as though it had been rehearsed. I was not surprised; Craig was well beyond your every day average control freak. I recalled with misery the days when I was fully into an affair with him—when he would call when he felt like it—come around when he wanted me—then disappear for days without a word. I recollected the agony at being ignored when I needed him most—when my obsession with him was at an all-time high. I would recklessly roll from one day to the next—neurotically checking my phone for texts and voice mails which would never appear. Craig was masterful at ghosting his lovers. When he decided to return, there was never an apology or excuse. Craig did not believe in excuses. He would just return to my life in an offhand way, resuming the dogged flirtation and sexual advances like no time had lapsed since the last interaction. Whenever I expressed emotion—when I stupidly confessed to having strong feelings for him—he would turn off like a light switch. It was like he put me into a little compartment and if I ventured outside it, he would squash me back in like a ball of dough.

Each time a team was taken back, the rest of us squirmed in the lobby, waiting for Cassandra's return. My team hovered around me fretfully as though we were a pack of orphans awaiting our foster home assignment.

When Cassandra returned, my group was next, and we were led down the long hallway toward HR. When I passed Jeffrey's office, I instinctively glanced inside to catch his eye, but he was distracted by a couple of the other partners.

Cassandra was a leggy Latina, with long brunette hair, big brown eyes, and tanned skin. She wore a short navy skirt with a pale pink blouse and walked with a confident stride. I immediately thought about the hemline policy and Cassandra's flagrant disregard. I caught myself wondering if Craig had an affair with her, too, as it seemed he did with every female who worked for him. I pictured Cassandra in his office, short skirt pulled up to her waist, with those long legs wrapped around Craig as he pounded her on his desk. The thought turned my stomach.

After making the stop at HR and picking up our paperwork, Cassandra returned to show us to our offices. My office was located on the opposite side of the building away from the partners, and my directors had smaller offices next to mine, so we were all in the same area. There were more than 350 employees, and Craig owned the entire office building. The art department, accounting, media services, etc. were all on different floors—it seemed like a multi-level maze.

When we arrived at my office, Cassandra gave me the keys and told me IT would be by to hook up my computer and give me access to email, internet, and the cloud where they kept all pertinent files. When she was finished showing me around the office, she asked if I had any questions.

"I don't think so," I answered looking around at the empty white walls and thinking I needed to find some artwork. The office was so plain and dreary.

"Good," she replied. "Mr. Keller said he would like to

meet with you today. Does 3 p.m. work?"

"Sure," I agreed, realizing I had nothing on my calendar because it was day one.

"Great—please check in with me about five minutes before so I can let him know you're there."

I nodded. "Of course." I imagined I would leave early just to find my way back to Craig's floor and office. As soon as she left, I perused the downtown skyline through my office window. It was an impressive view. The office had its own bathroom with a shower, something I had recalled when I toured the office a couple of years earlier. I wondered vaguely whether I would ever have the necessity to take a shower in my office. I felt exposed at the mere thought of it. I envisioned being naked and soapy with nowhere to hide, knowing Craig had the master key to every office. Five minutes had not passed before I began feeling homesick for Warren's agency, which no longer existed. I wondered what was on Jeffrey's agenda today and if he were meeting with Craig. I longed to call his office, but felt like I needed to leave him alone for the time being until he got settled in. I hoped maybe he would stop by at some point—just for moral support. He was like a security blanket that had been ripped away.

I ventured down the hall to see how my team was doing in the new work environment. Elli, Ashley, and Kevin were still waiting for IT, but it appeared that Nichol and Harlan were all set up. I invited the group to have lunch with me. We took the elevator together to the floor where the employee cafeteria was and quickly noticed its superiority. It was a dimly lit bistro that resembled a real restaurant. There were dozens of dining options, including vegan.

"Wow," Harlan exclaimed, gawking at the food selections. "This place is unreal. It must cost them a fortune to run."

I shrugged and ordered a Niçoise salad. Once seated, I glanced around the bistro and noticed the Keller employees all seemed cut out of a specific mold—one that didn't allow much of a margin for error. The women wore all-black outfits, wholesome smiles, and long shiny hair. I also recalled hearing that there was a waiting list at most of the major universities to get an interview at Keller Whitman Group. They recruited young men and women right out of college and paid them better than most of the other agencies in the city. I suddenly felt much older than any of them and, even though I was a VP and outranked them all, I felt small and insignificant in their presence.

I sat back and surveyed my team, comparing them to the employees at Keller Whitman Group and wondered how they would fit in. Kevin was a tall, lanky African American, dressed in ill-fitting suits from Banana Republic. He had extremely big ears. Harlan was a well-groomed young man with spiky blond hair and a goatee. Nichol and Ashley were like clones, nerdy chic with their horn-rimmed glasses and long straight hair. Elli, who was of Asian descent, was slightly overweight and wore floor-length skirts and a cape almost every day. They were a motley crew, I concluded; however, they were all smart and capable. I hoped this new world wouldn't swallow them whole.

They were suddenly all giggling at something. "What are you laughing at?" I asked, spearing a green bean with my fork, putting it into my mouth and crunching on it.

Nichol leaned forward. "We saw Craig Keller today—in *person*. Oh my God, he's so gorgeous—and his body. I can't believe he's managing partner of this place."

Ashley giggled and added, "I've seen lots of pictures in magazines but, up close, he's a total stunner."

I sighed and shook my head. My prediction had been

correct: they were all infatuated with Craig. "Did he say hello at least?" I asked out of curiosity. I speculated as to whether he would be kind to Warren's refugees.

"Yes," Harlan answered with a lustful gleam in his eye. "He looked right at us and smiled. He said, 'Welcome aboard.' I thought I might fall over because his teeth are so perfect—right out of a Crest White Strip ad. Do you think he's straight?"

Uh—yeah. He's definitely straight. Uncontrollably straight.

I noticed a group of perfectly coiffed men seated at a booth in a corner off to the right and realized they must be Craig's partners. Jeffrey was not with them. One of them was gazing rather intently at our table. From a distance, he was blond and seemed attractive. I wondered if he were checking out the newbies from Warren Mitchell & Partners.

ᴌ

AROUND 2:45 P.M., I headed for the front lobby to check in with Cassandra. She was on the phone, so I waited on the white leather couch in the ultra-modern lobby. The calla lilies were freshly cut, and the flat-screen television was tuned to CNN. I sat and watched absent-mindedly for a few minutes, notepad, and pen in hand. And, although I knew Craig intimately, I felt my heartbeat quickening and a bead of sweat trickling down my back in anticipation of having an official meeting with His Highness. I tugged at the neckline of my sweater just to get some air.

When Cassandra finally acknowledged me, she dialed Craig's office and announced, "Your three o'clock is here." Then she stood and led me to Craig's door, which had a plaque on it that read 'Craig A. Keller. Craig Axel Keller was his full name, and it earned him the nickname 'the Axe,' in town, which was self-explanatory. The last time I was in his office was not exactly pleasant. In fact, he had asked me to leave. Cassandra knocked at his door, opened it, and held it open for me.

I entered and saw Craig sitting at his desk in a charcoal suit with a lavender tie. He stood up as soon as he saw me and walked to where I stood, holding out his hand. My group was right, he looked cruelly handsome today, which was not unusual.

"Ms. Mercer," he greeted me, smiling, and shaking my hand. "How's day one?"

"Wonderful," I responded, unsure of how to act in front of him now that he had the power to fire me.

"Please have a seat," he offered, gesturing toward the orange suede chairs opposite his glass-topped desk. I had a quick flashback of having sex with him on that very desk more than two years earlier. I cringed at the thought and wondered, at that moment, if he remembered, too. My high heels clicked along the marble floors until I reached the chair.

He sat back down at his desk and studied me. "Now that you're here, I need to make you aware of a few things," he began as though he were about to get into an uncomfortable conversation.

I didn't respond, just watched his green eyes and thought about Warren's cautionary words to never trust anything Craig said.

"I'm not sure how much Warren told you," he stated, as though reading my thoughts, "but I have a slight challenge because there are now two VPs of accounts at my company."

"Warren mentioned that," I replied, thinking that it was always the acquiring company who took precedence over the one being acquired and, if that rule held true with Craig, I would not have a job for long.

"So, you understand, Jane, that I'm going to have to make a rather difficult decision because I don't need two people doing essentially the same thing with the same title."

He had an uncharacteristically cold and professional demeanor today, which was a radical departure from his usual playful taunting and sexual innuendos. I was not sure which mode I preferred.

"I understand perfectly," I replied. "What criteria are you planning to use to make that decision? Or does it matter at this point?" I gave his desk a quick glance—it was completely clear except for a lone file. I squinted and could tell that my name was typed on the tab, along with today's date.

"Of course, it matters, Jane," he answered with a slight smile at my directness. "I just haven't worked with you, so I don't have the answer yet. Warren said you were up for a partnership, but the woman with your job title is also up for a partnership. If I were a betting man, I'd say that one of you will end up with a partnership and the other will stay as VP of accounts. But I just can't make that decision until I give you a fair amount of time in your position."

"You mean to prove myself," I pressed, noticing he had a photo of his two children on the credenza behind his desk. A boy and a girl, around ten and eight years old, Axel and Anabel, I remembered. Axel had Craig's green eyes and dark hair—a mini-replica of Craig; however, Anabel had blonde hair and what looked like brown eyes. It was hard to determine from where I was sitting. They appeared to be miniature movie stars in their preppy, perfectly coordinated outfits.

"That's one of the things I love about you, Ms. Mercer," Craig said laughing. "You don't mince words."

He stood up from his chair and strolled to the floor-to-ceiling windows, which offered a panoramic view of downtown L.A. He paused to reflect for a minute, and I caught myself staring at his body from the back.

I couldn't help but notice what a perfect ass he had—anyone could tell that by just looking at him in clothes, but I knew it for a fact because I had seen him naked several times. He was never shy about showing off his body when we were together.

He turned to face me. "I'm going to have you meet Hayden, our other VP of accounts. She's a great woman—I think you'll get along very well together."

"Right, even as we're pitted against each other for a partnership?" I fumed, thinking this was just the type of thing Craig would do. He hadn't changed one bit from the shark I'd met years ago. And what really got me is that I knew Craig would enjoy it—enjoy watching two women compete for the same role.

"Now, Jane, that's not the way to look at this," Craig protested, now looking amused. "What would *you* do if you were managing partner of this agency?"

"I'd do the same exact thing you're doing, but I wouldn't act so damned excited about it," I shot back, knowing I was bordering on insubordination. "Tell me, Craig, how are you planning to evaluate me, given you don't know my work effort? Will there be some sort of test? Or will you simply give me goals to accomplish over a certain amount of time? What's the process?"

I knew I was putting Craig on the spot and couldn't care less. He deserved it for placing me in this position. He knew who he was going to make partner and I was unshakably certain it would not be me.

Craig looked unfazed as he sauntered over to where I was sitting and took a seat in the chair next to me. He leaned forward so his face was close to mine, an intimidating move. "Young Jane," he started, "I really think you should drop the chip on your shoulder and remember that I'm on your side. You're right, I don't know your work effort, but I'll make this process fair and even. And, no, there's no test. I just need to see how you do with your clients, how you manage your direct reports, and how you relate to the rest of the partners. It's all about leadership. That's what makes a partner here—not politics."

I watched Craig's handsome face as he spoke completely rational words. If this was what Warren meant by not trusting a word he said, it was going to be tough. I wanted to believe him, especially when he said all the right things and looked as good as he did. As always in the past, I wanted desperately to overlook his cunning character and make him into the prince he resembled—but on the exterior only.

"That's great to hear," I remarked, folding my hands over my chest, and taking a deep breath. "And I don't mean to have a chip on my shoulder—I just know how this works. But if you say you're going to make it fair, I'm happy to prove to you that I'm the right person for the partnership."

He smiled warmly. "You see—we'll be just fine working together. Now, here's what I was thinking about the clients. You'll continue managing the accounts you had at Warren's agency, and we'll meet once a week to go over their status. I'd like to have those meetings with Hayden, so you can get familiar with each other's accounts. How does that sound to you?"

"That sounds fine," I answered, thinking I needed to get some intel on this Hayden and fast. I needed to see what kind of competition I was up against.

"Good," he concluded. "Then it's settled. Cassandra will set up a weekly meeting and we'll use the time to go over your accounts. I normally would delegate these types of meetings to another partner but, in this special situation, I'll conduct them with you directly."

"Thank you," I replied, trying to figure out where the hitch was—there had to be one—that's just how Craig operated.

Craig leaned back and observed me from head to toe, like I was a piece in a jigsaw puzzle he was trying to find the right place to fit into the overall picture. At that moment, his office line rang, he stood and moved back to his desk so he could put the call on speaker.

I heard Cassandra's voice. "Mr. Keller, I have Mr. Whitman here to see you," she said. Benjamin Whitman was Craig's partner and the other half of the agency. I'd never met him.

"Send him in," Craig replied. I started to gather my things to leave the two partners alone, but Craig motioned for me to stay.

"It's okay," he assured me as his door opened and a tall blond man entered the room. He was around the same age as Craig and I remembered hearing that they went to Stanford together. As soon as I saw his face, I recognized him as the man who was staring at our table in the bistro earlier.

"I didn't realize you were with someone," he ventured to Craig and then turned his attention to me. "Who do we have here?"

"This is Jane Mercer," Craig announced, gesturing to me but not bothering to stand up. I immediately detected a level of familiarity between Craig and his former college mate. "She's a product of our acquisition."

I stood as the blond man approached me, noticing he was indeed good-looking. He had light blue eyes and an even tan that had begun to ravage the skin on his face in the form of crow's feet and wrinkles. Like Craig, he dressed sharply in a suit and tie. He held his hand out and gave me the once-over with a covetous grin, like he was getting ready to bite into a juicy steak. He wore a Rolex with diamonds—and a wedding band.

"Hi, Jane," he offered, shaking my hand. "I'm Ben Whitman. I saw you earlier having lunch. I was wondering who the attractive redhead was."

"It's a pleasure to meet you," I answered, giving him a princess smile but ignoring his inappropriate comment. He was reluctant to let go of my hand.

"The pleasure's all mine," he responded. "Did you call her an acquisition?" He glanced at Craig when he said this but held onto my hand with a firm grip. Craig laughed like he was in on a private joke. "Talk about a bonus on that deal," Ben commented. "Welcome to our agency, Jane." He finally released my hand and took a small step back, so he could assess me more thoroughly. I felt like a topless stripper, hired to entertain at a frat party. I stole a glance at Craig, whose eyes were fixed on Ben's, both wearing smirky smiles as though they were reading each other's perverted thoughts.

"Thank you," I said politely to Ben, secretly dying to get out of there. I found it interesting that Ben did not even want to know what I did for the agency. He was clearly the same make and model as Craig, which made me cringe at the thought of meeting the rest of his male partners. I turned to Craig, "Are we finished here?"

"Unless you have any more questions for me," he responded, back in his professional mode.

"Nothing for now," I answered, leaning over to grab my pen and notepad from the chair. "Nice meeting you," I called to Ben, whose eyes were now glued to my ass.

I turned to leave and took a quick look around Craig's office. There were all the familiar trappings: the fireplace with the Marc Chagall painting hanging above it, the animal print rug, the fully stocked bar, and the white leather couches where he held his 'casting calls.'

Craig rose and walked me to his office door. He opened the door for me and stood to the side. "And Jane," he asserted, voice deepening. "My door's always open." As he said this, his eyes lingered on my breasts a little too long.

"That's what I've heard," I remarked giving him a

princess smile and exiting his office. *Still the same pig as always.* The place was evidently one rather large pig pen.

⌐

I SCURRIED BACK DOWN the hallway, frantically searching for Jeffrey's office and saw, with relief, that his door was open, and he was alone. I stood at his doorway. "Hey, stranger," I broke in, like I had located a long-lost relative after being separated for years by war.

"Oh, hey … how's it going, Jane? Did you live through the first day?" His office was much bigger than mine but about half the size of Craig's. His artwork was leaning against the walls in different places as though he had them staged for hanging. His desk was already covered with papers and files—like he'd been working there, long term. Jeffrey leaned back in his chair and tossed his pen on his desk.

"Yeah—sort of." I answered. "How about you?"

"A lot to process, but I'm trying to be positive," he answered, looking around to make sure no one was outside his door.

"Did you meet with Craig?" I asked, slumping down in a chair across from his desk.

"No—I met with all the other partners. Why—did you?"

When I nodded, Jeffrey looked a little miffed that someone junior to him would be meeting with the big boss on the first day.

"I just finished with him. He informed me that there are two of me here and that I'm to compete with the existing VP of accounts for a partnership. If I don't make it, I stay in the job I'm in."

Jeffrey groaned and made a face. "That has to feel lousy."

"It's par for the course," I said wryly. "I just have to

find out about my competition … some woman named Hayden."

"I actually met her today—her name's Hayden Towne," Jeffrey said. "What do you need to know?"

"Everything," I replied. "First of all, is she pretty?" I knew this was a petty question, but I had to know, especially given how Craig was.

"Um, well, you know, I'm a guy—I think she's attractive—definitely a Keller type—tall, blonde—seems sharp but I don't really know her yet." I must have looked deflated because Jeffrey quickly changed his tune. "Come on, Jane, you're going to kick her ass," he added.

"Why do you think he's making a woman partner in the first place?" It just was not like Craig Keller to promote a woman into such a powerful position, especially when the rest of his partners were men. Sexist men.

"There's a woman who heads a big corporation they would love to have as a client," Jeffrey responded. "She's chairman of the board and an advocate for women. She basically made it clear that she won't consider Keller's agency unless he has at least one female partner."

Of course, Craig had been strong-armed into it. "Which company?" I inquired.

"Jalisco Foods," Jeffrey responded. "They supply all the major Mexican food chains with products. Big-budget corporation. Look them up—it'll give you ammunition when it comes time for Keller to make a decision."

THE NEXT DAY, I made it my mission to seek out Hayden Towne, whose office was not far from mine. But every time I walked by, either the door was closed, or it was open, but she wasn't there. I decided to send her an email introducing myself and asking if she had time available to meet, but she didn't respond. At around 5 p.m., I ventured down the hallway again and stopped at her office door, which was closed.

I knocked on the door and waited a few minutes. Finally, the door opened, and a woman appeared. As Jeffrey said, she was indeed tall, and she was also slender. Her long blonde hair draped in loose curls around her incredibly pretty face. But it was her eyes that struck me immediately. They were a breath-taking blue, bordering on violet. I could not think of anyone I'd ever met with eyes the color of hers, and they were arresting.

But her look was unwelcoming. She stared at me icily. "Can I help you?"

"I'm Jane Mercer," I said smiling. "I came from Warren Mitchell & Partners, and I just wanted to introduce myself."

Her face registered a glimmer of recognition, but she did not smile. "Oh, yes. You're the new girl," she said furrowing her brows. "I've seen you somewhere before." She was now studying my face with narrowed eyes. "I saw you in a magazine or something, right?"

I swallowed hard, now certain that, unlike Craig's optimistic assertion that we were going to 'get along well,' this woman hated my guts on impact. "I'm not sure what you're referring to," I answered. "But since we're going to be working together, I thought it would be nice if we got to know each other."

Hayden was not about to let the whole magazine thing go. "You *know* Craig, right?" she asked with a sarcastic smile. "I mean, you two are, like, *friends?*"

"I've known Craig for a while," I replied, "but I've never worked for him. He said very nice things about you and that we'll be working together closely."

"Yes, well, I've been at this agency for two years and I'm up for a partnership," she declared, eyes moving up and down my body as though she were sizing me up.

Naturally, Craig didn't tell her what was happening with me. Knowing Craig, he put it out of his mind as soon as I left his office because my future was so minuscule in the scheme of his day. I noticed Hayden wore a tight-fitting black sweater dress that hugged her sleek curves in just the right places. She had long mascaraed eyelashes and wore dark purple lipstick—a color I personally would only wear at night. In the bright office lighting, it made her look like a vixen. I imagined what Craig must think when she strode into his office. There was no doubt he was attracted to her. *Who wouldn't be?*

"Um, well, I guess we'll see about that, won't we?" I finally commented, getting the distinct impression that this woman would be a nasty opponent. I was now done being nice. It was war and, based on this first meeting, it was going to be a bloody one.

"What's that supposed to mean?" she demanded, purple glossy lips parting slightly at my boldness. I noticed her teeth were as straight and white as Craig's. She reminded me of the slutty-chic L.A. model-types we hired for nightclub ads.

"Maybe you should talk to my *friend* about that," I retorted, turning on my heel and marching away. *Unbelievable.*

THE MOOD AT KELLER Whitman Group was notably more serious and corporate than what I had experienced with Warren's agency, even with the rampant sexism. I quickly surmised that Craig was like some sort of royalty or a demigod, seen only rarely roaming the hallways and never in the employee bistro. He was reputed to have frequent power lunches at L.A.'s trendier restaurants, or he ordered food to be brought into his office and sometimes the conference room when he was meeting with clients. Jeffrey informed me that, when he was at the office at all, he would mostly hold court there—partners, top-tier VPs, and high-level clients being his subjects.

He traveled a lot on business, too. Sometimes I would see him exiting the building with his cocky gait, carrying a garment bag and briefcase with purpose. Craig never did anything without purpose, I had come to find.

Occasionally, I'd pass the large conference room and, if the door was open, I'd quickly glance inside and see Craig at the head of the table, dynamic and confident, making some point in brilliantly executed ad-speak. It was a glossary we all knew, but few of us could deftly maneuver around it and shape the conversation the way Craig could. He was an expert orator with a powerful, booming voice and certain charisma that drew everyone into his orbit. No one ever walked out of a meeting with Craig without loving all his ideas—being in love with him. That was his forte. And he used that adoration to maximize his profits.

I noted every woman at the office both revered and admired Craig, going on about him like he was an exclusive celebrity, a rock star only flown in for special occasions. They often did not even say his name, only 'He' or 'Him'. "*He* prefers this version of the ad," or "I would check with *Him* before you do anything."

The women clamored to get airtime with Craig and often talked openly and inappropriately about wanting to have sex with him someday, as though it were a career goal. In one meeting with several members of the accounts department, I overheard two young women discussing who they wanted more, Ben or Craig, and they finally landed on Craig because he was so aloof. Ben, as they pointed out, was 'too easy.'

I happened to be at a vending machine while several women from the art department speculated about the size of Craig's manhood.

"He's so tall and, you know, his feet are huge," said Julia Griffin, who had frizzy blonde hair and always wore a black headband. "I'm thinking he's, you know, pretty big in other places, too. What do you think, Jane?"

As all the heads turned in my direction, I felt my cheeks burning. I could have confirmed their theory first-hand but thought it best to remain silent on the topic. The worst thing is that these women did not care who heard them, including the men. That is how prevalent the sleaze-factor was at Keller Whitman Group.

The remaining partners, Steven Richards and Martin Strong, both former VPs at Warren's agency, were always walking around barking out orders to their next-in-command. They almost never acknowledged my presence unless it was something related to my clients. If that were the case, they would usually approach Jeffrey first and then, after Jeffrey referred them to me, reluctantly ask. It was never in person.

I'd get a call on the office line and they would put me on speaker, say something like, "Where are we on this? *He's* asking." They were obviously Craig's yes-men—the lower-level partners who had not yet earned the stripes to deserve having their names etched into the building's facade.

The one thing they all had in common was leering openly at the throngs of eager young women who comprised more than half the agency's staff. The partners acted like it was a buffet, bursting with succulent seafood and juicy prime rib. There were so many choices, they were not sure which to devour first.

There was one woman, however, who did not fit into the prototypical Keller mold. Her name was Bobbi Silverstein and she ran the media department. I knew of her long before joining Keller Whitman Group because her reputation in the industry was legendary. A short, crusty woman in her mid-sixties, Bobbi was the only woman in a protected class within the entire organization. Her nickname was "The Silver Dollar," referring to both her long, silvery hair, as well as her reputation for nailing media rates for clients that were well below what every other agency was paying. Jeffrey told me Craig went after her as soon as his agency was established and paid her a handsome sum to leave her previous job with Ogilvy in New York.

For whatever reason, Bobbi had taken an immediate liking to me, perhaps because I was Jewish, but she became the only friend I had on the Keller Whitman Group side of the agency. I met her while working on the media plan for Brave Harlots. I remembered being nervous to be in her personal space the first time I met with her, because she was reputed to be so formidable. Bobbi wore long, flowing black skirts with baggy sweaters, spoke in a raspy New York accent and eschewed everything that went on at the agency—especially where it concerned the partners. She caustically referred to Craig as *Sheyna Punim,* Yiddish for "handsome man" or "pretty boy." When it came to their shameless womanizing, Bobbi just rolled her eyes.

"How do you handle the nonsense that goes on at this agency?" I asked her candidly during one of our earlier meetings. I tilted my head toward her and raised my eyebrows. "You know what I'm talking about."

"I keep my head down around here," she answered, mouth a straight line with barely traceable red lipstick on her perpetually chapped lips. Bobbi was a heavy smoker and, because office policy prohibited her from lighting up indoors, she was constantly popping Nicorette gum into her mouth and chomping loudly. She had a habit of putting her chewed-up gum pieces on the side of her desk, in a row. She had just placed a fresh nugget on her desk before adding, "You should do the same, kiddo. You want someone to notice you? Then stay away from the *schmucks.* This place is crawling with them."

"Do you think Craig's a *schmuck?*" I asked, more to see what her reaction would be than for any other reason.

"I have to be careful there," she responded. "The man's no boy scout, that's for sure, but he pays me good money. You never want to piss him off, Jane. Trust me."

"Why do you say that?" I asked, with personal knowledge of how fierce Craig could be but wanting to hear it from Bobbi, who had worked for him over a decade.

"You know about his family, right?" she asked, searching my face for some level of recognition.

I shrugged. I had done enough online research to know Craig came from a well-off family with lots of connections but that was about all I could remember.

"His father is Donovan C. Keller—the famous criminal trial lawyer in San Francisco," she explained. "And he's not only loaded, he's *connected*, if you know what I mean. He's defended all the biggest mobsters."

My eyes widened. "Really?"

Bobbi looked around her office like someone might have heard me. "You don't want to piss him off, do you understand?"

I nodded, thoughts swimming. *What was she implying?* That Craig's father could have us bumped off? That sounded like something out of a Martin Scorsese movie. This job was just getting better and better.

ON FRIDAYS, BOBBI WOULD always bring fresh bagels from Farmer's Market or Canter's Deli on Fairfax. She would invite me to her office to share, along with her own employees, who would file in and out of her office, digging into the bagels and *schmear* with gusto. I quickly gathered that most of Bobbi's employees were young Jewish men.

"Kiddo don't shoot me for saying this, but most women don't have a head for math," Bobbi would croak, while slathering cream cheese and piling lox on her 'everything' bagel. "Sometimes you need a pair balls in this business, literally."

I wondered whether Bobbi had a pair of balls growing under those long skirts. She had no qualms about saying some of the most unfiltered things to me—to everyone.

One afternoon, she waltzed into my office to bring me a copy of a media plan. Bobbi didn't believe in emailing—she had no trust that people would resist saving a copy of her proprietary media rates and passing them along to a competitor—and insisted on handing off hard copies of everything, all stamped with 'CONFIDENTIAL' in bright red ink. Craig must have tolerated it because she was national media royalty. After tossing the plan on my desk, she looked at me with a funny expression. "Kiddo," she began. "Do you have a boyfriend?"

When I blushed without responding, she simply shrugged. "Nothing to be ashamed of if you don't, kiddo—it just helps to have someone to go home to when you work at this joint," she remarked before walking away.

I thought about Derek and fantasized that we were still together. I imagined heading out of the office and passing Craig, Ben and the rest of them—leaving them in their morass of greed and decadence—but having a fiancé to share the madness with—someone to protect me. I sighed and stared at my computer screen, feeling my eyes burn.

Fifteen

I HAD BEEN WITH KELLER Whitman Group a full month when it finally came time to meet with Craig and Hayden for our first weekly status meeting. I went over my accounts thoroughly and drafted a detailed update. I still was not sure how Craig worked, so I thought it best to over-prepare.

The meeting was set for 11 a.m. every Friday and, it seemed, this was the only time I would see Hayden. Despite Craig's initial pronouncement that she and I would be working closely, she avoided me at every turn. I had run into her one time at the employee bistro and she didn't acknowledge my presence. I wondered how she would act in front of Craig since we were forced to spend an hour together.

When I proceeded to Craig's office for the meeting, his door was closed. I knocked and when the door opened, it was Hayden. I thought it odd that she was already there, with the door shut. She was wearing a tight black pencil skirt and pale blue button-down blouse, unbuttoned one too many, so I caught a glimpse of the lacy blue bra she wore underneath. I also noticed her skin was California-tanned. Her long blonde hair was pulled into a tight ponytail. The overall effect was attractive in a cheap way. I had chosen a black dress with white cuffs and collar, what I thought to be a chic choice. Again, unlike Hayden, I had the sex appeal volume set on low. I spotted Craig at his desk on the phone. Hayden yielded to let me in but did not smile nor did she offer a greeting.

Craig hung up the phone and called, "Good morning, ladies." He rose from his desk, straightened his jacket lapels, and gestured for us to sit at his conference table. He was wearing a navy pin-striped suit with a crisp white shirt underneath but no tie. Then he did something that disarmed me. Instead of sitting at the head of the table as I expected, he chose a seat with his back to his office window. I was not sure where to sit so I took a seat directly across from him, facing his window. Hayden sat to his immediate right. *Great. Two against one.*

Seeing Craig sitting right next to Hayden was quite a sight to behold. They were both so physically perfect, so striking together that I caught myself thinking Hayden was the female version of Craig. I imagined what their kids would look like. I also tried to read their body language, but it was just too early to tell what their relationship was like.

"So," Craig said to start the meeting. "Since this is Jane's first meeting, why don't we begin by going through Hayden's accounts. I'm assuming you two have been spending a good amount of time together already." Craig glanced at me and I looked directly at Hayden, who was staring down at her phone, purposely ignoring me.

"Your assumption is incorrect," I confirmed, still staring at Hayden, who refused to look up at me. "I'm certain it's because Hayden's so busy that she hasn't had a moment to spare."

Craig turned to Hayden and his light jade eyes met her shimmering chips of blue-violet ice. "I asked you to reach out to Jane a long time ago. Why hasn't that happened?" Craig's voice sounded stern, like a father admonishing his rebellious teenaged daughter.

Hayden finally spoke, only acknowledging Craig. "It totally slipped my mind," she said with an insouciant grin.

"Well, you need to make it a priority," Craig answered, now visibly annoyed. "You two can't work in silos when you're managing accounts this big—especially if there are conflicts—accounts that are too similar. Jane needs to understand how things run here and she can't do that if you don't make time to meet with her."

I could not help but smile inside that Hayden was the cause of Craig's frustration. I was also a bit surprised that he would flog her right in front of me.

"Fine," she replied sullenly, pulling a sheet of paper from her notebook. "Do you want me to go through my accounts now?"

"Yes," he responded and glanced at me. "We only have an hour to get through a lot of information, and I want there to be sufficient time to go through Jane's accounts."

I nodded to Craig and he gave me a closed-mouth smile. Hayden went through her list of accounts, rattling off such blue-chip brands as Warner Brothers, BMW, Amazon, and UFC, while I studied her body language and mannerisms and listened to her voice. She came off smart and articulate, but especially haughty. Craig just sat back and listened while examining his phone here and there. There were a lot of major accounts at Keller Whitman Group. I was impressed at just how many high-level clients they had. When Hayden had finished, she turned to Craig for his reaction.

He shot me a glance. "Jane, do you have any questions?"

"I have many," I replied. "But since we only have an

hour, I'm happy to ask them when I meet with Hayden in person." I threw Hayden a princess smile as I said this, and she just gave me a distasteful sneer.

Craig nodded. "That's great, Jane. Now, why don't you give us the run-down on your accounts?"

I went through my list, being careful to include information I thought would be relevant to Craig. I felt uncomfortable in his presence because he was still attractive to me and, with the ardor that had been brandished upon him by almost every woman at the agency, I was seeing him in a different light. He was even more omnipotent than I'd ever thought in the past and it unnerved me to feel him listening intently and studying me as I spoke. I wondered what he was thinking, having me there as his employee and whether the professional Craig would at some point disintegrate and give way to the other Craig I knew—the one who took me behind the Ritz Carlton with the clear intent to have sex.

I also wondered about the nature of Craig's relationship with Hayden. He had to have been with her. There was no way a man like him would have a woman that beautiful in his presence all the time without having gone after her at least once.

Craig interrupted me several times with pointed questions but seemed to be impressed by my knowledge and assessment of each account. Hayden just gave me a blank look, her purple lips squeezed together unpleasantly as though she had just sucked on a lemon wedge.

When I mentioned a brand of cough syrup, Kibosh, from my accounts, Craig stopped me. "Hold on, Jane— we represent Relief cough syrup and that directly conflicts with Kibosh. What are your billings?"

I knew exactly what Kibosh brought in and was not afraid to boast about it. I tossed my hair. "Well, you know we won the Addy for the television commercial—the kid with the baseball hat playing in little league—Kibosh—Stops Coughs Cold," I said proudly. "Billings are $100 million."

Craig's eyebrows raised and a smile tugged at the corners of his mouth. He turned to Hayden. "What about Relief?"

She scanned her worksheet as though thinking of a rebuttal. "Actually, we are at $80 million today, but analysts have estimated tremendous growth over the next five years, unlike Kibosh, whose earnings are slowing down—probably due to its lackluster ad campaign." She turned to Craig triumphantly.

Craig looked from Hayden to me and then appeared to be thinking it through. "There are a lot of factors that could turn around in a five-year analysis. Let's drop Relief. I'll break the news to them. Anything else?"

I inwardly gave myself a high-five. I already won one over on Hayden. And I loved how Craig was so decisive. He was the opposite of Warren, who would take weeks to figure out which account to fire. I watched Hayden's face turn from sullen to furious. She stared at Craig like she wanted to kill him. I frankly did not understand how Craig put up with her attitude. But he seemed to ignore it.

When the meeting was finished, Craig stood up dismissively and went to his desk to review emails. Hayden immediately followed him and stood in front of his desk with her back to me. That's when I caught it. Craig's eyes moved from his computer screen to Hayden for a split second and I saw a trace of lust—I knew the look well.

Of course, he's had her. That whole routine with him scolding Hayden for not working with me was an act. The dropping of Hayden's client in favor of mine. I can't believe I didn't see right through it. I knew exactly what Craig was doing. He was going to make it seem like he was being objective so that I would have no reason to think Hayden was getting the partnership and not me. He had pitted us against each other in more ways than one.

I left his office in huffy silence, marching down the hallway, so fast that I almost ran into Jeffrey, who was just returning from his meeting.

"Do you have a minute?" I asked, voice almost shaking.

"What's wrong?" he said searching my face.

We went in his office and I shut the door, quickly turning to face Jeffrey. "I can't work here."

He cocked his head. "Hold on, Jane—you want to tell me what happened?"

"I just met with Craig and that bitch, Hayden. He's got to be sleeping with her." I was so incensed I could barely catch my breath.

"What makes you think that?" he asked, obviously puzzled by my emotional outburst. "I mean, I know the guy sleeps with everyone but what did he *do*?"

"It was the way he was looking at her," I explained, suddenly realizing what was happening and it was not just about the partnership. *I was insanely possessive of Craig.* I couldn't stand the thought of him giving his attention to anyone but me and he knew it. That's what he wanted. I hated myself for feeling the way I did about him—the constant seesawing of emotions. And I prayed Jeffrey did not catch my vibe and figure things out.

"Jane, the guy looks at every attractive woman that way," he explained. "You're going to have to get used to it. I'm sure he looks at you that way, too. But is that what you really want? If I were you, I'd be thrilled he's not coming after you."

How could he understand? He didn't know the history.

Jeffrey was now sitting at his desk casually shuffling through his mail. I stood there frozen, watching, considering his words and my own troubling emotions. Jeffrey had already decorated his office with framed images of some of his best ad campaigns. I surveyed the selection fondly, remembering how things used to be. Jeffrey pulled a small box from the pile of mail and began to slit it open. He pulled out a bag of Starbuck's coffee with a note attached to it. He read the note and then looked up at me, grinning. "It's from Warren," he said, reading the note aloud: "I hope this keeps you going."

The mere mention of Warren's name made me smile, and my shoulders relaxed slightly. "I wonder why he sent that."

Jeffrey shrugged. "No idea, but it's sort of nice. I hope he's keeping himself busy."

I thought about Warren and Veronica and my eyes misted up, thinking about all the sudden changes in my life—Derek leaving, Warren leaving. I missed my old life and it was hitting me hard.

"Are you okay, Jane?" Jeffrey asked, studying my face again. "I mean, you're not still upset about the Craig thing, are you?"

I shook my head. "I guess not," I answered. "It's pointless."

Jeffrey stood and moved around his desk to face me. He wore a caring expression, which caused my eyes to mist up again. "Good, because we have to stick together. Don't worry about Hayden or the partnership or what she does with Craig on her off time—just do your job. Remember, if *you* leave, *they* win."

⌐

When I returned to my office, I found a box just like Jeffrey's on my desk. I opened it and it was the same—a gift of coffee from Warren with a note. I carefully placed it in my messenger bag and picked up my phone to make dinner plans with Kat.

On my way out of the building, I stopped by Cassandra's desk to drop off paperwork and Cassandra was not there. I looked around and saw an attractive woman sitting in the lobby reading a magazine. She glanced up at me briefly and there was something about her that felt vaguely familiar. She had shiny shoulder-length dark hair, big brown eyes, and full red lips. She looked to be in her mid-thirties. She wore a white silk blouse, faded skinny jeans, and high-heeled red suede pumps. She had a red Hermès Birkin Bag with silver hardware.

Cassandra returned to her desk at that moment and I handed her the paperwork. "For Mr. Keller," I said, as she accepted the files, but she was not paying attention and, instead, looked beyond me at the woman on the couch.

"Well, hello there," Cassandra greeted the woman, smiling. "Let me get him for you."

"Thank you, Cassandra," the woman responded politely and returned to her magazine.

Cassandra picked up the phone and typed in numbers, her long, acrylic nails clacking against the keypad. "Mr. Keller, I have Mrs. Keller here to see you."

Mrs. Keller! It was Alessandra—someone I'd never seen in person, just in photos. That's why she looked so familiar. I turned to examine her again, trying not to stare but I couldn't help it. I had for so long wanted to see who she was—to see the woman who inspired Craig to marry her, no matter how disastrously it ended.

"Would you like water or coffee, Mrs. Keller?" Cassandra offered.

"No, thank you," said Alessandra, without even looking up, as though she did not want to be there.

I just stood in the lobby for another few minutes but, once I realized I had no business standing there, I abruptly turned to exit the building. I approached the exit, but something made me turn back to have one more look at Alessandra. Instead, I saw Craig enter the lobby to meet his ex-wife. He had an impassive look on his face and didn't appear to notice me as I scurried out the door.

That was weird, I thought, once I was in my car. I

knew they had to be in touch over their two children, but I never thought I'd see her at the office. She was pretty in a classic way, I had decided. I thought back to the time when I was seeing Craig while he was married and felt a pang of real guilt. That's the thing with illicit affairs— you never see the other side of the equation—the person or people you're hurting.

INSTEAD OF MEETING ME for dinner, Kat invited me to her house and, when I pulled up to her home in Laurel Canyon, I noticed an unfamiliar car in her driveway—a newish Audi.

Kat answered the door and seemed a bit embar-rassed. She was wearing a black silk robe and high heels. Her long blonde hair was matted in back and her blush-colored lipstick was smeared. "Hi, Jane," she said smil-ing sheepishly. "I didn't think you'd get here this quickly since you were driving from downtown."

"Am I too early?" I asked, realizing I must have barged in on her late-afternoon romp with the young boyfriend.

"He's still here," she leaned over and whispered, obviously referring to Caleb. I whiffed the sour essence of red wine on her breath.

"Oh … sorry, Kat. I … um, do you want me to come back later?" I took two steps backward.

"No, come in. I'd like you to meet him," she coaxed, standing aside and gesturing for me to enter.

I awkwardly stepped over the threshold and observed the most boyish of young boys I could possibly have imagined, a mere stripling who looked barely legal. But she was right. He was very good-looking. He had long, wavy brown hair and big almond-shaped green eyes. They were what Grandma would call 'bedroom eyes' because they slanted down in the corners, making him look slightly sleepy. His skin was so fair and smooth, it looked like he had not even begun shaving. He was settled on her couch playing a game on his phone when I entered. He did not look up.

"Hi, I'm Jane," I called, smiling, and waving to get his attention.

He briefly looked up from his game app and exclaimed, "One second—I've got aliens on my ass."

I rolled my eyes, thinking he must be playing *Alien Rage*, which I was only familiar with because some college intern at work was always talking about it. Kat and I exchanged glances and she smiled, like we shared a little secret.

"Jane, this is Caleb," Kat announced. I could not help but think Caleb looked like a young Craig Keller, with the hair and eyes. Kat must have a thing for that type.

He finally looked up, grinned at me, and then stood, placing his phone in his suit pants pocket. I noticed he was around six feet tall and very slender—almost too thin—and angular. His suit was ill-fitting—a bit too baggy and the arms of his jacket too long—almost as though he were only *playing* office. He moved toward me with an awkward gait, like a young colt.

"Nice to meet you, Jane," he said, shaking my hand. "I was just about to take off."

He turned to Kat and said, "I'll see you tomorrow." He leaned over and kissed her on the lips, which was tough for me to watch. I just could not shake the feeling that it was an incestuous relationship between mother and son—or aunt and nephew—or something else that felt strange and unnatural.

As soon as he was out the door, Kat excused herself to change, calling over her shoulder to me, "There's cold wine in the fridge."

I made my way into her kitchen and noticed a strip of photo booth black and whites stuck to Kat's fridge with a magnet. It was of Kat and Caleb, in various stages of playful poses. In one photo, they were both laughing like they just heard the most hilarious of jokes. In the next, they were both puckering up for the camera and, in the next, Caleb was kissing Kat on the cheek. I had mixed feelings. On the one hand they were sweet, and on the other, bizarre.

I inhaled the scent of coconuts and realized Kat was burning a candle. Two bubble wine glasses, one with lipstick on it sat next to the sink. I opened the refrigerator, immediately spotting the open bottle of chardonnay. I pulled it out, poured myself a glass, found a *Vogue* magazine and sat on her sofa. When Kat returned, she looked fresh-faced and happy, in a peach camisole, and cream-colored cashmere sweatpants. She located the open wine bottle I had set in the kitchen and returned with a glass, setting the bottle on the coffee table.

"Well? Isn't he cute?" Kat's cheeks were slightly flushed, I noticed, as she settled down next to me and poured herself a glass of wine. "Doesn't he look like a Greek god?"

"As in Oedipus?" I quipped without even thinking. I set the open magazine on my lap and looked over at her.

"That was your outside voice, Jane," Kat scolded, looking wounded.

"Okay, yes, he's cute. But he *is* young, Kat. Does anyone at the office know?" I still had a tough time believing she would fool around with this boy.

She shook her head. "We've been very discreet."

"How long are you going to keep this up?" I asked, flipping through the *Vogue* pages with an anxious jerking motion, now not even looking at the content.

Kat shrugged again. "As long as we make each other happy. How's everything with you?" she asked, pulling her feet up onto the couch and sitting with them tucked underneath her. She took a sip of wine. "Have you settled in at work?" She then made a face. "What's it like working for Craig?" She said 'Craig' in a way that made him sound like an evil bastard—with an undeniable rasp in her voice.

I sighed. "Awful."

"How awful? Like, do you want to resign?"

I explained the situation to Kat with the partnership and how Craig was making me jump through hoops to get it.

Kat groaned. "Jane, you're right, that *is* awful. Do you know anything about the other VP?"

"I know she's a bitch from hell—a beautiful, sexy one—and she's most likely doing him," I bitterly complained, pitching the *Vogue* magazine onto her coffee table in disgust. The pages fluttered when it landed. "She's been there two years."

Kat seemed to be thinking through the situation. "Well, I'm sure he *has* done her before, but whether he's doing her now is debatable. Two years is a long time to keep Craig interested. He usually moves on to the next one after a few months."

"Well, this one's gorgeous, Kat. And what's worse is I'm jealous of her—I'm also insanely possessive of him."

"I'm sure she's jealous of you, Jane. You're not exactly unattractive and we know how Craig feels about you." Kat refilled my glass with wine and topped off her own glass.

"What do you mean, how he *feels* about me? How do you think he feels about me—about anyone? The man's never been anything but a mystery to me." I detected a note of sadness in my voice and lifted my eyes to meet Kat's. She had an empathetic look on her face. Of course, she did. She had been there before—with him. She knew exactly what I was feeling. "You know I ran into his ex-wife on my way out of the office earlier—that was interesting."

Kat's expression suddenly turned from somber to gossipy. "What was she like?"

"She was beautiful and well-dressed," I responded flatly. "She definitely made out in the divorce—she was carrying a Birkin. All I got was a Prada."

Kat giggled. "Prada is not exactly low-end, my dear. But you know the rumor is that was an arranged marriage anyway. Supposedly, Craig's parents hand-picked her for him, but they never got along and that's why they divorced."

"How do you get along in a marriage when one partner cheats incessantly?" I shook my head, thinking of Craig's relentless sexual appetite and abundant bed partners—and those were just the ones I had heard about. "His bedroom probably has a revolving door."

"When's he going to make the final decision on the partnership?" she asked, abruptly. I could tell she wanted to change the subject. I forgot sometimes that her experience with Craig had been painful, too.

"In a few months after he's had a chance to review my *performance*."

Kat suddenly broke out laughing uncontrollably.

"Kat, there's nothing funny about this," I protested, frowning. She was now laughing so hard, her shoulders shook, and she rocked back and forth on the couch.

"I'm sorry, Jane—it's just that this is so typical of him. This is Keller 101—at his most devious."

"What would *you* do?"

"I'd be looking for another job, Jane. But then, I *despise* the man. I wish you'd wake up and despise him, too. But it sounds like you're still in that place where you're attracted to him. I honestly don't get it. I mean, you lost your fiancé over that guy. You really do have grounds to hate his guts." She took a sip of wine and put her glass down.

My thoughts went back to Derek and it felt like a

lifetime ago that we were living together and engaged to be married. *How did my life get so screwed up so quickly?*

"Have you heard from Derek?" she asked, sensing my melancholy.

"Not a word," I said. "It's like he departed the planet."

"Do you still think about him?"

"Of course, I do," I admitted. "But it's so painful, I have a hard time going back there. Plus, with the new job situation, I've been preoccupied. I guess that's a good thing—keeps my mind off all the depressing elements of my personal life."

"I'm hungry," Kat interrupted suddenly. "Let's get takeout. What are you in the mood for?" she asked. "I'm thinking Italian."

"Sounds perfect." I smiled, thinking that I lost everything important in my life, but at least I still had Kat and Marisa. They would always be my closest friends, and I needed them more than ever now—needed them to get me through what would undoubtedly be tough times ahead.

Sixteen

FTER TWO MONTHS, I was beginning to get the hang of working at Keller Whitman Group. I had by now met and begun to understand all the partners; they were cut from the same cloth: aggressive, chauvinistic, and serious about making money. It was a hostile environment in general, but especially for the women. It's not like the partners were unfriendly to me; they just viewed me as an object and took nothing I said seriously. Ben Whitman was the worst, though. He did nothing to hide his lewd behavior.

Sometimes, he would show up at my office unannounced, under the guise of some client issue. He nicknamed me 'hot stuff' and never called me anything but that. I assumed he did not remember my real name. His office visits would always start with a quiz down about what was happening with a client; however, when I would give him the updates, he would clearly not be listening. I would see his eyes move to my breasts. The other thing he loved to do was stand behind my desk and lean over me, so his head was only a few inches from mine. He pretended to be looking at the client file I had open, but I knew he was only trying to look down my blouse. I would experience the unexpected attack of aftershave at such close range. It was like being around a horny dog who sensed I was in heat. Only it was all the time.

"Hot stuff, what are you working on today?" he would greet me every day, standing in my doorway.

"A little bit of everything," I would respond, holding files over my chest so he couldn't look.

I sometimes wondered what he would say if I just told him to get away from me. I never had the nerve. It's like these partners were untouchable and above any normal laws outlining sexual harassment. We were there for their visual and physical pleasure only.

One time, I passed both Craig and Ben heading down the hallway, an extraordinary sight given Craig was so rarely seen walking around in the building. They smiled simultaneously, and Craig beamed at me. "Hi, Jane." Then, each gave me his own brand of sexually charged stare-down. When they thought I was out of earshot, I overheard Ben say to Craig, "Is she a natural redhead?" I couldn't hear Craig's reply but the two erupted in laughter, which made my face burn with humiliation. *So disgusting, these men!*

I was surprised Jeffrey could deal with them, given he was so clearly different. They were all married but Jeffrey was probably the only one still loyal to his wife. Because Craig was likened to some type of god at work, the women all wanted his attention and the men wanted to be just like him. He had his own kingdom—or fiefdom—however one wanted to perceive it.

Hayden stayed her usual bitchy, sullen self, but I remained a stone-faced professional, determined that I was going to get the partnership in the end. I started to want it more than anything and was willing to work harder to get it. I still felt uncomfortable in Craig's presence and watched for signs of what he might have going with Hayden. And while there was no perceptible chemistry between them in the office, I often saw them walking out to the parking garage together, leaving for the night. And Hayden was almost always already in Craig's office before our Friday meetings. I had a hunch they were having an affair, but I simply had no real proof.

With Craig, it was hard to see him as a colleague, instead of the gorgeous ex-lover he was. Whenever I entered his office, or saw him randomly, I felt a shot of adrenaline, like I was seeing him for the first time. It was weird, but, even though I met with him once a week, I could never quite get used to him being my boss.

The other person I had a hard time getting used to was the creative director, an odd, temperamental artist who was unbending when it came to his work. When we met, I immediately recalled Warren's comment that he was an 'infamous prima donna'. His name was Alonzo Costa and he dressed like a teen-aged rapper with baggy pants, black hoodie sweatshirts, and a baseball cap worn backwards. He was Latino, with long, straight black hair past the middle of his back. His sideburns were dyed a peacock blue. He was unnaturally thin, and his veins protruded from his arms like a wiry labyrinth of cords underneath a coating of thin tattooed latex. He had obviously not read the employee handbook's policy regarding tattoos. I suspected Craig gave direct orders as to who would be given preferential treatment—obvious double-standards. He must have a list of who the agency would tolerate violating policies—the superstars could get away with anything they wanted.

The creative department was on the fourth floor of the building and the joke was that anyone who got off the elevator on that floor got an immediate contact high. There was so much pot and alcohol being consumed in that department that it was impossible to fathom. I remembered the environment at Warren's agency, and there was no comparison. Warren had a zero tolerance for substance abuse of any kind, especially at the office. But Craig and his partners appeared to be tone-deaf when it came to substance abuse on the fourth floor. They only cared about the ideas and, given the ammunition, there was plenty of creativity to go around. The place was brimming with stellar concepts.

Whenever I approached Alonzo who, by no coincidence, occupied suite number 420, he threw me a distasteful stare, as though I were an unwelcome intruder there, forcing him to compromise his art. Sometimes, when he saw me, he would just hold up his hands as if he were a gargoyle staving off evil spirits and say, "No more changes."

Alonzo was such a far departure from Craig, I wondered how they even got along. I tried to picture them sitting in a pitch meeting with a client and for some reason, it made no sense. Craig looked from head to toe the polished corporate professional and his creative director a gangster. I had to admit, however, that Alonzo's artwork was outstanding, by anyone's standards.

One day, while I was in Jeffrey's office, I asked what he thought of Alonzo.

"He's one of those L.A. creative directors," Jeffrey responded, rolling his eyes, and shaking his head.

"What do you mean by that?" I asked.

"He's a creative genius who likes to throw his weight around," Jeffrey explained, leaning backward, and stretching his hands above his head in a 'V' and then placing them on the back of his head.

"So, you think he's a *genius*? I thought you were the only creative genius in this town," I teased, plopping down in the seat across from him. Sometimes, I wished my office was right next door to Jeffrey's, so I would feel protected in some way.

Jeffrey laughed. "There are a lot of us in this industry.

He's an odd guy, Jane, but you need to stay on his good side."

And speaking of odd things, Jeffrey and I were receiving mail from Warren at least once every couple of weeks. And there was always a cryptic note accompanying a gift. We had already received three additional gifts after the Starbuck's coffee. Once he sent a pair of red dice with a note saying, "Don't take any crap." Next, we received a Mercedes Matchbox car with a note saying, "Hope he's not driving you crazy;" and then a pair of Mickey mouse ears with a note that said, "Greetings from the happiest place on earth."

Each time we received something, Jeffrey and I would confer, and explore possibilities as to why he was sending these things. Jeffrey concluded he was just bored and missed us. I pictured Veronica putting the packages together for him, as his personal assistant. No matter what Jeffrey said, the whole thing puzzled me.

∿

I WAS INVITED TO my first creative concept pitch meeting with Craig and Ben, which had me unnerved. It was with Noel Marques, who had always been my client, and they knew Noel's loyalty to me was boundless, hence the invitation to lead the meeting. I wondered whether Alonzo's unfiltered attitude would come across as offensive to Noel. He had made a special trip from London to be at this meeting and it was the first time he was meeting Craig. We were doing an ad campaign for their new U.S. runway collection, in advance of New York Fashion Week. I had been working with Alonzo for weeks on the creative, which I felt was truly a fine representation of the clothes.

The night before the meeting, I took great care in planning my outfit for the next day. I pondered wearing one of my Noel pieces, but something told me I would appear a kiss-ass if I did. *Overkill*. But I needed something that would make me feel confident and in control of my audience. After sifting through the contents of my closet, I selected a black pinstripe sleeveless coat dress that buttoned down the front, and I wore a smart white button-down shirt underneath. I picked out a pair of Christian Louboutin black leather high heeled pumps and carried a red leather bag to match the red soles of the shoes. Smart and confident. That was what I needed to impress this crowd.

I practiced the presentation at least eight times in front of the mirror before washing my face, brushing my teeth, and going to sleep.

I ENTERED THE CONFERENCE room the next morning and felt my hands shaking as I held the printed version of the presentation deck. This meeting could make or break me. Craig had never seen me present and I felt pure apprehension at the thought of how he might react. He was a creative genius who knew how to work clients better than anyone I'd ever seen, including Warren. *How would I look in his highly attuned eyes?*

Cassandra appeared in the doorway. "Jane, Noel Marques and Meredith Sheen are in the lobby."

I nodded. "I'll be right there. I took another long look at the empty conference table and imagined myself facing the clients and partners with confidence. *I had to be perfect.* I met Noel and Meredith in the lobby, and they greeted me warmly, like I was an old friend, not their account VP. Noel kissed me on both cheeks and Meredith gave me a big hug.

"Welcome to L.A.," I said, grinning at them.

Once I had them seated comfortably in the conference room, I ventured toward Alonzo's office to make sure he was ready with the presentation. He was not there, and my stomach lurched in panic. I quickly returned to the conference room, thinking maybe we had crossed paths, and he was not there either. Just as I was about to call Alonzo on his cell phone, Craig and Ben sauntered into the room together.

Ben looked me up and down predictably with a lustful gleam in his eye, and Craig just nodded to me with a curt smile. "Ms. Mercer," he acknowledged. "Are you going to introduce your guests?" He wore his cold, professional demeanor, which I was now accustomed to seeing all the time, not just in client meetings.

Noel regarded Craig with immediate admiration. He had obviously heard of Craig and seen him in magazines—he saw Craig in the magazine with me—in his dress. I hoped he didn't remember Craig in that context. Luckily for me, he didn't seem to recall that particular magazine. Still, it was always the same when anyone glimpsed Craig in person. He took their breath away at first, he was so visually stunning. Today, he had on a sleek navy three-piece suit with a pail blue shirt and navy tie printed with silvery palm fronds.

"Certainly," I answered Craig. "Noel and Meredith, this is Craig Keller and Ben Whitman, both partners at our agency," I said with the utmost professionalism. "Craig and Ben, Noel Marques and his CMO Meredith Sheen."

I watched as they all greeted each other, and Ben and Craig took the head of the table at opposite sides, like good-looking book ends.

Craig glanced at his watch and then at me expectantly. "Well? Where's Alonzo?"

I eyed him uncomfortably and gave him a slight shrug, not wanting to clue in Noel that the infamous creative director was MIA.

A brief look of annoyance crossed Craig's handsome face before he rose from the table. "Excuse me one moment," he announced coolly and strolled out of the conference room into the hallway.

I made small talk with the group but overheard Craig's booming voice in the hallway, obviously on the phone with Alonzo. "Where are you?" There was silence. "I don't care. Get in here now."

I suddenly got the connection between Craig and Alonzo. Craig was like a parent with a problem idiot savant child who never followed rules nor stayed on course. Craig's role was to discipline him regularly but balance it with enough encouragement to keep his productivity high.

When Craig re-entered the room, he gave Noel a dashing smile and seated himself again. "Creative's running a few minutes behind but why don't we start by hearing a bit about your Spring line—I've heard nothing but amazing things from Jane here, who loves your clothes."

As he said this, he smiled and winked at me. No matter what I thought about Craig personally, professionally, he was always so polished and buttoned up. Ben had effectively checked out, looking up blankly while staring at his phone intermittently, like he barely knew which client he was meeting and didn't really care either. I realized then that Ben was useless to Craig, other than as an attractive ornament, there to agree with everything Craig said, rather than to express an opinion of his own merit. He was the proverbial dumb blond.

Noel spoke about his line, what he was doing with fabrics and dresses, silhouettes, hemlines, and sleeves. By the time he finished, Alonzo miraculously showed up with red, glassy eyes, obviously stoned as usual, lugging an LED widescreen projector to show the creative presentation.

Craig gave him a stern look. "And here's our creative director, Alonzo Costa," he introduced brightly, and then muttered under his breath, "Glad you could join us."

"Sorry boss," Alonzo mumbled. "Hello everyone. Let me get this set up and we'll run through it." As he said this, he swiftly fudged with the equipment and connected his tablet to the projector. One thing that always surprised me was Alonzo's natural talent for putting together electronic equipment. I often saw him fix glitches on the spot in creative presentations.

Once the audiovisual equipment was in place, I stood and made my way to the head of the table, near where Craig sat. It was where we all stood when presenting in the large conference room. Ben had moved around to the side of the table in order to see the presentation clearly even though his expression was one of boredom—like he was going through tedious motions that were of no interest or consequence to him.

"In a market saturated with disposable imagery, sustained success is coming from an exciting new source," I began. "It's based on advertising with aesthetic longevity." I felt the pressure of Craig's eyes on me but did not look in his direction. He intimidated me so; I tried to pretend he was not even in the room.

Instead, I focused my attention on Noel and Meredith, and was suddenly struck by the irony that my own team was far more daunting than the client. "In an ever-expanding luxury market, the trend has changed drastically from flashy, logo-driven glamor to a more understated way of manipulating the market."

I signaled Alonzo to change the introductory Keller Whitman Group logo slide to the first page of the deck content and then continued.

"As you can see, mega-brands like Prada, Gucci and Valentino have shifted their focus to the idea of editorial life-style photography as a way to showcase fashion in a setting that evokes an emotional response."

The next slides were examples of this type of photography, so I cued Alonzo to change slides quickly as I paused to elaborate on the new advertising trend.

"With this style of imagery, you have the freedom to create any number of situations and feelings—take this ad for example," I said as a slide with a Michael Kors Ad appeared on the screen. The ad featured an androgynous looking model dressed in a long sequined gown, ensconced in a luxurious seat of a private plane with a glass of champagne and a vase of flowers on the table, her stiletto heels casually strewn on the floor next to her and her handbag placed neatly behind the seat.

"What are we seeing?" I asked the group. "Literally, we see a Michael Kors gown, matching slippers, heels and a handbag. But more importantly what are we *feeling?*"

I moved my gaze around the room and caught Craig Keller leaning back in his chair now, swiveling it lazily from side to side, resting his chin on one hand, studying me with intrigue. I tried not to let my eyes linger on him too long, so I would not lose my train of thought.

"We're feeling luxury, aren't we?" I proposed. "We're feeling upscale, VIP treatment, relaxation and comfort. We put ourselves in this model's place and want exactly what she has. We want to be there with her. The dress, heels and handbag are part of the overall lifestyle. We want it all."

I signaled Alonzo to change the slide to the first ad concept. The first two concepts were always the less attractive option than the third, which was the one the agency usually favored.

I had coordinated with Alonzo to run through the first two concepts and turn the floor back to me when we reached the final ad. Alonzo was not too thrilled about giving me so much air-time in the presentation; however, I had convinced him it was appropriate, considering I had represented their account long before he ever touched the art, and he finally relented.

After Alonzo had done his preamble on technique and gone through the first two concepts, I moved in for the conclusion. "As you can see, the feeling can be anything we want it to be—it can be soft and intimate or rough and controversial. It's all about creating a feeling and a mood—one which sells clothes."

I gave Alonzo a nod to move to the final concept. It was a mock-up of several models on a street in New York. One was seated on the curb wearing pieces from Noel's casual collection, which featured shiny silver pants and a pair of shirts layered over one another, a mixture of prints, solids, and textures. The second model was walking near her, wearing all red—jacket, sweater, pants, and sneakers and the third model was in a rose-colored velvet slip dress, searching her handbag as though she may have forgotten something.

"In this ad, we have a New York street scene that could be any day of the week, but each of these models has a different plan—a different agenda—and high fashion to match. I envision a style of imagery that feels a bit like Wes Anderson if he were to do documentary photography. I also think this concept captures Grace Coddington's *Vogue* editorial legacy with the unexpected combination of urban angst and fairy tale fantasy. Either way, we're transported somewhere—anywhere—that makes us feel special."

I paused to get reaction and finally had the nerve to steal a glance at Craig. He was sitting up straight in his chair now and his expression had changed from intrigue to awe. I quickly turned to Noel and Meredith, who were both smiling and nodding.

"This whole concept should feel very familiar to you both," I commented directly to Noel and Meredith. "It's based on all the elements contained within your Spring line and, based on the research we've discussed at length, it plays right into your target audience."

I paused to look around the room. "Well," I said. "Initial thoughts?"

Noel was first to speak. "Jane, your team has outdone themselves. These concepts are all brilliant. But if I had to pick the one that sums up our brand, it would be the third."

Bingo. This was going to happen just as I had planned. I took the seat to Craig's left and held my head high.

Noel glanced in our direction and asked, "Mr. Keller, do you fancy the third ad? What's your opinion?"

Craig paused for several second before responding. "I think you're absolutely right. The team nailed it with the concepts, and the stylistic imagery moves them into a different class of experiential marketing," he explained. "That said, I agree with you, Noel—the third concept is the one that resonates with the most emotion—the most profound feeling, as Jane described. It's also true to your brand."

As he uttered the last line, he gave me a look. *Was it one of admiration?* I noticed Ben was back to scrolling through emails on his phone, like a completely superfluous, non-participatory drone in an expensive suit.

"Then, I think we have a winner," I announced, smiling. "Alonzo will begin sourcing photographers and talent for the ad. Of course, we'll shoot in New York to retain the authenticity of the scene."

WE FILED OUT OF the conference room and, just before I was ready to ask Noel and Meredith to lunch, Craig caught me in the hallway. "Do you have a minute?" he asked, gently pulling me aside by the arm.

"Of course," I responded, subtly removing my arm from his grasp.

"You were incredible in there," he commented, moving his body so close, my eyes were level with the palm frond print on his tie. I caught a quick whiff of his soapy scent as he moved even closer. "It's rare that an account VP can take the ball and run with it alone on the creative side, as well as drive a hard pitch."

I felt my heart bursting with pride as I gazed up at him. I had just received a real compliment from Craig Keller—and it was not physical. It was about my intelligence and ability. "Thank you, Craig," was all I could think of to say.

"You have a lot of talent," he added, backing up slightly, eyes lowering to the rest of my body and back to my eyes. "I'm glad I was able to see it in action."

Well, it was mostly not physical. I was still thrilled to be praised by His Highness.

"You're really on the fast track," he concluded, turning to walk away from me.

The fast track—to what? He was so cryptic all the time. All I wanted was for him to say I was headed for a partnership—that I was leading Hayden in our quest for the holy grail of advertising. But, as usual, Craig loved to play games and keep me in the dark.

L.

THAT NIGHT, I WENT out with Marisa and Kat to celebrate my coup at work. We met at The Old Man Bar in the back of Hatchet Hall in Culver City and ordered Old Fashions.

Marisa was all keyed up because she had just landed an interview on her show with a famous actor she had longed to meet since she was a kid. He had racked up numerous Oscars and other awards and she was busily preparing for the interview. "This is going to make our ratings during May sweeps," she declared, taking a sip of her Old Fashioned and grinning widely at us.

"How exciting," Kat commented without enthusiasm. She looked subdued tonight in a black shift dress, worn with black pumps and no stockings.

I wondered what was going on with Caleb, if perhaps he was the one causing Kat's mood swing, but I didn't want to bring it up in front of Marisa because I wasn't sure how much Kat had shared with her. Maybe she would bring it up first. I decided to be vague. "Are you okay, Kat?"

She frowned and made a face. "I started my period today—horrible cramps and bloat," she said shifting and patting her normally flat stomach, which I noticed was slightly distended today. "What about you? You said you had some news."

"Well, I just did my first creative pitch in front of Craig, and one of the other partners, and it went so amazingly well, Craig pulled me aside after the meeting to tell me." I smiled triumphantly. Kat and Marisa went silent like I told them someone died. "What's wrong?" I asked, frowning. "Isn't that good news?"

Kat and Marisa exchanged glances and Marisa spoke first. "Jane, it's not like we aren't happy for you, but don't forget what a monster that man is—if he complimented you, it's because he wants something."

I sighed. "Come on, you two—I've worked there quite a while now and this is the first time that he's ever paid me a compliment. Can't you just be happy for me?"

"What happened to being cautious around him?" Kat questioned. "I'm sorry, Jane, but you're letting yourself fall under his spell again. It's shameful after everything he's done."

"No," I protested, shaking my head. "Craig's the most important partner at the agency—I've only just now figured that out. You wouldn't believe how busy he is—how much power he has. He has no time—that's why he'd never seen me pitch. But today was different. I really felt like he noticed me—like he finally knows I'm capable and should be made partner."

"Then why hasn't he offered it to you?" Marisa challenged. "What's he waiting for?"

"He needs time to evaluate my performance," I countered defensively. I picked up my Old Fashioned and took a huge slug, feeling the bourbon burn my throat. "He made that clear right when I started."

"Sounds to me like you're drinking the Keller Kool-Aid," Kat snickered. "He knows who's getting the partnership. Trust me. That man decided the day he made the deal with Warren. He could have awarded it to you then if he wanted because, as you said, he does have *all the power*."

I knew my friends were being protective of me for a reason, but I was not in the mood to hear yet another smear campaign against Craig. There was something about what happened today that changed the way I felt. It's like he finally woke up to the fact that I was smart and valuable as an employee and he hopefully now saw me as partnership material. I had finally caught his attention from a professional standpoint, and it felt good—so good it made me temporarily forget his true character.

Seventeen

WITH THE PARTNERSHIP CARROT dangled in front of me, I wondered if Craig was ever going to decide. Even after the success with the Noel Marques campaign and Craig's compliments about my presentation abilities, he was still considering who should be made partner. I had even brought in a new account: the Hollywood Bowl. Derek and I had been to so many concerts and events there, and we had become good friends with the marketing director, who was ready to change agencies. I had run into him at an industry mixer and, while I conveniently left out the fact that Derek and I were no longer together, I convinced him to take a meeting with me.

When I brought the news to Craig during one of our Friday meetings, he was impressed.

"That's fantastic, Jane," he expressed, smiling. "I had no doubt you'd be as great at new business development as you are in pitch presentations."

As he said this, I noticed Hayden's hostile eyes on me, scanning my outfit as though she were taking a mental inventory. I had on a simple cream-colored silk blouse and red wide-legged cropped pants. She was wearing a tight, low-cut yellow wrap dress and I could see her perfectly tanned, rounded breasts struggling to free themselves of the restrictive fabric. My eyes darted instinctively to Craig to see whether he noticed but he was busy studying a spreadsheet and seemed unaware of Hayden's exposed body parts.

"What do you estimate to be their annual billings?" she asked shrewdly.

"Billings are modest, but it's very prestigious—I mean, it's Hollywood Bowl—a Los Angeles icon," I declared, victorious. There was no way Craig could deny my contribution to the agency. Hayden snickered, like it was small potatoes compared with the ideal Keller Whitman client she worked with. Still, I was proud of my acquisition.

"That's great, Jane. Hollywood Bowl *is* iconic. Keep up the good work," Craig complimented as Hayden shot him an evil stare.

THE FIRST WEEK OF June, Cassandra canceled my weekly status meeting two weeks in a row because Craig was out of the country. I thought perhaps he was on vacation and found myself wondering who he took with him. When I inquired with Jeffrey as to where Craig was traveling, he informed me Craig was in Nice, France, trying to negotiate a deal to acquire another original painting directly from the Chagall museum.

"You know how crazy he is about his Chagalls," Jeffrey commented. "Supposedly, he's trying to procure one he's been after for years."

I pictured Craig in Nice, strolling the quaint streets, hordes of French women gazing at him with amorous eyes, wondering who the stunning American was with all the money and glamour. I was sure women went after him wherever he went.

One thing that bothered me in a visceral way was

that as soon as Craig had gone, Hayden's office remained dark and her door locked. I imagined she was cavorting all over the French Riviera with Craig and it made me sick with jealousy. I even ventured to Bobbi's office one day and casually brought it up to obtain intel.

"You know Craig's in Nice purchasing another Chagall," I began tentatively, testing the waters.

"That's what I heard," she answered in her usual gruff, New York accent, not even looking up at me.

"And you know, Hayden's also out of the office," I added to see if I could get a reaction out of her.

"Hayden," she repeated with a look of revulsion, peering over her glasses at me. "That one," she added, just shaking her head.

"That one ... *what?*" I asked, now curious as to what Bobbi thought of her.

"It's a relief whenever she's out of the office. Watch out for that one, kiddo," Bobbi warned. "She's a real viper. She'll trample all over you and wipe her feet with you when she's finished."

"Yeah, no kidding—found that out on day one," I responded, still obsessing over the fact that Craig could be in such a romantic place with her. "Do you think she's with Craig right now?" I knew I was pushing my luck implying that Craig and Hayden were together, but I could not help it. I was dying to know.

"What?" she replied, leaning back in her office chair, a few wisps of silver hair flying out of her bun and landing on her left cheek. She twisted her jaw and blew the strands away. "Why would you ask that?"

"I don't know," I said, pausing. "I just thought maybe ... since they were both out of the office ..."

"That man messes around a lot at the office but he rarely takes his *zoynes* with him on trips, especially when he's after a painting. He takes that stuff seriously, you know—the paintings, that is."

"So that means you think something's going on between them when they're in the office—between Craig and Hayden." I noted a hint of panic in my tone.

Bobbi reached into her skirt pocket, pulling out a piece of Nicorette and popped it into her mouth, chomping loudly. "I don't know what he has going with who, and I don't pay attention." I could tell she was getting impatient with my interrogation. "Neither should you, kiddo. These men, you know, they just do what they do."

I turned and left her office. Bobbi just did not want to call out Craig on anything. I got it. It was smart of her, especially in her position.

ONE WARM SUMMER EVENING after he returned from Nice, Craig surprised me and stopped by my office. I was absorbed in paperwork and about to leave for the night.

"Ms. Mercer," he said, standing in my doorway. "You're working awfully late this evening."

I jumped with the usual shock wave that hummed through my body whenever I saw his savagely handsome face. With the trip overseas and the cancelled meetings, it felt like an eternity since I'd seen him. It was seldom I caught a glimpse of him outside of our weekly meetings anyway. He looked striking dressed all in black, with a white shirt and periwinkle silk tie. His face and neck were tanned from his trip to the French Riviera, a slight blush lingered over his well-defined cheek bones.

"I still have a lot of projects to finish," I responded.

"Do you have dinner plans?" he asked, leaning against my doorframe casually.

Several women passed by my office on their way home for the evening, staring, awe-struck at Craig standing there in the flesh, and then spying the name on my door in envy, trying to get a peep of the woman behind the nameplate. "Not really," I replied, thinking I hadn't eaten since breakfast.

"Then let's have dinner," he suggested matter-of-factly. "I'll make reservations at Patina. Sound good to you?"

I regarded him doubtfully. Patina was a romantic, pricey, and exclusive downtown L.A. French restaurant. I instinctively scanned my outfit, which was appropriate for Patina: a sky-blue suit by Virgil Abloh with a long jacket and shorter skirt. My hemline was in violation of the agency's policy, but it was such a killer outfit, I couldn't resist wearing it. Besides, I had no idea Craig was back from Europe and would invite me to dinner. I still felt uncomfortable being with him socially and was suspicious of why he would so suddenly want to take me out—especially after the low vote of confidence Kat and Marisa expressed at our last get together. These were the types of overtures they warned me about. "I'm not sure that's such a good idea," I responded finally.

"Why not?" he asked, now looking amused. "I can't take my hard-working VP out for a nice dinner after a long day?"

I set my elbow on the desk, rested my chin in my hand but said nothing. I was marveling at how elegant Craig looked, leaning against my doorframe with his hands in his pants pockets, like it was the most natural thing in the world for him to ask me to dinner at an expensive restaurant on a school night.

"Come on, Jane. It'll be fun," Craig urged, smiling warmly with those teeth.

"Okay," I agreed reluctantly. "What time do you want me to meet you?"

"We'll drive together," he answered. "Meet me in the lobby in a few minutes."

I was always struck by Craig's ability to get what he wanted. I wondered what Hayden was doing this evening. Maybe she was not available, and I was a cheap stand-in. Maybe she had jet lag after their long vacation together in the Côte d'Azur. I felt queasy at the thought.

I met Craig in the lobby and, after I caught him predictably eyeing my legs in the short skirt, we walked silently to his car. His Bentley was parked in the reserved space right next to the elevator, so you always knew whether he was in the office. He opened the door for me, and I got in, immediately smelling his soapy essence, and feeling that familiar sense of desire return. It had been a long time since I had had sex and I did not trust the way I was feeling. I hoped he would be on his best behavior tonight, for both our sakes.

As Craig drove closer to Patina, which was on South Grand Avenue, burrowed in a corner of Walt Disney Concert Hall, I thought immediately of Derek and wondered whether he was performing that night. I spent so many evenings there, watching as he drew his rosined bow across his violin, his entire body pitching in concert with the music. He was first chair, which was one step away from concertmaster, and was always graceful, so effortlessly artful in his movements. And, just like that, I felt tears in my eyes at the thought that we could be so far apart—such total strangers now.

Craig did not notice my sentimentality as we drove in silence. He was cranking songs from his iTunes library. A song by Alt-J was playing and I remembered Derek and I listening to the same song—only on the floor of our apartment living room, volume set at its highest level.

When Craig pulled into valet, the attendant opened my door and I stepped out, being careful not to give the valet guy a crotch shot based on the length of my skirt. I took a few steps behind Craig toward the restaurant entrance and he opened the door for me. He strode right up to the maître d' like he owned the place.

"Mr. Keller," said the maître d'. He obviously knew Craig and feared him. "I have your table." He wasted no time leading us to a rather large booth on one side of the restaurant. When we sat down, the waiter immediately came to our table.

"Mr. Keller, which menu would you like tonight?"

He turned to me and asked, "How hungry are you?"

"Pretty hungry," I replied, surveying the room. The lighting was soft, and the walls were awash with an undulating wooden texture that reminded me of swirling curtains. The restaurant was filled with beautiful L.A. people chattering, laughing amid the noise of clinking glassware and silverware banging against dishes.

"We'll take the seven-course tasting menu," Craig directed the waiter.

"Right away, Mr. Keller. Would you like us to pair the wine?" the waiter asked.

"Yes, of course. But bring us two martinis to start. Grey Goose up with olives." Craig gave me a devilish grin.

"And you expect me to come in on time tomorrow?" I asked, eyebrows raised.

"Jane, you know I don't care when you come and go. That's up to you. As long as the clients are happy." He gave me his seductive slow blink as he said this.

There was no way I was going to stand a chance tonight. I could not help but think, as we were served our vodka martinis, how irresistible he was.

"*Salut*," Craig said as he clinked his glass against mine and smiled his dashing smile. "I'm so happy you agreed to have dinner with me."

"I'm sure you have no problem finding dinner companions," I remarked, taking a small sip of my martini. Craig just studied my face without responding. With a few drops of vodka, I started to relax. Several of the restaurant-goers gawked at Craig, like he was a movie star. He certainly looked the part. "How was your trip?" I asked, thinking it was best to keep the conversation light. Plus, I was dying to know what he did in Nice—more importantly, who he was there with.

"It was productive," he responded, spearing an olive from his martini, and popping it into his mouth, chewing while watching me intently.

"What did you end up buying?" I thought I would attack it from the painting angle in the hopes he would give up more information about the trip in general.

"Something for the gallery," he answered, placing his perfectly manicured fingers on his tie to adjust it slightly. "It's called 'Le cheval Roux.' One of the classics—lots of rich reds—my favorite color."

Of course, his favorite color is red—one full of fire, power, and energy. I should have guessed. "What made you such a fan of Marc Chagall?" I could not help but be curious—I never had the opportunity to talk like this with Craig—not since I'd gone to work for him. It's like he had purposely wedged an arm's-length barrier between us.

"His works just speak to me," he commented reflectively, before taking another sip of his martini. "I knew it the minute I first saw one of his paintings when I was about eight years old. I was at the San Francisco Museum of Modern Art."

The waiter interrupted our conversation to serve the first course—bluefin tuna and Kagoshima Hamachi. Craig took a small fork and placed a few pieces on my plate. I wanted to press him for more details about his childhood—I couldn't help it, I was fascinated—but he shifted the conversation back to work, almost as though he felt uncomfortable sharing anything personal with me, as though being intimate with me beyond sex would crush some invisible armor he bore.

"So how do you like working for my agency?" he asked casually. "And be honest, Jane."

I took a deep breath. I was not sure what to tell him. "Well, it's certainly challenging," I said, trying to appear neutral. And that was the truth. Working for Craig was like swimming with sharks, desperately trying to keep up or be torn into bloody pieces and left saturating the sea.

"You don't like it," he assessed immediately, as if reading my thoughts.

I laughed, watching as he elegantly impaled a small piece of the tuna with his fork and inserted it into his mouth. "I guess that was the wrong answer."

"How can I make it better for you?" he asked, running his fingers up and down the martini glass stem and squinting his eyes at me thoughtfully.

"You can make me partner," I responded.

"Is that what you *really* want?" he asked, slow blinking his green eyes at me, his expression turning seductive—it was the same look I saw him give Hayden that day in his office and I bristled at the memory.

"Yes," I answered in a sober tone. "I'm working seriously toward that goal and I know you see it."

At that moment, a young woman appeared at our table and I recognized her right away as Chelsea, a long-time friend and former music student of Derek's. She was young, beautiful, and a soloist with the Los Angeles Ballet Company. I always thought Derek had an affair with her despite his numerous protests to counter my theory.

"Jane … hi," she greeted me. "I thought it was you sitting here. How've you been?"

Craig turned his attention to the pretty intruder, whose long, silky dark tresses cascaded down past her shoulders. She had big brown eyes and dewy skin. And she wore a light pink off-the-shoulder sweater over a black leotard, her slight body framed by tight jeans and high heels.

"Hi … Chelsea," I replied awkwardly, wondering when she last spoke to Derek. Maybe they were in contact again since he moved out, another thought I hated to consider.

Craig, who normally disliked being interrupted, was suddenly interested. "And which agency are you from?" he asked, giving Chelsea one of his most dazzling, white-toothed smiles.

Naturally.

She responded in like fashion, batting her eyelashes, and blushing slightly. "Oh, I'm not from an agency. I'm a ballerina," she revealed, smiling proudly. "I'm a principal with the Los Angeles Ballet Company."

She had obviously moved up from soloist since the last time I saw her. Craig could not have been more impressed. "Really?" he responded, giving her the once-over to determine whether she had a dancer's body and, by the look on his face, seemed satisfied she was telling the truth. "That's refreshing to hear. What did you say your name was?"

"Chelsea," she announced, giving him a little curtsy. I thought I might throw up in my mouth. One thing was certain, with Chelsea in the room, I was entirely invisible to Craig. I silently cursed her.

Craig looked charmed and amused. "Craig Keller," he said with a nod. "And where are you performing, Chelsea?" he asked, still fascinated by the waif-like girl-child in front of him.

"Dolby theater this week. I just came from rehearsals. This place has the best vegetarian menu and I need to get a carbo-load for tomorrow. I have rehearsals for eight hours straight to look forward to."

I was getting more flustered as these two blatantly flirted with each other right in front of me until an ethereal-looking blonde fluttered over to our table, wearing a hot pink low-cut backless dress. She was so thin, her ribs protruded underneath the thin material of the dress. Her breasts were non-existent. "Chelsea, we need to head out—the car's in valet," blonde princess girl said.

Chelsea turned to me. "Nice seeing you, Jane," and then to Craig in a flirtatious voice, "Nice meeting you. Come see one of our performances—you won't regret it."

Craig smiled again. "Maybe I'll do that." And his sparkling eyes followed the pair out of the restaurant. *Such a scoundrel!* My humiliation was complete.

Left alone with me again, he took a bite of the fourth course, foie gras, chewing carefully. "How do you know her?" he asked after swallowing. Clearly his wheels were spinning after meeting Chelsea.

"She's a friend of my ex," I explained. "And he probably got the news that I'm here having dinner with you right about … now."

Craig shrugged. "What does it matter? You're with your boss and you're single. Why do you care what he thinks?"

Because I'm not a machine like you, Craig. I still have feelings for the man you made sure I lost. I obviously have some twisted feelings for you, too, based on my jealousy of your relationship with Hayden and the fact that you would chat up Chelsea—a woman I've always been jealous of— right in front of me. I said nothing.

The fifth and sixth courses arrived, black truffle risotto, red snapper, and wagyu beef. I wanted to sway the conversation back to the partnership, but Craig seemed more intent on making small talk and eating.

The seventh course arrived, a dessert called Gianduja Crémeux, a delicate passionfruit, chocolate, and hazelnut mousse; Craig took a spoon and scooped up a small amount, leaned over and held the spoon to my mouth. I was taken aback. *What was he trying to do now?*

"Open up, Jane," he commanded with a mischievous grin. "This is the best part."

Knowing the restaurant was full and that all eyes were on us, I backed away slightly, glancing nervously around the room, but finally opened my mouth just to get it over with. He promptly inserted the spoon. I let the creamy custard fill my mouth and swallowed as he watched with amusement.

Then, he scooped more of the mousse on the same spoon and licked it off, slowly and suggestively, eyes fixed on mine. *He's doing it again ... he's trying to publicly seduce and humiliate me.* Before I knew it, Craig had moved closer. His leg brushed up against my body and I felt the warmth of him pushing against me. I felt a stab of lust, which resulted in further confusion about how I was going to react. *No, Jane, stay in control. Don't let him go there.*

"Tell me, Jane," he whispered. "How *badly* do you want that partnership?"

There it was in all its debasing glory. He moved in closer and touched my skirt, sliding his hand down my thigh to where the skirt ended, so his fingers were just underneath the material. I felt the pressure of his fingers against my skin.

"What are you doing?" I hissed, grabbing his hand, and holding it tightly so it would not wander further. His mouth was close to mine now.

"Trying to find out how serious you are," he answered, giving me a rakish grin. He then put more mousse on the spoon and held it to my mouth, which I hesitantly opened. I felt my eyes watering. Instead of inserting the spoon, he leaned in further and dipped his tongue into my mouth, grabbing me roughly by the back of my neck and pulling me toward him. I heard the spoon drop onto the plate with a loud clanking noise as I tasted saliva from Craig's probing tongue. I tried to resist, turning my head to the side, and pushing him by his shoulders, but I was afraid to make a scene at Patina. I was now also excruciatingly aware of what I was up against with the partnership. He had plainly spelled it out for me. I felt his lips on my neck and his hand sliding up my skirt, and then realized someone was standing at our table. *Thank God!*

It was the executive chef and owner of Patina, there to rescue me, whether he knew it or not. Craig immediately released me and put his hands on the table. Free of Craig's grip, I pulled a mirror out of my handbag and checked my face, which wore a thoroughly mortified expression.

Craig spoke first. "Hey, chef," he said coolly, like he had not just been busted trying to maul me. "How've you been?"

The chef smiled, leaned over to Craig, and said in a low voice like Craig was his fraternity brother. "Hey buddy—I just wanted you to know one of the local gossip columnists is having dinner here in a few minutes, so if you'd like to get out of here, now would be a good time."

"Right," he responded quickly. "If you'll just have your guy bring me the check. I think we're done here."

"It's taken care of, my friend," the chef replied. "I hope you enjoyed."

It dawned on me that Patina was one of Craig's clients, so they comped the meal out of respect. I also saw quickly that Craig had everyone in his pocket, and they knew to help him dodge cameras and reporters. He was such a big shot, they all wanted to protect him—especially the good old boys' network, of which the chef was obviously a member.

Craig pulled a few hundred dollar bills out of his wallet and set them on the table to tip the waiter. "Thanks, man," he offered, standing up and patting the chef's arm. Craig put out his hand to help me out of the booth and when I took his, he gently pulled me along with him toward the front entrance, like I was his chattel. My thoughts raced because I knew what was coming next. *How was I going to get away from him if I were stuck in his car? If I said no to his advances, would he take the partnership off the table for good?*

Craig's car was already waiting in valet and, after he tipped the attendant, he opened the door for me and watched intently as I got in, lowering his gaze to my short skirt and bare legs, likely hoping for the shot robbed of the valet attendant earlier. Before I knew it, we were driving away.

"It must be tough to always be in the limelight," I mused, trying to change the subject from what had just gone on in the restaurant. "Does it ever bother you?"

"It's part of the turf, Jane," he returned with a bored expression, abruptly changing three lanes, and moving to a side street with which I was unfamiliar. Once we were far enough away from the restaurant, to my chagrin, Craig pulled over and put the car in park.

He turned to me. "Let's go to my place. We have some things to sort out, wouldn't you say?"

"I need to get home—I have an early meeting tomorrow," I replied quickly.

"I'm your boss, Jane. I already told you to arrive whenever you feel like it. Cancel your meeting. I don't care what you do. I just need to have you—*now.*" His voice was so direct, I caught my breath nervously.

"I can't do that—my team needs me there," I countered, feeling sweat trickling down the back of my neck. "Working at your agency is a big deal to them, and they want to succeed."

"Tedious details involving your employees mean nothing to me," he asserted dismissively. "And quite frankly, those people are lucky they're all still employed. Warren made that a point of his deal, but it's not like I need any of them."

"So, we're all dispensable to you," I retorted, swallowing hard and feeling my stomach burn. "Is that what you're saying?" This was the behavior Kat and Marisa warned me about. *Why was I always willing to believe he could be a better person? How could I possibly think the cad who was at this moment coercing me to have sex could ever take me seriously?*

"I would *never* say that about you, Jane," he replied. "That's why I allowed you to throw your hat in the ring for a partnership."

"*Allowed* me?" I repeated. "You know, Craig, I've worked really hard at this job trying to impress you that I'm the right person for the partnership. I even brought in a new client within my first three months."

"Oh, I'm aware of all that," he replied with an arrogant laugh. "So why not come to my apartment so you can impress me even further? You'll help me make a better-informed decision about your ability to be a partner at my agency."

"Did you really just say that, Craig?" I felt my cheeks heat up. *How could he be this egotistical and underhanded?*

"I'm not letting you do this again, Jane," he replied sharply. "You can't keep teasing me. Do you know how many women want to be *you* right now? You're making me crazy."

"If you're that intent on getting off tonight, why don't you just call Hayden?" I shouted now glaring into his green eyes, which were aglow in contrast with the pinkish car lighting.

"Hayden?" he repeated, drawing in his chin, and looking at me sideways. "What does she have to do with this?"

"I'm sure she has everything to do with this, Craig," I snapped, voice now raised. "You think I don't *know* you? In case you don't remember, this isn't our first dance."

"What do you want me to say?" he asked, brows furrowing slightly but his tone remaining level.

"You've made it abundantly clear that the partnership hinges on whether I sleep with you—isn't that what you just said, or was that my imagination?"

He calmly turned and stared straight ahead, hands on the steering wheel. He took a deep breath and blew it out slowly, like steam from a hot tea kettle, but remained silent to my allegation.

"So, tell me, Craig, what's the score between Hayden and me? Does she willingly go back to your apartment? Because if that's what it takes to become a partner at your agency, we might as well part ways now."

"Is that a threat?" He turned his head and stared ruthlessly into my eyes as he said this, yet his voice remained as calm as a stone wall.

"You can't force me to do something against my will."

He reached over and grabbed my chin, pulling it up slightly. "You want me so badly, it hurts. Just admit it and stop playing games."

"It's *not* consensual, Craig," I cried, slapping his hand away. "Do you get that?"

He glowered at me in pure frustration, lips pursed. The man was not used to being told 'no'—by anyone. "Yeah, I get it," he finally muttered, pulling out onto the street, and doing a choppy U-turn, a sure indication that I had thoroughly pissed him off. The Bentley skidded slightly as he overcorrected the turn.

We rode in silence and, when we finally reached the agency parking lot, he turned to me and put his hand on my arm, gently but firmly. "Tell me one thing," he said coldly, eyes penetrating but calm. "Are we going to keep this up? Because it's getting kind of old now, don't you think?"

I jerked my arm away from him without responding. Then, I cracked the door and pushed it open, immediately exiting the car. I was careful not to slam the car door, even though he had me incensed.

I drove home sickened by what had transpired. It was an old, familiar combination of anger, humiliation, frustration, helplessness and, yes, lust. I caught myself wondering how bad it would be if I had just said yes and gone to his apartment. It's not like I was engaged to Derek or even dating anyone. I was completely single and so was Craig. I was still deeply attracted to him and longed to feel the weight of a man's body, so what was stopping me? I tried to remember what it was like to be with Craig. That's when I remembered Craig's special perversion was biting, which always caused pain and left a discolored chain of bruises that took forever to heal. I thought back to the first night we were intimate at Shutters on the Beach in Santa Monica. He preferred me on top, and always wore condoms even when he wanted me to perform oral sex on him. I'm sure it was because he was still married then and trying to avoid STDs or an unwanted pregnancy. Right afterward, he would immediately get up and shower. This always killed me. His obsessive, careful cleanliness made me feel like I was a flagrant whore, tainted with filth he didn't want near his pristine body.

Whatever the case, he made it clear to me tonight that I could either join his expansive club of women who slept with him to get ahead or stay stagnant where I was as VP of accounts.

He was right about one thing, and it's what bothered me most. I did want him. And, just as he said in the car, I wanted him so badly it hurt. It hurt not to be able to relieve myself with him. But even if I agreed to his proposition, it would never be enough for me—I would become obsessed. I also knew Craig only wanted things he couldn't have and that once it was over, he would be on to the next. I was in a no-win situation. I went to bed that night tossing and turning for two hours trying to decide my next move with him. *Should I, or shouldn't I?*

Eighteen

U PON ARRIVAL AT THE office the next morning, I pulled up emails and immediately noticed Cassandra had canceled all the Friday meetings with Craig and Hayden. *What?* I thought quizzically as I began accepting the cancellations, thus removing the emails from my calendar. I wasted no time in dialing Cassandra's extension to pose an inquiry.

I pounced on her, as soon as she answered. "Cassandra, what's going on with the Friday meetings?"

"Mr. Keller asked me to cancel them," she explained. "He said he no longer needs to hold those meetings."

"But ... why?" I felt my pulse quickening. "Is he there now? I need to talk to him."

"He said you already know the reason."

I caught a glimpse of myself in the mirror that hung across from me and saw that my face was flushed with anger. "Cassandra," I said, trying to keep my voice in check. "I'd like to get on Craig's calendar as soon as possible today. Will you please tell me when he's available?"

There was silence on the other end. "Jane, his calendar is booked through the rest of the month and beyond.

I'm afraid you'll have to wait until early August to get a meeting."

I hung up with Cassandra and immediately dialed Craig's cell phone, which went directly to voice mail. I didn't leave a message. Instead, I typed a text to him. "I need to talk to you right away," which did not get an immediate response.

I knew exactly what Craig was doing. He was punishing me because I had crossed him. I had no idea how to react. I felt like I was playing a harrowing game of chess and Craig just moved to check mate. So, this is what happens when you say no to Craig Axel Keller. *Damn him!*

At that moment, Jeffrey was calling me. I snatched up the phone.

"Jane," he said. "Why is Keller asking me to do your one-on-one meetings?"

I inhaled deeply, feeling the sting of being brushed off. "I don't know. Tell me what he said."

"Nothing. He just called me and told me you were reporting to me on all of Warren's previous clients moving forward and that he would be managing Hayden."

Obviously, he did, that double-crossing bastard.

"I mean, I'm happy that we're going to be officially working together on everything," Jeffrey said, "but I didn't expect it to be this soon. Did anything happen that I need to know about?"

I sighed. "No Jeffrey." I was just not ready to bring Jeffrey into the whole sleazy situation.

ᑋ

THAT NIGHT I MET Marisa for dinner at Josie on Pico in Santa Monica. I was so frantic about the whole situation at work I couldn't even wait to sit down without starting in on her with the story, flailing my hands, eyes flashing wildly with anxiety.

"Jane, take it easy," Marisa objected as we were handed menus. "You're almost foaming at the mouth—I want to hear the whole thing, but I need a drink first. Today's been a rough one."

"Tell me about it, Marisa, he all but spelled everything out for me," I blurted, while flagging down the waitress to get our wine order. "The bastard took me to dinner last night and told me the only way he'll consider me for a partnership is if I sleep with him."

"There's no way, Jane," Marisa exclaimed. "Are you sure you didn't misinterpret him?"

"Oh, please, Marisa," I protested, shaking my head. *How could she think I may have heard him wrong?* "You know how he is. You and Kat were just harping on me for trusting him in the first place. I'm such a fool. He attacked me right there in the restaurant—had his hands all over me—tried to kiss me. Then he went after me in the car."

"What?" Marisa demanded in disbelief. "Did he think he wandered on to a set of *Mad Men* or something? I mean—he could get sued blind. Did he try to force you?"

"He never forces anything—he always tries to either seduce or bully me into consenting," I said thinking about how many times we were at the brink and when I said no, he backed off. He would pout like an impetuous child, but he would not force me. He was too smart for that.

"That must be some kind of legal thing, so he doesn't get accused of sexual assault," Marisa mused.

"I think it has more to do with his arrogance," I responded. "He finds it unfathomable that any woman would ever say 'no' to him. He told me that in not so many words last night."

Marisa shook her head. "What a first-class pig," she remarked.

"That's not even the worst of it," I returned. "It's been

so long since I've had sex that last night, I was actually considering doing it with him."

"No, Jane!" Marisa shot me a look of alarm. "I won't let you. Don't give him the satisfaction."

"It's too late anyway," I explained, detailing for Marisa how he cut me off and put Jeffrey in charge of me.

"That mother fucker," Marisa shouted, slamming her fists on the table. "You need to go to HR."

"You see, that's just the thing, Marisa. I have no witnesses to corroborate what happened at Patina—except for the executive chef, but he's in Craig's pocket, too—and if I go to HR, what am I going to tell them? That Craig no longer has time to meet with me? No one will care. I'll just appear to be another disgruntled former employee of Warren's. Plus, someone in the office informed me that Craig's family is, like, mob-connected or something, so it's useless for me to do anything that might get him into trouble."

"*Mob-connected?*" Marisa asked, eyebrows raised. "Who told you that?"

"Someone who knows him pretty well, Marisa. His father defended mobsters in San Francisco his whole life—this is not a person you want to mess with."

Marisa sighed and rested her forehead in her hand. "You really are in a mess, Jane."

"Yeah, you're not kidding," I agreed, shaking my head. The waitress delivered our wine and I immediately grabbed the glass and took a rather large gulp.

Then Marisa's demeanor suddenly changed, and she got this gleam in her eye, like she was on to something. "Does his father still practice law?"

I shrugged. "No clue."

"What if I did a story on him?" she asked, taking a sip of her wine.

"What? Why?" I asked, now bewildered. "What story is there to do?"

"You know, do a story about his father to establish a connection between Craig and the mob—there's an easy way to do that."

"I don't know, Marisa," I said doubtfully. I had already downed half my glass of wine in exasperation.

"What if Craig used his father's dirty mob money to fund his agency? Or to purchase all those original art pieces? Now, that would turn some heads in his direction and not in a good way."

"Oh, Marisa, that's a total stretch. How would you ever find out? You'd have to get into Craig's financial records and you're never going to do that—legally, that is."

"He runs a publicly-traded company—so most of those records are already out there. I would just have to dig deeper." Marisa grabbed her phone and immediately began a search on Craig's father. "Here we go, Donovan C. Keller, Esquire," she announced triumphantly. "He still lives in San Francisco and he's definitely still practicing law."

"But why would you want to do it?" I asked, slurping down the rest of the wine and contemplating ordering another.

"Well, number one, for ratings. And, also, to get him back for torturing you like this—more as revenge than anything else." Marisa shook her fists. "Come on, Jane, that man deserves some bad publicity. It's the least I can do for you."

I sighed. "Do what you want, Marisa. But it's not going to change anything."

BY FRIDAY, JEFFREY AND I had received two more cryptic gifts from Warren in the mail. One was a post card from a Marriott hotel with a note that read, "Hope you're able to sleep at night," and another a red candy apple with a note reading, "Ready to take a big bite out of life?" We were so busy with everything that we did not have time to confer on the latest of Warren's odd gifts.

I was more focused on the fact that was that Craig was still ignoring me. I happened to walk by him in the hallway while he was with Martin Strong and tried to get his attention, but he stared right through me, like I didn't exist. It left me fuming.

Another two weeks went by and I never saw Craig. I knew he was around, but he avoided me like I was in quarantine. The one who could not stay away from me was Ben Whitman, who had begun visiting my office once a day for no good reason. He would sit down in one of the chairs across from my desk and give me that leering smile, asking how my day was—or worse—how life was. I always wanted to answer him with something like, *'You mean how is life since your dick-head partner cut me off and decided I'm damaged goods? Not great. In fact, it really sucks to be here.'* It was almost as though Craig had said something to him … like he was checking up on me and reporting back to his frat buddy. I pictured Ben texting Craig daily to let him know I was still showing up like Bartleby the Scrivener, even after being shunned by His Highness and deemed useless to the agency's mission.

I dutifully reported to Jeffrey, who was consistently supportive and kind. But I was still bothered that Craig wouldn't talk to me, and that he never got back to me about the partnership.

One day, in Jeffrey's office, I asked him openly about it. We were going over Brave Harlots, who were doing an album release party, and I casually asked if Craig were attending.

"Not sure," Jeffrey answered. "But I can't imagine he'd miss it. Remember, Brave Harlots was originally his client until we stole them."

"Yeah, I know," I replied, trying to find a way to segue into the partnership discussion. I decided to just flat out ask him. "Jeffrey … have you had any conversation with Craig regarding the partnership and whether he's made a decision?" I knew my voice sounded uneasy but there was no way I could control it. I had been miserable ever since the night at Patina. There was a part of me that hated to be ignored by Craig and a part of me that felt relief to be away from him. It was hard for me to admit to myself that I needed his attention—wanted his accolades—that there was still that insecure side of me that was in desperate need of his approval.

"He didn't say anything to me," Jeffrey responded, tapping his pen against his desk, and giving me a contemplative look. "Do you want me to ask him?"

I sighed. "I don't know. I just find it weird that he's been silent on the topic ever since he moved me over to you."

"Well, he's a weird guy. Haven't you figured that out yet?" Jeffrey searched my face. "Jane, what happened between you and Craig?"

I looked down into my lap but said nothing.

"You can tell me. Did he hit on you? Did something happen? What?"

I looked up at Jeffrey but had no words. He had this concerned look on his face, and I knew he had figured out exactly what happened.

"It's no secret how he is," Jeffrey acknowledged. "He doesn't begin to hide it—he never has. I told you a long time ago to watch out for him."

I just kept my eyes on Jeffrey's pen, which he continued to tap against his desk nervously, awaiting my big reveal. But I just could not bring myself to say it out loud. Not yet.

⌐

OVER THE WEEKEND, I fretted over my next step with Craig. By Sunday afternoon, a thought suddenly occurred to me and I pulled my phone out of my purse. I scrolled through Craig's texts and found it. It was his address and apartment number, along with the note that I had full access to get into his building whenever I wanted. *What would he do if I showed up unannounced?* Would he welcome me, so we could talk frankly about what happened at Patina? *Or would he throw me out?* There was, of course, the chance that he was not at home—or even in town. But I could no longer wait. The more I pondered the whole fiasco, the more anguished I became. Craig knew exactly what he was doing—he had done it in the past. As soon as I said or did anything to cross him, he would do a disappearing act to punish me. He was an artful dodger—an escape artist, and he did it out of maliciousness.

After pacing in my kitchen for a half hour, I got into my car and drove recklessly to Brentwood. It was around 2 p.m. and I drove with trepidation, my hands shaking as they clung to the steering wheel. I was not sure what I was going to say to him when I got there. I was afraid of him now, but, one thing was certain, I had to break the ice between us. This was the only way I knew how to do it. He gave me no other choice in the matter.

When I arrived at his apartment, I drove up to a gigantic wrought iron gate and an attendant approached my vehicle. My heart was pounding as he asked for my ID and returned with a parking pass to put in the windshield of my car.

I drove to the guest parking and slowly got out of the car, feeling faint and wobbly as I walked. When I approached his building, I was floored by its opulence. His apartment building was a palace. I rode the elevator up to the penthouse and, when the door opened, I saw his apartment front entrance. Of course, he had the whole floor to himself.

With trembling fingers, I rang the bell next to a set

of shaded, tall double glass doors and waited. A couple of minutes went by and I rang the bell again. A small shadowy figure appeared through the glass and my heart raced. The door opened, and a dark-skinned woman stood there in a blue housekeeping uniform.

"I'm Jane Mercer, here to see Craig Keller," I asserted.

She gave me the once-over and then replied. "He's expecting you?"

"Why, yes," I lied. "I work for him at Keller Whitman Group." I officiously flashed my business card at her but did not allow her to take it out of my hand. "He asked me to bring him some papers from the office." I gestured toward my handbag as though I had them stashed there.

Shockingly, she believed me and stood aside to let me into his apartment. When I stepped over the threshold, she closed the door and said, "He's outside at the pool."

I almost gasped aloud at Craig's apartment. There were thirty-foot vaulted ceilings and the décor was mostly white, grey, and black, with pops of red and other bright colors here and there. The housekeeper led me through his dining room where I saw a long table with more than twenty chairs—enough for a banquet. There were expensive pieces of art and sculpture everywhere. It was the ultimate bachelor pad tailor-made for a multi-millionaire. *So, this is the place he kept pressuring me to visit. Not bad.* A vague feeling of regret passed quickly through me. *What woman would resist coming here—to visit a man like him?* I followed Craig's housekeeper past a wall that appeared to be nothing but framed family photos, some of his children, some of his parents and other family. The family all appeared to be attractive, smartly dressed, and serious looking. There was a photo of a young blond man who looked like the pictures I had seen of Craig's daughter. I wondered if he were perhaps Craig's brother. I also saw a photo of a younger Craig, in a black cap and gown with a red sash, graduating from Stanford University. I paused a moment to examine it more closely because he looked so positively striking. But there was a somber, almost sad look in his youthful green eyes that had me curious.

I followed along and, when we passed through a markedly spacious, minimalist kitchen, I glanced around and spotted a colossal glass cabinet above the stove area. It was filled with colorful bottles of booze and seemingly limitless stemware, in every size. There were bar stools everywhere, and I pictured Craig throwing large parties, filled with sophisticated, beautiful L.A. people.

We turned a corner to the living room area. A modern sectional took up most of the room, along with a trio of square zebra-print ottomans. An enormous multitiered chandelier hung from the middle of the room and served as the centerpiece, with its long undulating limbs stretched out like octopus legs, holding up lighted tips that resembled actual flames. The room looked out to the back patio which I could see through massive floor-to-ceiling glass windows. While peering through the glass, I noted a rather large infinity pool outside.

I saw them and froze in terror. It was unmistakably Hayden, laying on her stomach on a yellow raft, wearing a bright pink Brazilian bikini that left nothing to the imagination. Her perfectly bronzed ass was exposed, along with her willowy legs, which spanned the entire length of the raft. She held a magazine as she drifted along from one side of the pool to the other, seemingly without a care in the world.

Craig was reclining on a chaise lounge, also reading a magazine. He looked insanely handsome and tanned in an olive-green silk robe opened to the waist with only swim trunks underneath. His dark hair was wet and slicked back away from his face like he had just been swimming. He wore tinted aviator sunglasses. I felt the familiar shot of adrenaline pulse through me as he leaned back, completely unaware that I was spying on him. The most troubling reality was that he seemed so comfortable and familiar in Hayden's presence, almost to a level of boredom—as though they had been an item for a long time.

I gawked at the scene as though in a daze and watched Craig put his magazine down and stand. He removed his sunglasses and unknotted the tassel tie that kept his robe fastened, exposing his six-pack abs. Once the robe was off, he dove gracefully into the pool and swam over to where Hayden was. When he came up for air, he was right next to her raft and he glided his hand down her back and onto her ass, pausing there before moving his hand down her smooth, tanned legs. I thought I might vomit on the spot. Then I saw Hayden look up from her magazine with a predatory sneer on her pretty face, almost as though she were merely tolerating Craig's caresses, rather than enjoying them. She was facing the opposite direction, so Craig could not have seen her expression.

The housekeeper, who was trying to get my attention, gestured for me to go outside, but when I snapped out of my stupor, I gave her a look of panic and retreated. I began to back my way out of the living room area so there was no chance Craig and Hayden would discover my uninvited presence.

The housekeeper had a bewildered look on her face. "I thought you had papers ... for him," she said.

"I—um—I forgot something important at the office," I declared, lips quivering. "I have to go now."

Again, she looked puzzled. "Are you sure? Do you want me to tell him you were here?"

"Oh, no—please don't. I—um—I'll come back another time. Thank you for your help."

I quickly side-stepped her and walked past, then

sprinted toward the front door. Once there, I exited and ran like hell to the elevator. As soon as I was in the elevator and the door closed, I promptly burst into tears. It was all true, every shred of it and, whether I wanted to be, I was deep in the middle of Craig's bizarre love triangle. Alone with my thoughts as the elevator descended, my shock turned to anger—crazy, stupid anger. *I hate you, Craig Keller, I hate you!*

I WENT HOME THAT night, unsure of my next move. Craig was having an intimate relationship with Hayden and was trying to have one with me, too. There was no question, Craig had made up his mind about who would be made partner and it had nothing to do with talent or hard work. She was clearly the winner on every level. *But was she?* I knew what it was like to have an affair with Craig and I knew enough about his personality— the controlling, sadistic Craig, who would appear warm and gracious at one moment, brutal and self-serving the next. I wondered how she handled him. My thoughts went back to the image of her sailing blissfully along on the pool raft and I wondered again about the sneer I saw on her face. There was only one way she could handle him—she had to be even worse than he was. I had not thought that was possible. I considered all my interactions with her, and remembered Bobbi describing her as "having ice in her panties" because she was reputed to step on people regularly, firing anyone who got in her way. Perhaps Craig had met his match in Hayden.

Nineteen

TRAFFIC WAS THICK ON Monday, and I was still annihilated by my discovery at Craig's apartment Sunday afternoon. I pumped the brakes amid loud honking and thought about what I had witnessed. I did not know why I was surprised at all. It was just like him to have both Hayden and me going at the same time. The only difference was that I said no. She was craftier than me by far. She knew what she had to do to get the partnership and would stop at nothing. I guessed blowing her boss was probably something she did all the time anyway. After all, she had already been there two years dealing with his bullshit. She probably had the skin of a rhinoceros by now.

On my drive downtown, I got a call from Marisa. "What's going on?" I asked. "You sound upset."

"I just got a call from Derek," she said apprehensively.

I felt my pulse quicken. "Derek? What did he say?"

"I'm not sure how you'll take this, but his father passed away last night from a heart attack."

The words felt like a punch in the stomach. "Oh my God, Marisa … no. Please tell me it's not true."

"I'm afraid so, Jane," she replied sadly. "He told me

not to tell you, but I knew you'd want to know."

"He told you *not* to tell me?" I demanded, feeling wounded that he specifically asked that Marisa not inform me. I imagined Derek with his sister Carey, debating who to call and Carey winning out, telling him, 'make sure you don't tell Jane.' I felt a pain rip through my abdomen—that I could be so far away from Derek now—so far away that I wasn't even on the call list for when a parent passed away.

"I … told him I couldn't promise anything—I mean, after all, you're my best friend," Marisa reassured me.

"Oh Marisa," I returned, heart sinking with sadness, "I want to call him. I still love him—more than anything. I'm not over him and I want to be there. What should I do?"

"Jane, I would try to call him but, if you do, know that he might not answer, and he might not return your call. Don't push it. Just let him know that you're thinking about him," she cautioned.

"Is there a funeral service planned?" I asked.

"Yes, he plans to go to Seattle for the services. They're scheduled sometime on Friday,"

"Listen, Marisa, if you can find out where the services are and let me know, I'd be forever in your debt."

"You're not going to show up, are you, Jane? I don't think he'd want that."

"I promise I won't. I just need the information."

⌐

WHEN I ARRIVED AT the office, my heart felt heavy with regret. I decided there was no way, no matter what Derek had said and the fact that we were not on speaking terms, that I could not acknowledge his father's death. After all, David Lowell was the one I bonded with immediately in Derek's family. He was a kind man who exhibited nothing but optimism. I pictured Derek, numb with grief and

I could no longer hesitate.

I picked up my phone and dialed Derek's number. It rang more than five times and then hit voicemail. When I heard the beep, I left a message: "Derek, it's Jane. Listen, I know you probably don't want to talk to me, but I heard some sad news about your dad. I'm so … sorry, Derek." My voice shook as I said this, and I realized I had tears streaming down my cheeks. I took a deep breath. "Um … I don't know what else to say, but if there's anything you need, *anything* at all, please let me know. I … I love you."

I hung up and put my head down on my desk, chest heaving with deep sobs. I realized the "L" word just slipped out naturally, but I didn't care. I had nothing more to lose with Derek. After all, I had been engaged to him once—we had planned to marry—to spend the rest of our lives together. There was no more pride left in me when it came to him. I just wanted him to know how I felt, even if he didn't feel it in return.

When I finally composed myself and dried my eyes, I noticed there was a box sitting on my desk. I opened it and found, to my delight, a box with a pair of Christian Louboutin shoes. They were tall black pumps with stiletto heels and the heavenly red soles, miraculously, in my size. I located the note and was astonished to find that once again, Warren was the culprit. The note read: "Don't sell your sole to the devil."

I wasted no time running down the hallway to find Jeffrey, who was not in his office. My eyes went to his desk and I discovered the same sized unopened box waiting for him. *What was all this with Warren, anyway?* It was like Warren had become the non-villainous version of the Riddler from the Batman comic, leaving riddles and puzzles as clues to a larger plot, of which we were completely in the dark. One thing was certain, if Warren could afford to buy Jeffrey and me such expensive gifts, he was not at all hurt financially after the loss of his agency.

When I returned to my office, I caught Hayden bent over my desk, going through my files. I couldn't help but examine her ass, which was now covered in snug-fitting black pants, and recall that only yesterday, I saw it swathed in a skimpy pink bikini—with Craig's hands all over it.

"What do you think you're doing?" I confronted her.

She straightened up and turned to face me. The ruthless bitch didn't even flinch. "Just looking for something," she retorted, snobbishly eyeing the open Louboutin box on my desk. "You know Craig has a policy about accepting swag over two hundred and fifty dollars. Those are worth at least a grand so it looks like you're going to have to return them to the vendor who sent them."

"Are you the gift police now?" I remarked, fixing my green eyes on her rhinestone-like blue pupils. "They're from a friend, not a vendor. But I'm sure friendship is a concept you can't grasp."

"And partnership is a concept you can't grasp," she responded with the same sneer I'd seen her give Craig behind his back yesterday. "Don't you see the writing on the wall?"

I took a step toward her, so I was only a few inches away, blocking her path to the door of my office. I noticed her skin was not as smooth as I expected at such close range—it was marred by oversized pores—especially around her mouth and nose. "Oh, I've seen much more than writing on the wall, Hayden. In fact, you'd be surprised at how much I *have* seen. But if I ever catch you in my office again…"

"You'll what?" she interrupted, face contorting into a scowl. "Tell Craig? He won't even take your calls and you're in the same building." She let out a mean-spirited laugh. "You're on the same floor and you have zero access to him. How does that make you feel?"

"Like I've been totally *blown off*," I retorted, glaring at her. Then I couldn't resist adding, "And I'm sure that's something you do well." I stepped aside to let her through the door and out of my office. She took the opportunity to march out immediately.

I searched my desk wildly trying to determine what she was looking for but could not find anything. Everything on my desk seemed to be in the same place as I had left it. A few client job jackets were sitting there, but it looked as if they had remained unmolested by Hayden.

LATE IN THE AFTERNOON, I had an unexpected visit from Noel Marques. He appeared in my doorway looking slightly befuddled, his long hair illuminated like a ginger halo under the office lights.

"Noel," I stood up immediately and approached him, stretching out my hand to shake his. "I didn't know you were in town."

"It's a quick trip but I'm glad to find you still in the office," he said in his proper English accent. "Do you have a minute?"

"Of course," I assured him, ushering him to my conference table. "Please sit down."

"Would you please close the door?" he asked, glancing at my office door anxiously.

My heart rate began to accelerate. *What now?* I prayed he was not there to fire us. He was the one client who had been loyal to me ever since Warren's agency dissolved and we moved to Keller Whitman Group. I had convinced him he would have the same level of service he enjoyed with Warren, and that his account and creative team would not change. That was what made him stay with the agency in its new incarnation.

I shut the door and sat across from him. "Would

you like something to drink?" I asked apprehensively. "Water ... coffee?"

He shook his head. "No thanks, Jane. I wanted to make you aware of a strange call I received this morning." I shot him a quizzical look before he continued. "Someone named Hayden Towne called my personal cell phone to ask if I was happy with your service."

I swallowed hard but let him go on.

"She implied there were changes coming and that she was calling the clients to get a feel for how loyal we are. I felt like she was hinting Keller Whitman Group was going to be changing hands. Now Jane, you know I love you to death, and you've been nothing short of amazing to work with, but I really don't fancy another change to our account management. Part of the condition that I would continue with your new agency is that there would be no shift in the day-to-day operations or staff."

He paused reflectively and then said, "I'm here to ask you straight away, what's going on with your agency? I know you'll tell me the truth."

That's why Hayden was in my office snooping! She needed Noel's contact information. "That's very interesting," I responded, feeling my face flush with anguish. "I don't suppose she mentioned what exactly the changes were, did she?"

"No, Jane," he replied. "That was what was so odd about the call. It was like she was fishing around for information about our account. Who is she, anyway?"

"She's a colleague here," I responded, feeling sick inside. She was fishing around knowing her partnership offer was around the corner. Maybe she already had it. She was preparing to take everything over. Craig probably gave her the partnership at the pool the day before but did not bother to tell me. That was just Craig's way. I had seen him do this very thing before—in another lifetime, another chapter when I was a different person—at least I thought I had become a different person. But if that were true, why did I feel the same level of indignity and distress at having been undone by him yet again?

"Listen, Noel," I began carefully. "I'm not aware of any changes but if you'll give me a day or so, I'll get to the bottom of it." I was not sure how I was going to do this, but I needed to reassure Noel that there was nothing to worry about—that his account was safe in my hands as it always was.

"I'd appreciate it, Jane," he answered. "Even if it's not what I want to hear—I know you'll be straight with me." He smiled, gave me a quick hug, and disappeared down the hallway. When he had gone, I immediately rose and made my way to Hayden's office, which was closed and locked. I banged on the door several times but there was no answer. I looked at my watch and it was past five. She had obviously left for the evening.

I locked all my files in a cabinet and gathered my things to leave for the evening. As I bolted down the long hallway past Craig's office, something made me stop and linger. I heard barely audible voices coming from inside but could not make out who or how many people were in there. The thought crossed my mind that Hayden was at that moment in Craig's office, having sex with him on his pristine glass desk, further cementing her partnership. I thought back to the time when it was me on his desk and a chill went up my spine. The place was so tawdry, it made my skin crawl.

THE NEXT MORNING, WHEN I arrived at work, I knew what I had to do. I had thought about it all night and had not slept at all, tossing, and turning and watching the clock. And the rawness I now felt over the news of Derek's father's death only made me more fearless—more apt to stand up for myself. I locked my handbag in my file cabinet and immediately headed down the hallway to Craig's office, feeling like I was on a slow death march.

I stood at his door, which was closed, and heard muffled male voices inside. I did not even knock, I just twisted the doorknob, which was unlocked, and opened the door.

I saw Jeffrey seated at Craig's conference table, with his back to me. Craig was facing me, but he had not yet noticed my intrusion. His expression looked inordinately serious. They were the only two in the room. Jeffrey twisted around, and his eyes widened, eyebrows upturned when he spotted me.

When Craig realized it was me, his expression immediately became peeved. "Ms. Mercer," he said, rising from the table and approaching where I stood. "I don't think we have an appointment, do we?" His tone was terse.

I shook my head. "No, we don't. You've made that impossible. But I promise not to be long." Craig eyed me with a look of caution—like he was concerned about what I might say. He glanced anxiously back at Jeffrey, who had now stood and was moving to where we were standing.

Jeffrey shrugged at me and mouthed the words, "What's going on?"

Craig turned to Jeffrey and said, "Would you excuse us for a minute, please?"

"No," I protested. "I prefer that Jeffrey stay."

"Fine," Craig said quickly, looking more uncomfortable with each passing second.

"I'm here to inform you of my resignation," I announced, looking him squarely in the eye. Jeffrey's expression turned to shock while Craig looked unmoved.

"I think you should sit down so we can discuss this, Jane," Craig responded. "You have a lot to lose if you leave now."

"I know exactly what I have to lose and, frankly, if it means never having to see you again, I'm perfectly happy with my decision. In fact, I consider it a *huge* win." There was a cold symmetry to my tone—one I didn't think I was capable of in the presence of Craig.

A slight hint of embarrassment crossed his face because I was saying this in front of Jeffrey, whose mouth had jutted open at what he was hearing. Craig and I locked eyes for a moment and then Jeffrey interrupted.

"Craig, would you mind if I stepped outside your office with Jane? I'd like to talk to her for a moment."

"Please," Craig responded flatly, his eyes not leaving mine.

Jeffrey gently put his arm through mine and corralled me out the door. Once it was closed, he interrogated me in the hallway. "What are you doing?" he said in a loud whisper. "Don't leave before the movie's over. What about the partnership?"

"Jeffrey, we both know the partnership's a joke. I know Hayden Towne is getting it and there's no use in my staying here and pretending any longer."

"Jane," Jeffrey said, looking up and down the hall to make sure we were alone. "I know for a fact she's *not* getting it. She resigned early this morning to start her own agency and evidently took a bunch of Keller's clients with her."

"What?" I uttered in disbelief. "But ... I—Jeffrey, I know for a fact she and Craig are having an affair. Don't ask me how, but I know it."

"Then she was obviously using him," he responded. "She had this planned for months, maybe ever since she started working for him. There's no way she could take so many clients without a lot of planning. That's why I was in there meeting with him—he just told me what happened. He's trying to regroup and strategize the entire agency's future. The clients from Warren Mitchell and Partners now make up the largest percentage of the business."

"What?" I was reeling at the thought that I had been right about Hayden Towne. She had gotten one over on Craig. She had used his own tactics to manipulate him. And she had won.

"Listen, Jane," Jeffrey was now pleading with me. "Don't leave without a job ... that's just not smart. Even if you aren't getting the partnership, you can still be VP of accounts, and for a major agency like this, that's a huge job."

"I don't care about being broke," I argued. "I have some savings I can live on while I look for something else."

"Well, you'll hardly be penniless. You got a significant number of shares upon Warren's closing of the deal with Craig—over a million dollars. If you stay the full two years, you'll get another three million. Do you really want to give that up?"

I was shocked at the numbers Jeffrey was quoting. I had no idea I was worth that much money upon my resignation, let alone if I stayed two more years. I considered my options but kept landing back at the same place. It was Craig. I could not bear to be around him another day. The game was over. "I'm sorry, Jeffrey, but yes, I'll give that up."

"But with Hayden out of the way, you have everything to gain," Jeffrey reasoned. "Plus, now that Warren's former clients make up the majority of the agency, our stock just went up—literally—and in everyone's eyes."

I put my hand up to stop him. "Jeffrey, there are some things I haven't told you about Craig ... about Craig and me ... our history."

Jeffrey cocked an eyebrow at me in curiosity. Then his mouth dropped open. "No ... you, too?" He sighed, lowering his eyes to the floor. "I guess I'm not really surprised. I sort of had a hunch that something had happened. I mean, you were with him in that magazine."

"You saw that?" I asked, suddenly recalling the magazine photo and my level of anxiety about what Jeffrey and Warren might think if they saw it.

"We all saw it," Jeffrey admitted. "Warren was super concerned about you coming over here—especially after he saw the magazine. He knew Craig would try to manipulate you, so he asked that I protect you as much as I could. I guess I failed."

I watched Jeffrey's reaction. I couldn't tell whether he was feeling anger at Craig or disappointment in me. "You didn't fail. I never wanted you to know, but a lot has happened between us and … well, I just can't work for him. It's over, Jeffrey. Please understand."

"Damn it, Jane—I told you there are laws to protect you from that kind of stuff—laws that'll protect you now," he cried, desperately trying to change my mind. "Are you just going to quit when you can save this to your best advantage?"

"It's not just him," I explained, shaking my head. "I don't want to be here any longer. This place makes me sick—the way the men are—the way everyone is—it's a toxic environment and I just can't do this anymore."

Suddenly Jeffrey's eyes widened, like he was having a revelation. "Jane, was Keller the reason you and Derek split?"

I shrugged and slowly nodded. He might as well know all the lurid details. I had reached a point where I had nothing more to hide. "He was a major factor in the breakup," I confessed.

Jeffrey's expression turned to one of ire, but he said nothing. After a few minutes of silence, he took a deep breath. "Are you ready, then?"

I nodded, and Jeffrey opened Craig's door for me as I walked past him. Craig was at his desk, calmly typing an email. When we walked in, he looked up and motioned for us to sit across from him. Craig leaned forward, elbows on his desk, watching me carefully. I couldn't help but notice how handsome and serene he still looked, even after a woman like Hayden had made a fool of him and cost him a fortune in client revenue. Or maybe I could just never read what was behind his impenetrable expression—no one could. He must have nerves of steel to keep that kind of game face up in the middle of all the turmoil.

"Well, Jane," Craig began. "I'm hoping Jeffrey was able to convince you that an early departure from your current position would be foolish, if not a career-killer."

Before I could respond, Jeffrey spoke directly to Craig. "I couldn't change Jane's mind if I wanted to, and now I fully understand why she's leaving." As he said this, he gave Craig the once-over with an air of disgust.

Craig's gaze shifted from Jeffrey to me and back. "I don't know what Jane's told you, but I can assure you, I want her to stay. She's a highly valued executive here."

I wanted to vomit. He could not possibly be serious after everything that had happened. The only reason I was now valuable is that, along with Jeffrey, I held the key to holding on to the remainder of the clients—the ones Hayden was not able to scuttle off with.

"Jane didn't have to tell me anything," Jeffrey retorted. "I just know you, Keller. Remember? We worked for Warren at the same time. Some things just never change."

"I don't know what you're talking about," Craig addressed Jeffrey, the color of his eyes becoming a shade darker.

"You know exactly what I'm talking about," he shot back, shaking his head.

"What if I offer Jane the partnership she so squarely earned?" Craig proposed, now focusing on me.

"There's nothing you could offer that would make me stay," I replied. "What you don't understand is that none of this means anything to me anymore. I'm leaving, and that's that. You can walk me or accept my two weeks' notice. I won't try to steal your clients because that's not in my DNA. I'm happy to end this on a professional note if you are."

His eyes tapered slightly at the corners. I was surprised at my ability to keep a straight face and confident demeanor in front of him. He also kept a straight face, but I could tell he was seething underneath it. He never expected such a bold move from me.

After several minutes of uncomfortable silence, Craig finally relented. "Okay, Jane. I accept your two weeks," he said. "Jeffrey will work with you to transition the accounts to your employees while we look for a replacement."

"Right," I responded. "The employees whose tedious details mean nothing to you—the employees who are lucky to still have jobs."

Craig pursed his lips and frowned at me, his jaw rigid. Jeffrey and I stood up to leave and Craig's eyes followed us as we filed out of his office.

Twenty

KNOWING I WAS ABOUT to leave a negative situation removed every ounce of pressure because there was nothing more to lose. My last days at Keller Whitman Group were relatively calm. And, although my employees were saddened that they were losing their leader, I assured them they would be okay—that everything would turn out fine. I did caution them to watch their back when it came to the partners.

The clients were another story. Craig warned me not to call the clients to tell them I was leaving—that he wanted full control over that process—but I had given my word to Noel Marques. I called him a few days after I resigned to let him know. And while he was disappointed that he would no longer work with me, he was grateful I called him personally and he appreciated my honesty. We vowed to keep in touch after my departure from Keller Whitman Group.

With me, I was not so sure of what I was going to do with my life, but it didn't matter. I only cared that I would be free to pursue another opportunity, whatever that would end up being. I went home every night, thoughts focused thoroughly on Derek. Marisa had provided the information about his dad's funeral service. I had wracked my brain trying to think of a way to remember him without breaking Derek's established boundaries and it finally came to me. I withdrew a large amount of money from my savings and donated it anonymously to a fund that had been established by Carey and Derek in their father's honor. It somehow made me feel better, even though I knew I would never get to see or speak to Derek again. I had come to a level of acceptance regarding the matter.

ON MY LAST DAY at the office, Jeffrey brought a cake and invited my team to the conference room to say goodbye. We gathered in the board room at around 3 p.m. and Jeffrey made a toast to me, one which brought me to tears. I was going to miss working with him, after all these years.

That afternoon, Bobbi stopped by my office as I was fitting the last of my belongings into a box. I looked up and smiled. "Hi Bobbi."

"Kiddo, I just heard you're leaving," she noted with a glum look on her face.

I nodded. "Yes, it's true. This place just isn't a good fit for me."

"What happened?" she asked, eyes flickering around my empty office as though it were haunted.

I shrugged, not knowing how to answer Bobbi. I knew she was a staunch defender of Craig's and I had no reason to bad mouth him. I just wanted to get out of there as quickly as possible and free myself of his influence. "It was a lot of things—not just one," I said finally. "I don't belong here—I never really did."

"Well, you got the *sheyna punim* all worked up," she commented, shaking her head, and sinking into a sigh.

"What do you mean by that?" I asked, thinking there

was not much that could get Craig 'all worked up.'

"Are you kidding?" she asked, plunking down in the seat across from me. "He's devastated to lose you."

I laughed. "*Devastated?* You sure about that? He didn't appear to have a care in the world the day I gave notice."

"That's all a façade, Jane," she protested, shaking her head, silver strands of hair swarming her face. "I know him well and he's not at all happy you're leaving. Neither am I, for that matter. You're one of the good ones, kiddo."

I smiled. "Thanks, Bobbi. I'll miss you."

It was no surprise Craig never showed up to the going away party, although there was a distinct possibility Jeffrey never invited him. And Craig never stopped by my office to say goodbye. It was just as well, I thought, as I carried my box of belongings down the hall toward the parking garage.

When I was in the garage, I happened to spot Craig out of the corner of my eye walking the opposite way. He must have seen me because he changed direction and was now heading toward me. "Hey, Jane," he called out. "May I carry that for you?"

"I've got it," I replied, looking up at him with a half-smile. He appeared as attractive as ever, in a cream-colored light wool suit with a white shirt and brown and white houndstooth tie. His elegance never failed to give me goosebumps, even now, after everything he had done to make me hate him.

"I insist," he offered, and took the box from me. I caught myself wondering whether Craig would sully his pristine suit by carrying the box, but he didn't seem to mind. When we got to my car, I opened the trunk and he squatted down, placing the box gently down. I shut the trunk and turned to him.

"Thank you." I looked up into his eyes, thinking no matter how beautiful they were, in all their jade-imbued murkiness, I never wanted to see them again.

"You know, Jane," he said slowly, searching my face. "I realize how badly I treated you, but I never wanted you to leave."

I shook my head and smiled. "Please, Craig. You don't need to say any of this."

"But I do," he replied. "For whatever it's worth, I'm sorry." His luminous green eyes looked genuinely disappointed that I was leaving. In fact, it was the most human I had ever seen Craig look—like there may be a kernel of a heart and some level of compassion in his soul. But it was a little too late.

"Apology accepted," I responded without hesitation. I looked down awkwardly and adjusted my shoulder bag because it was digging into my collarbone.

"What will you do now?" he asked, putting his hands in his pants pockets.

I shrugged. "Maybe I'll go to the beach and think about things for a while. Then, I'll probably find a job somewhere."

"How old are you, Jane?" he suddenly asked, with a look of mischief on his face.

"It's illegal for you to ask a question like that of an employee," I responded, suppressing a grin.

"You're no longer an employee," he returned with a smile in his voice.

I rolled my eyes. "I'll be twenty-nine soon."

"Ah," he nodded as though he had suddenly solved a deep mystery. "Women your age never know what they *really* want."

"And men your age?" I asked, curious as to where he was going with this conversation.

"Us? I don't think we ever find out until it's too late," he replied with a contemplative expression. "Regardless, will you do me a favor and please keep in touch? I'd like to help you, if you'll let me. Jane, you're just … you're different."

At that moment, he took his hands out of his pockets and moved them up to my face like he wanted to touch me one last time. But he visibly stopped himself, jerking his hands away and dropping them like a thief trying to fight his innate urge to steal hot property.

I nodded slowly, thinking I would never feel comfortable having him help me with anything. But one aspect in our relationship had finally changed. He saw me in a new light. He did not have to explain why he thought I was different. I understood completely. It took losing half his clients and being shredded by an unscrupulous woman to make him understand. I turned to walk away from him.

"Jane, wait a second," he called to me.

I turned back, and he took a step toward me. We just stood there by my car door, staring into each other's eyes for a full minute as though some unspoken dialogue was taking place until finally, he took my hand, stooped down, and kissed it tenderly. Then, he opened the door of my car and waited for me to get in.

"Good-bye, Ms. Mercer," he said before shutting the car door. I gave him a little wave, backed out and drove away. In my rearview mirror, I could see his towering silhouette as he watched, waiting until my car was out of sight.

⌐

I MET MARISA AND Kat for dinner that night at Milo and Olive on Wilshire Boulevard in Santa Monica. Upon learning of my resignation, they congratulated me and insisted on buying dinner to celebrate my new status of unemployment—and the fact that I could no longer afford to dine out.

Milo and Olive had a Southern California feel, with its white marble tables and cheery bouquets of orange tulips. There were always crumbs and half-empty wine glasses left over from some previous customers' revelry. Marisa had requested it because she was craving their wood-fired pizza. When we were all seated and had full glasses of Chianti, Marisa held her glass up to toast.

"To Jane, who is now unemployed, but who has integrity and we love her for it," she toasted as we all clicked glasses.

I laughed. "Integrity doesn't pay rent and it certainly doesn't buy couture." I couldn't help but be proud that I *did* have integrity.

"You won't be unemployed for long, darling," Kat maintained with sincerity. "Your perfect job is out there ... I can feel it."

"Yes, well, I hope you're right, or you might find me on your doorstep," I responded, still amazed that I had over a million dollars in equity shares to cash out. That should hold me over for a while—a long while.

"How much fun would we have?" Kat replied smiling. "You'd be a great roommate."

"I doubt Caleb would appreciate that." I could not resist the comment, even though I still was not sure how much Marisa knew about him.

Kat just laughed. "Speaking of men, how's your hot Brit?" she asked Marisa.

"Not great," Marisa revealed tentatively. "I got a call from him last week—some electrical issue caused the band's show in Austin, Texas, to black out completely—and Ewan said he was close to getting electrocuted. They had to cancel the show and refund all the ticket money because they couldn't get anything to work—no lights, no sound—complete darkness. Cost him a boat load of cash."

"That's terrible, Marisa," I said, picturing the chaos that must have ensued.

"Wait, I'm not finished—he got a call the next day from some thug who told him his girlfriend was causing problems by nosing into Craig Keller's financial records and that the blackout and near electrocution was no accident."

My jaw dropped at that news. "Oh my God."

"The thug implied that the same 'accident' would happen again and the next time, it wouldn't end as well, if Ewan didn't silence me for good," Marisa added.

"Holy crap," I exclaimed. "I guess the Keller family really is connected—thank God I never pissed him off." I wondered if Hayden's client-stealing machinations would earn her a call from this same thug, and I smiled inside if that were indeed the case.

"Is Ewan okay with everything?" Kat asked. "I mean, he's not mad at you for creating the drama in the first place, is he?"

"Oh, sure, he's okay," Marisa replied, grinning. "He just told me he wrote a song about me for the next Brave Harlots album."

"Maybe he should do a cover of that song "Live Wire," I commented with a smirk. "But it must be pretty serious now for him to be writing songs for you—you're so lucky."

Marisa must have remembered my shattered romance at that moment because she looked a little gloomy. "You still haven't heard from Derek, have you?" she asked me.

I shook my head and sighed. "No. But I'm in a good place. I'm honestly looking forward to starting fresh … with everything." I looked from Marisa to Kat and they appeared so sorry for me, I added, "Come on—everything's fine. I really *am* okay."

A familiar voice resounded from across the room and I turned to look in its direction. *It was Hayden Towne!* She was holding court with a group of people, likely clients she stole from Craig. *So much for starting fresh.*

I leaned over to Kat and Marisa and whispered, "Don't look now, but that woman I told you about—the

273

one who stole the clients from Craig—is sitting over there," I revealed while nodding discreetly in Hayden's direction.

Kat's eyes widened with curiosity. "Is that the one you saw at his apartment that day? The one he was canoodling with?"

I nodded. Kat and Marisa turned their attention inconspicuously toward the woman in question and turned back to me.

"She's pretty hot," Marisa instantly assessed. "That's the woman you were competing with for the partnership?"

"She's not as beautiful as you are, Jane," Kat interjected. "She looks like an iceberg ready to crack."

I giggled. "Thanks, Kat."

"Although she did the unthinkable," Kat remarked. "She screwed Craig Keller in more ways than one and, for that, we should applaud her."

Later that night, once we were sufficiently toasted on Chianti, I made my way to the ladies' room. Once I had used the toilet and was washing my hands, someone came out of one of the stalls and was washing her hands next to me. It was Hayden.

"Oh, it's you," she said, as soon as she recognized me. "I didn't expect to see you here."

"Likewise," I responded, picturing her having sex with Craig Keller in his palatial apartment, their two pairs of striking eyes locked on each other in fascination.

When Hayden finished washing and drying her hands, she turned to face me at the mirror. "You must be happy," she contended, "now that you have Craig all to yourself."

I frowned at her. "Do you actually think that's what I *wanted*?"

"I know it was *you* he really wanted," she muttered resentfully. "I knew it the day I saw you with him in that magazine."

I stared at her curiously, wondering why she was choosing now to tell me this. "I highly doubt that," I responded, the memory of Craig in his pool massaging Hayden's ass in her pink bikini coming to mind.

"You don't have to believe me, but it's true. He told me point blank when I questioned him. But you kept putting him off. Guys like him don't like that game and then ... they do. You played hard to get."

"Oh, come on, Hayden, everyone knows you're the one who *played* him. I just wanted to do my job, but I found out the hard way that's impossible when you work for him."

She let out a high-pitched, wicked laugh. "He was so easy. You could have gotten exactly what you wanted from him. He would have given you everything. He told me. And that's why I hated you with a passion. You were in my *way*."

I suddenly realized why Hayden had a sneer on her face the day I saw her at Craig's pool. He had settled for her when he really wanted me. There was nothing special or exclusive about their relationship, and she knew it. He was using her because the person he really wanted had told him to get lost.

"So, is that why you plotted against him and took all his clients?"

"I robbed his clients because he deserved it. And I slept with him, so he would never suspect me. It's a long-standing family vendetta. And I won," she concluded, triumphantly. "But he'll survive. Craig has real money in case you didn't notice—he won't feel a thing. But I suppose you're getting all protective because you still work for him."

I shook my head. "You don't have to tame your words for me—he's no friend of mine," I said, thinking that Craig was an utter mystery. I never thought he cared one bit for me, other than as a sexual conquest but, based on this woman's assessment, it was a different story altogether. I thought back to how he tried to get me to his apartment that night after the scene in Patina. He was so intense about his desire to get me there, too, openly holding the partnership over my head unless I did what he wanted. Then I remembered his bored, resigned look that day I spied on him at his pool with Hayden. She was the cheap stand-in, not me. And though it was somewhat of a compliment, it was still shrouded in the slime that was Craig Keller. I sighed.

"He *is* your friend, Jane. No matter what you might think," she responded after a few moments of silence. It was the first time she called me by my name. "As much as that man can be anyone's friend."

"Well, I guess neither of us has to worry about that now," I remarked emphatically, no longer wanting to discuss Craig Keller with his former concubine. "I resigned. Today was my last day. So, I don't have to see either of you again."

She stared at me in awe, like she hardly expected me to deliver that news. "You watch," she commented, now smiling. "He'll come after you again. He'll keep coming back and coming back until you say yes."

And with that, she turned and exited the bathroom. I took a long hard look in the mirror and thought about what she said. *He had wanted me and not Hayden the whole time.* I thought back to what he told me in the parking lot—about finding out what he wanted after it was too late. *Was that some sort of hint about his feelings for me?* The whole thing made no sense.

I returned to Kat and Marisa and reported what happened in the bathroom. "Do you believe that?" I asked, incredulous.

"Yes, I do," Kat replied, giving me a maternal look. "I told you. You need to watch out for him. Always be on guard when it comes to him."

Marisa nodded in agreement. "She's right. Now, more cocktails, anyone?"

I SPENT MY FIRST unemployed weekend painting the apartment. I decided to make three walls in the living room camel and one orange, just to be avant-garde. I did not have a lot of experience painting, but I had plenty of time and enthusiasm. I set about to update the place and perhaps remove a bit of Derek from the equation. No matter how hard I tried, I could never quite shake what happened. And there were so many things about the apartment that reminded me of him. New colors on the walls were just what the place needed.

Once I had covered two walls (and my T-shirt and jeans) with a coat of camel paint, I heard my cell phone ringing. It was Grandma.

"Pigeon," she crowed into the phone, "how's my sweet girl?"

"I'm fine, Grandma," I replied. I had called them the night I resigned, and they were full of support. They even offered me money to hold me over in case I didn't get another job right away. I had also shared the news of Derek's father, which troubled them to no end. They still held on to the thought that someday we would reconcile, but I assured them that was a fantasy.

"What are you up to this weekend?" Grandma asked. I could hear the faint whoosh of her exhaling smoke into the phone.

"Painting the apartment and then … I don't know what," I answered cheerfully.

"Would you like to come over for dinner tomorrow night?" she asked. I knew it was because she was worried that I might be lonely, and I loved her for it.

"That's okay, Grandma. I'm fine being on my own this weekend. I have tons of things to do."

"All right, sweetie, but please come over if you get bored."

"I shall, Grandma. I love you." And I hung up the phone.

I SPENT THE NEXT two weeks meandering without a schedule of any kind. I went to the beach and lay in the sand, I body-surfed, and I walked, endlessly. I checked out books from the Santa Monica public library and read titles that I'd never had time to read before, works by writers like William Carlos Williams and Lawrence Ferlinghetti. I immersed myself in everything as though I was a young child, a porous new sponge, able to absorb every detail and consider different interpretations. I felt like I was a new student of life and that leaving the advertising industry, even if temporarily, had freed me to be someone different—someone of depth. I did not consider updating my resume or calling recruiters. I was experiencing something of a transformation, and I needed to let it play out.

One day, after having been to the beach for three straight days and nursing a bad sunburn, I rifled through my refrigerator and found the last of its contents: A Hostess Ding Dong, left over from—I don't know when.

I sat on the sofa in ripped-up overall shorts and a T-shirt, and mindlessly bit into the chocolate-covered cake, licking my lips, and tasting the sweetness of the cream filling. I heard a sudden knock at the door. I stood and went to the door, not even looking through the peephole. I had gotten sort of loose over my time being unemployed. I was less concerned about home intrusion, less self-conscious and more spontaneous. I opened the door, still chewing a huge mouthful of Ding Dong, and there stood Derek.

"Hey," he said, observing me curiously in my overalls.

He was probably shocked at finding me at home on a weekday and dressed the way I was. I cocked my head in disbelief. *What was he doing here?* He looked the same, handsome, and boyish, but something had changed—his hair was longer, almost shoulder-length, and looked like it had been bleached with blond highlights from the sun's rays. He looked like one of the hot surfer guys I saw early every morning, catching the ocean waves.

"Derek," I mumbled softly, still chewing, and swallowing Ding Dong cake. "Is it really you?"

"May I come in?" he asked.

"Um … sure," I said, thinking I was not at all ready to see Derek. My hair was pulled into a high ponytail, tangled and sandy from the beach, my skin was red, I wore no makeup, and I had Ding Dong cake stuck in my teeth.

He entered the apartment and looked around cautiously. His eyes stopped at my orange wall. "Damn Jane," he said, "That wall is … um, really orange."

"You don't like it?" I asked, scrunching up my nose. The place still reeked of fresh paint, too. I had no idea what to say in this situation, one I had dreamed of for the past six months.

He shrugged, turning his attention to the half-eaten Ding Dong, sitting in its crinkled foil wrapping on the coffee table. "I see you've abandoned all decent nutrition."

"That's because my personal chef went away," I responded, smiling. "I'm dangerous with food, left to my own devices, as you're aware."

"Oh, I'm definitely aware," he replied, returning my smile.

I observed his clear, hazel eyes and felt like I was imagining them. I had only pictured those eyes in dreams but when I woke up, they disappeared. "Derek, what are you doing … here?" I asked, almost not wanting to hear the real answer.

"I tried to call your office and they told me you resigned," he answered with knitted brows.

"Why would you call my office when you have my cell?"

"I tried your cell phone a couple of times and it went straight to voice mail," he replied, glancing around my apartment as though trying to figure out what was really going on. Maybe he was looking for evidence that I was involved with someone new. Regardless, his look was one of distrust. "I didn't want to leave a message and, knowing how much you work, I thought the best place to catch you live would be at the office."

I nodded, realizing he must have been calling while I was painting or at the beach. I turned the phone off during those times—so Derek's phone number would not have showed up on the phone log. I shifted my weight from side to side. "What can I do for you?"

"Well … I heard something about you … about something you did," he said blinking at me, his voice slightly uneasy. "You gave a lot of money to my dad's fund and I wanted to personally thank you."

A tinge of disappointment fell over me. "Oh, you weren't supposed to know it was me."

"I know that's what you wanted, but I found out." He cast his eyes to the floor. "What made you quit your job, anyway?"

"Guess."

He looked me in the eye and shrugged. "I thought you'd like it there, you know, being with *him* all the time."

I thought back to my sordid relationship with Craig, everything that led to my break-up with Derek and my final resignation. A shiver rolled up my spine. "Now, why would you think that, Derek?"

"I just heard stuff, okay, Jane?" He was starting to get defensive. I could tell by the way his eyes widened at me. He only did this when he was ready to get into an argument. "I heard stories that you were all over town with that guy."

I thought back to the time at Patina when we ran into Chelsea and I knew who authored the 'stories'. "Derek, that's not true," I responded, feeling angry tears forming. "I know who told you that and she's wrong. I went to dinner with Craig once the entire time I worked there. He tried to go after me exactly the way he did at the charity dinner. Only this time, I wasn't drunk. I was furious. And not long after that, I resigned. So please stop saying there's something going on between us—between Craig Keller and me—because it's just flat-out wrong."

"You mean, you quit because of something he did to you?" Derek asked, eyes fixed on mine. He moved a step closer. "Why didn't you tell someone?"

"Tell who?" I asked, now incredulous that Derek was still accusing me of being with Craig. "He was my *boss*, Derek. He was the managing partner. There was no one above him to tell."

"There's always someone to tell—don't they have a human resources department at that agency?" His tone was stern. "You didn't tell anyone because you still have a thing for him."

I could not believe what I was hearing. "How dare you say that?" I answered, voice now guttural. "You have no idea what I went through working there. But I know it doesn't matter to you anyway—you didn't even tell me when your own father died. Do you realize how much that hurt? Or was that the intention?"

Derek shut his eyes and shook his head. "Jesus, Jane. What the hell happened here?"

"I guess life got really—you know, messy," I answered. "And I know you can't deal with that."

"What's that supposed to mean?" he demanded, cheeks slightly flushed as though anger was beginning to roil inside him.

"Let's face it, Derek, I didn't fit into your perfect relationship mold," I blurted. "I'm not perfect and I never will be. I can't cook and sometimes I do stupid things. Now I don't even have a job, but that doesn't make me a bad person. It just makes me imperfect."

"Now wait a minute, Jane," he argued. His hazel eyes were glowing—like a wild animal about to pounce. "None of this would have happened if you had just been straight with me about that guy in the first place. I never cared that you weren't perfect. No one's perfect. I just wanted you to be honest and true to me."

"You held the ring and the marriage proposal hostage while you dug up what was left of my past and threw it in my face," I shouted, returning his glare. "You couldn't get it out of your head that I have a past. We all do."

"It wasn't just about your past, and you know it," he shot back. "We both know what happened while you had my ring on your finger, Jane, so don't try to twist the facts."

I felt tears forming again. *Why was he torturing me about this?*

Derek saw my tears and sighed. "I don't know why I came here. I don't want to rehash what happened months ago. I just wanted to make sure you're okay."

"Why? Are you saying you still care about me? Tell me, Derek … tell me why you're really here." I took a step toward him, so my face was inches from his. He didn't move away.

There was a long pause. "Because I …," he uttered softly. "I … Jane, I don't know anymore. I just wanted things to go back to the way they were. We were so happy once. We had all these incredible plans and then—it's like everything just got destroyed—by your lies and betrayal, my dad's death … I wasn't sure how much more I could take."

I could not wait any longer. I threw my arms around

Derek's neck and pulled him into me. I felt his arms around my waist, and I lay my head on his shoulder and whispered, "I'm sorry, Derek. I'm so sorry—about everything. I never meant to hurt you. But you couldn't forgive me." I gripped his shoulders even tighter as tears flowed down my face. "Will you please forgive me, Derek?" I whispered, now breathless. "Please?"

After another long pause just holding each other tightly, Derek finally withdrew and looked me in the eye. His stoic expression had given way to sadness and he took a deep breath before saying, "Okay. I forgive you, Jane." He swallowed hard. "I forgive you."

My chest began to heave uncontrollably with sobs as I felt the last five months of stress flow out like lava from a volcano. I dropped to the floor, legs buckling underneath me, knees hitting the cold hard wood and bent my head down toward my lap. Derek knelt and tried to console me, stroking my hair. "Take it easy, Jane. It's going to be okay. We're both going to be okay."

Then we were both on the floor and he was holding me in his arms, sharing my pain—for it was clearly *our* pain—something we had not figured out until now. When our eyes finally met, I saw that he was crying, too. We had finally hit a breaking point. We hit it together. The war was over.

Twenty-one

ONE THING I LEARNED over years of stressing about things that have not yet happened is that it's pointless. Derek's return to my life was unexpected but it did not cause the type of anxiety it would have before I quit my job. I didn't think about how it would be with him, after our war of silence. I just accepted his return to calling me once a day and seeing me on weekends.

After a full six weeks, we still had not slept together, and that didn't bother me either. I knew to just let life happen a little at a time, until we were both comfortable moving forward. But the important thing is that we were moving forward—and that was all that mattered to me.

With work, I was half-heartedly looking for a new position. I had found a recruiter who brought me job after job at a variety of decent agencies; however, none of them resonated with me. I was still detoxing from what went on at Keller Whitman Group and the world that once excited and inspired me was somehow defiled by that experience.

On a warm September evening, Derek had taken a three-month sabbatical from the L.A. Philharmonic, so he could perform a lengthy gig with the Los Angeles Ballet's orchestra. He was scheduled to perform in Royce Hall at UCLA in a run of performances of *Coppélia*, and Derek had been in rehearsals for weeks perfecting the music of Léo Delibes. Derek gave me four tickets and I invited Kat and Caleb, and Marisa. Ewan was on tour in Australia, so Marisa would be my date for the evening.

The ballet was completely sold out and we had seats within the first three rows. I noted from the program that Chelsea was the principal, playing the part of Swanhilda. That did not thrill me, but I was mostly over her exaggerated report to Derek about my whereabouts with other men. And after all, I was only there to see Derek and would spend the evening straining my eyes to watch him play his violin. It had been so long since I had had the pleasure of doing it.

After the ballet, our group went backstage to wait for Derek. "What did you think?" I asked Marisa, who seemed entranced throughout the performance. She was just gazing around at the various props, left over costume pieces and ballerinas, strolling about in various stages of undress. "It was beautiful," she answered. "I forgot how talented Derek is. And the ballet was superb. I know you don't like her, but Chelsea is pretty amazing."

I lowered my eyes to the faded red carpeted floor, recalling how perfectly balanced and graceful she was. "I agree."

Kat and Caleb were right next to us, but they were not listening. They were instead leaning into each other like high school sweethearts, as though there were no one else in the room. I had to hand it to Kat. She had been with Caleb almost an entire year. He had long since left the company for another job (which Kat had secured for him) and they were free to date in public. I noticed

Caleb holding Kat's hand and, although it still seemed a little weird, it was kind of sweet how much he seemed to care for her.

Then I heard a familiar voice and turned my attention to its origins. I jumped, thinking I was seeing a ghost. It was Craig Keller approaching our group. He looked striking as always, in a black pullover sweater with a crisp white shirt underneath and jeans. I braced myself and grabbed Marisa's arm. She looked up and spotted Craig. "Oh Jesus," she exclaimed, turning her back on him and facing me.

"What's he doing here?" I hissed under my breath.

"Katherine Blakely," he greeted Kat, smiling, and immediately sizing up Caleb. It was almost funny to see Craig and Caleb together, because they looked so much alike. Caleb could be Craig's nephew. "What a lovely surprise. Are you babysitting tonight or was there a son I didn't know about?"

I was afraid Kat might kick him in the balls, but she remained cool and collected. Caleb looked puzzled as to what was happening. "I didn't realize you were a patron of the ballet," she answered, clinging to Caleb's hand.

"I am now," he responded, suddenly noticing me standing next to Marisa. He instantly sauntered in my direction with a dazzling smile on his face. "Jane." He sounded like he had just found the lost dead sea scrolls. "How've you been? You're looking well."

"Yeah, I guess unemployment agrees with me," I answered, looking around for Derek.

"It sure does," he remarked. "You know, I'm hurt that you never called me. I thought you might have dropped off the planet—but here you are. What are you doing here?"

"I'm waiting for my ..." my voice trailed off because I was not sure what to call Derek now.

"She's waiting for her boyfriend," Marisa interjected,

to save me. "He's first chair violinist in the orchestra."

"What a coincidence," Craig answered. "I'm waiting for my date, too."

"Oh, Derek's more than just a *date*," Marisa was not about to let it go. "They were engaged to be married until something came between them."

Craig narrowed his eyes at Marisa. After all, she was the one who blackmailed him years earlier to get him to leave me alone ... the first time Craig screwed me over. They were not exactly buddies and, with her latest stunt trying to get dirt on his father's mob connections, Craig could not have been happy to see her. He turned his attention back to me. "Well, I'm glad you're doing so well, Jane. It's nice to see you again."

Derek suddenly appeared in his tuxedo and, as he approached us, Craig turned to him and said, "Ah—you must be the lucky ..."

He did not have a chance to finish his sentence because Derek, who immediately recognized Craig, hauled off and gave him a sharp right hook in the jaw. Derek's coat tails wildly flapped behind him as he delivered the power blow of his life. The force of Derek's punch was so mighty, Craig lost his balance and tumbled to the floor on his back.

"Oh my God, Derek," I exclaimed.

Astonished, Craig put his hand to his jaw and sat up slowly, checking his fingers for blood. Chelsea appeared out of nowhere in her street clothes, stage makeup still heavily masking her face. "What happened?" she demanded, running to Craig's side, and kneeling to see if he were hurt. Chelsea was obviously the 'date' to whom Craig had earlier referred.

"Looks like your boyfriend finally got what was coming to him," Kat commented to Chelsea. Then she looked down at Craig, smiling. "Tell me, are *you* babysitting tonight or was there a daughter I didn't know about?"

With that, she grabbed Caleb's hand and stepped around Craig's body to exit the backstage area.

Meanwhile, Derek nursed his right hand and muttered to me under his breath, "Damn, that's my bowing hand."

Craig was now standing and staring oddly at Derek, like he was not sure whether to return the punch. Then he smiled broadly, white teeth gleaming. "I was going to ask if you were the lucky guy who's with Jane, but you hit me with a lucky shot instead. Touché."

Chelsea turned to Derek in bewilderment. "Derek, why would you do something like that? What did he ever do to you?"

I think that's when Derek suddenly realized Chelsea and Craig were dating. "You mean, you and he …?" Derek shook his head and glared at Chelsea like she was crazy.

"Are you ready for dinner, beautiful?" Craig hastily broke in, so Chelsea would not have to answer the question. "You were magnificent tonight." And they walked away, holding hands, while Derek looked on in amazement. When they had gone, he turned to me and I shrugged.

"She's in for a real treat," I said, picturing Craig taking her to his penthouse apartment and forcing her to do splits in a tutu and point shoes while swinging from his mammoth chandelier. He was such a complete pervert, I'm sure her agility was the first thing on his mind when he decided to infiltrate the ballet community in the hopes of landing a hapless new sex partner like Chelsea. The one thing absent when I saw them together was any form of jealousy on my part. She could have him— because having him was the worst thing that could happen to any woman and I knew it first-hand.

"But don't you think I should warn her or something?" Derek asked.

I shook my head. "Nah—let her find out for herself," I replied, now smiling sweetly. "It's a rite of passage in this city."

"Oh, yes," Marisa immediately agreed. "The poor girl has no idea what she's in for with that man." She chuckled in glee, obviously at the thought of Chelsea's unforeseeable demise.

Derek turned to me. "Shall we go home now?"

"Where's home?" I inquired curiously. "My apartment or yours?"

"Ours," he answered, taking my hand, and leading me away.

Twenty-two

DEREK MOVED BACK INTO my apartment—our old apartment—the next week and we started over. Only this time, we agreed that we needed a new place—somewhere we could start again fresh. With the raise Derek had recently received, an inheritance from his dad, and the money I had saved from cashing out my shares at Keller Whitman Group, we had plenty of money to invest in a home.

I also decided it was time for me to look seriously for employment and set about contacting my pool of recruiters to see what opportunities were out there.

Both my grandparents and Derek's mom were thrilled that we were back together. Of course, sister Carey was the last to come around and I still was not so sure she thought it was a great idea for Derek to be back with me, but I didn't care anymore. I knew Derek loved me, and that was all that mattered. Carey would have to get used to it at some point because we were going to be family.

I RECEIVED A CALL from Jeffrey out of the blue one afternoon and realized I had not spoken to him since I left Keller Whitman Group. We had exchanged texts a couple of times but that was all.

"Jane," he said when I answered. "How's life?"

"Life is much calmer," I responded. "How's everything with you?" I didn't want to ask about Craig or life at the agency because I still had mixed feelings about how I left.

"It just got a whole lot calmer for me, too, Jane," he said cryptically. "I was wondering if you could meet me tonight over at Philippe The Original."

"Why, are you craving a French dip?" I asked, laughing.

"I just thought it would be nice to catch up," Jeffrey replied. "I feel like I haven't seen you for years."

"Glad to know I've been missed."

"You have no idea, Jane. Seven-thirty?"

"See you then."

WHEN I ARRIVED AT Philippe The Original's on North Alameda Avenue downtown, I found Jeffrey planted at a table with his phone out, texting someone. "Hey, stranger," I greeted him, beaming.

Jeffrey looked up and immediately stood to hug me. "Jane—is it really you?"

"It sure is," I answered.

"You look great," he said. "I mean, you look so rested."

"Well, I've had a lot of time to rest," I replied, thinking it was good to see Jeffrey after so much time had elapsed. He had always been like a big brother to me and seeing him now reminded me that I had missed him terribly. I eyed his attire—jeans and a casual button-down shirt. "My aren't we dressed down for a workday—did His Highness relax the dress code?"

Jeffrey gave me a sly look. "Please sit down and order something. I have a lot to tell you," he prefaced before flagging down the waitress.

Once we had both ordered food, I leaned back and took a long look at Jeffrey, whose spiked hair looked a little wilder than normal. "So, tell me about the agency. Is it filled with the same old nonsense?"

"Oh God, yes, Jane," he replied. "It's run like a brothel, as you know. You definitely left at the right time." He toyed with the straw wrapper before tearing it and dipping his straw into the ice water.

"What happened to Hayden? Did she start her own agency with all of Craig's clients?" I still could not shake the image of Hayden at Craig's pool that day—she had to be one of the craftiest women on the planet.

Jeffrey nodded. "It's called Towne Ink. And I found out later you were right. Keller was having an affair with her, on and off, the entire time she worked there, but he wasn't the only one. Apparently, the partners passed her around like a bag of potato chips—she dated Whitman, Strong, and Richards, too. The grossest thing of all is that they all knew about each other—they nicknamed her 'Lay's'. They'd say, 'Who has Lay's this weekend?' Or 'I've got dibs on Lay's tonight.' Do you believe that?"

I shuddered. "Jeffrey, how do you think Hayden got away with stealing all those clients—you know, with everything rumored about Craig's family being connected?" I was testing the waters with Jeffrey. If anyone was going to get bumped off by one of Donovan C. Keller's 'friends', it was Hayden.

Jeffrey shook his head. "No matter what Keller's family connections are, Hayden has him one-upped—she's untouchable. Did you know Hayden's father, Stephan Towne, is the Attorney General for California? The Keller family's history with mobsters has always been on the radar with Hayden's family, and evidently the two factions have been warring for years. Don Keller ordered Craig to hire Hayden, so he could keep Stephan at bay."

So that was it. I recalled the comment Hayden made in the ladies' room that night—that she stole the clients because of a long-standing family vendetta. Hayden's connections out-ranked Craig's and that was why she could do what she did to him without retribution. I also realized that must have been the real reason Craig refused to decide who to make partner. He obviously knew I was the more qualified candidate, but his link to Hayden's family and his own father's corruption kept his hands tied. *What a mess.* I glanced up at Jeffrey. "Stories like this just reinforce what a great decision I made in leaving."

"Well, now you're not the only one. There's something I need to tell you, Jane, and it's why I called you to meet. I resigned this morning," he announced, pausing for my reaction.

"You did?" I was genuinely shocked. Jeffrey had a wife and kids to support. He was the last person I thought would resign, especially in the face of the two-year earn out. "But why?"

The waitress interrupted by placing our food orders in front of us. "Would you two like anything else?" she asked.

We shook our heads in unison. As soon as she was gone, Jeffrey leaned in. "When you left, the place just went downhill in my eyes and the clients knew it," he explained. "You remember Warren's former clients made up most of the business at Keller's agency, and I just felt like I was carrying the whole thing. Even the long-time partners like Martin Strong have started looking around." He picked up the saltshaker and aimed it at his French dip.

"What was Craig's reaction? I mean, he had to have been pretty upset to lose you."

"Oh, please, Jane," Jeffrey responded, rolling his eyes. "That guy never gets upset about anything. That's what happens when you have too much money. You could light a stick of dynamite up his ass and he wouldn't react. I swear, I've never met a colder bastard in my life. You know him."

The thought of Craig made my appetite wane. I picked at my Cobb salad without enthusiasm, turning the diced avocado with my fork and dipping it in dressing. "But where are you going? Do you already have another position?" I could not imagine Jeffrey remaining unemployed like I had. He must have something lined up.

"Well, that's what I wanted to talk to you about," Jeffrey said, eyeing me anxiously. "You see, I've done enough research to know for a fact that most of Warren's former clients want to leave Keller's agency right now. And, if there were an opportunity to work with you and me again, they would take it and go with us."

"You mean, start our own agency?" I asked. "But how? That would take a ton of capital and I just don't have it right now. Derek and I are looking for a house, so I need every dollar I have in savings as well as a steady income."

Jeffrey glanced quickly at my left hand, where my shiny diamond sparkled under the restaurant lights. "You're back with Derek—you have no idea how happy I am to hear that."

I smiled. "Thank you, Jeffrey. It wasn't easy, but we made it."

He just smiled. "True love always wins." Then he turned serious again. "Jane, listen, I've done the math and I know it can work. We would be partners and share in the client profits. I would take care of the capital on the front end and you'd be able to pay it back over time—however you want to do it. I just know this could be big, Jane. I really want you on board with me." He paused for my reaction.

"But what about the employees and hiring the right

candidates?" I asked, still skeptical. "We would need an HR expert, lawyers and accountants to set all that up … I'm not trying to be a downer, but have you thought all of that through? And have you thought about the fact that neither of us has experience starting up an ad agency?"

"Well, I haven't told you about the third partner," Jeffrey said mysteriously, looking over my shoulder, waving and summoning someone to our table.

Before I could turn to see the newcomer, he was standing next to us. I did a double take when I saw it was Warren Mitchell. "Warren?" I exclaimed, standing right away, and giving him a hug.

"Hello, Jane," he said smiling and hugging me back. He slid into the booth next to Jeffrey. I watched him like I were in a trance. *What was Warren doing here?* "I'm the third partner, Jane," Warren professed as soon as he was seated.

"But—I thought you retired," I threw back in surprise. I did notice he looked tan and rested, his greying hair a bit longer and greyer.

Warren shook his head. "No, Jane. I'm just getting started. I never intended to retire but I couldn't say anything until I knew I could secure the clients to start fresh."

"You remember all those gifts Warren sent us while we were still at Keller's agency?" Jeffrey asked me.

"Um, yes, of course," I answered, thinking back to the series of covert gifts and notes Warren kept sending.

"Those were all hints at the clients I've been racking up since my agency dissolved," Warren said. "We've got quite a list now and they're all ready to sign as soon as our agency is set up."

"You mean … those gifts were all about clients?" I asked, still trying to untangle what was happening.

"You got it," Warren replied. "We have Starbucks, The

Regal Oasis Casino Resort in Las Vegas, Mercedes-Benz, Marriott Hotels, Disney, Apple, and Christian Louboutin. That ought to be enough to get us started."

My mouth dropped open and I stared at Jeffrey.

"And that doesn't count all the clients who'll come with us from Keller's agency. He'll be lucky if he doesn't have to lay off half his staff, at least the ones who don't want to come with us." Warren's expression exuded a certain satisfaction in having brought his enemy down.

I shook my head. This is how Warren had been spending his time over the past year. He had been working his numerous connections, prepping to start a new agency and pay Craig back for everything he had done to eradicate Warren Mitchell and Partners. And now, I would be a part of it. Then another idea came to me. "I suppose we could add Noel Marques and Hollywood Bowl to our list, although I did promise Craig that I wouldn't personally try to steal any of his clients."

"Oh, come on, Jane," Jeffrey countered. "You and your damned integrity. After everything he put you through? I'd say that's well-deserved and you should make a run for them—Brave Harlots, too, for that matter."

"Do we have a name yet?" I asked, now excited at the proposition that I would be an equal partner with my two biggest mentors. "For the agency, I mean."

"Does that mean you're saying yes and coming with us?" Jeffrey asked me.

I smiled and nodded. "Are you kidding? Working with you two again? It's the chance of a lifetime."

"Then how about Mitchell Vance & Mercer?" Warren offered.

"I love it," I exclaimed, heart ready to burst with exhilaration. "It has a great ring to it."

"We already have our HR director hired," Warren added. "It's Veronica, and she's drawn up a plan for the initial department, so we can immediately start hiring as soon as we've gone through the legal process and established the business. Also, my former office building is still available, and I've put in an offer. It looks like the deal will go through in a couple of weeks."

I thought about Veronica and how perfect she would be at maintaining the HR department of our new agency. I looked from Jeffrey to Warren and felt, for the first time in the past year, that everything was working out perfectly—that my destiny was finally clear.

I drove home that night immersed in the possibilities that laid before me. Could it be that I was finally getting everything I always wanted? I never forgot the line from my favorite childhood movie, *Willie Wonka and the Chocolate Factory*, the one starring Gene Wilder, and couldn't help but feel like Charlie Bucket when Wonka leans down in the glass elevator and says to him, "And don't forget what happened to the little boy who suddenly got everything he always wanted: he lived happily ever after." Only I was not a little boy—I was a grown woman with a brilliant future ahead of me.

When I arrived home, I got into the elevator and pushed the third-floor button to the apartment I shared again with Derek, the love of my life. When I unlocked and opened the door, I saw candles burning, dimly illuminating the house in a cozy, sensual way. I smelled the savory scents of something gorgeous cooking and, when I got to the kitchen, there was Derek hunched over the oven in his apron, moving a pan around and stirring something inside. A glass of Cabernet Sauvignon sat on the counter, glowing with a deep crimson warmth.

I leaned against the doorframe of the kitchen and just watched in delight and comfort. This was my home and I was with the man I had always loved. We were going to have dinner and then we were going to listen to music and watch the news and then go to bed. We would make love and wake up together the next day, and the next, and the next. And I couldn't wait.

THE END

Acknowledgments

Thank you to my first readers, Mom, Jenni, Shirley, Doug, Pam, Carrie, and to my editor, Becky, for combing through my earliest draft for plot holes and other aspects. You all have been invaluable to the production of this book.

Many thanks to the members of Don's critique group, who took time out of their busy schedules to help. A special shout out to Lori, my most treasured writing partner, and to Pedro, who provided much unexpected insight from a man's POV.

Thanks, also, to Casey for educating me on the details of mergers and acquisitions.

My sincerest gratitude goes to my longtime friend and one of the most talented photographers I've ever worked with, Merrell Virgen, who shot the book cover on a cold day in London.

Thank you, most of all, to my family for always reading my work, giving me your honest opinion, and for supporting my literary endeavors. I love and appreciate each, and every one of you.

About Adele Royce

Adele Royce was raised in Los Angeles, and graduated *magna cum laude* from Arizona State University with a BA in English Literature. She survived the insanity of the Las Vegas Strip, where she worked for many years as an advertising and PR executive. Ms. Royce's personal experience with the industry's creativity and chaos gave her inspiration for her multiple-book series titled *Truth, Lies and Love in Advertising*. She lives with her husband in South Florida, where she is active in the writing community. Her short stories have won numerous first place awards.

Connect with Adele Royce online at adeleroyce.com.